Volume 2 of the Holy Spirit Series

Anne Church O'Planick

Carpenter's Son Publishing

The H.S.: Volume 2 of the Holy Spirit Series

©2025 by Anne Church O'Planick

All rights reserved. No part of this book may be reproduced or transmitted in any form or by any means, electronic or mechanical, including photocopying, recording, or by any information storage and retrieval system, without permission in writing from the copyright owner.

Published by Carpenter's Son Publishing, Franklin, Tennessee

Published in association with Larry Carpenter of Christian Book Services, LLC
www.christianbookservices.com

Holy Bible, New Living Translation (NLT), copyright © 1996, 2004, 2015 by Tyndale House Foundation. Used by permission of Tyndale House Publishers, Inc., Carol Stream, Illinois 60188. All rights reserved.

Cover Art by Anne Oplanick

Cover and Interior Design by Suzanne Lawing

Edited by Ann Tatlock

Printed in the United States of America

978-1-956370-96-6

Contents

Foreword	....	7
Chapter 1	Mack Gersham	9
Chapter 2	Santaya Woodring..................	17
Chapter 3	Mack Gersham	27
Chapter 4	President Santaya Woodring..........	33
Chapter 5	Ricardo Medina....................	39
Chapter 6	Santaya Woodring..................	43
Chapter 7	Mercedes Singleton.................	49
Chapter 8	Ricardo Medina....................	57
Chapter 9	President Woodring	65
Chapter 10	Mercedes Singleton.................	71
Chapter 11	Mack Gersham	77
Chapter 12	Mercedes Singleton.................	85
Chapter 13	Santaya Woodring..................	89
Chapter 14	Ricardo Medina....................	93
Chapter 15	Mercedes Singleton.................	99
Chapter 16	Mercedes Singleton	107
Chapter 17	Mack Gersham (Troy Griffins)	111
Chapter 18	Ricardo Medina....................	117
Chapter 19	Mercedes Singleton.................	123
Chapter 20	Mercedes Singleton.................	127
Chapter 21	Ricardo Medina....................	131
Chapter 22	Mercedes Singleton.................	135
Chapter 23	Ricardo Medina....................	141

Chapter 24	Santaya Woodring	147
Chapter 25	Mack Gersham (Troy Griffins)	151
Chapter 26	Santaya Woodring	155
Chapter 27	Mercedes Singleton	159
Chapter 28	Mercedes and Mack	167
Chapter 29	Arun Polysoing	175
Chapter 30	Ricardo Medina	179
Chapter 31	Mack Gersham	187
Chapter 32	Ricardo Medina	191
Chapter 33	Santaya Woodring	195
Chapter 34	Mack Gersham	201
Chapter 35	Mercedes Singleton	207
Chapter 36	President Santaya Woodring	213
Chapter 37	The Native Nations	221
Chapter 38	Ricardo Medina	227
Chapter 39	Mercedes Singleton	235
Chapter 40	Ricardo Medina	241
Chapter 41	Santaya Woodring	251
Chapter 42	Mercedes Singleton	257
Chapter 43	Reverend Singleton	263
Chapter 44	Mercedes Singleton	269
Chapter 45	Santaya Woodring	277
Chapter 46	Ricardo Medina	287
Chapter 47	Mack Gersham	291
Chapter 48	Mack Gersham	297
Chapter 49	Mercedes Singleton	303

Foreword

Who is this mysterious part of the Godhead, the Holy Spirit, and how does He figure into our lives as Christians?

Most people of my generation talked about Him as an addendum to God. We were not quite sure what to do with Him. We were focused on Jesus Christ, and that certainly was right.

But the Holy Spirit allows us to know the true Jesus and to fulfill His calling on our lives. Jesus Himself told us that He must leave so that He could send the Advocate, the Spirit, the Presence into our midst. Jesus sent the Spirit to enliven our minds and hearts to experience God in a whole new way. This way allows us to see, hear, touch, and know the Godhead.

And this certainly enhances our relationship with the Trinity!

This second volume of the H.S. continues the saga of those whose lives are caught up not only in human events, but the movement of the Spirit. The story began as the Spirit prompted me a decade ago to write about Him in a way people could relate to. When He talked to me in our car on Interstate 77 and said, "This is where your story starts," it was to write His story. The characters of this book continue to interact with the Spirit as He moves them into a life patterned on Christ. The Holy Spirit can be seen facilitating miracles, opening a view into the spiritual world, and providing presence and comfort in the difficulties of life.

He speaks, guides, cherishes, and holds those who follow Him.

Although the setting for the story is staged in the near future, this book is not intended to be a prophetic explanation of the days to come. The shift of time frame is simply a realistic setting for the Holy Spirit to pour His Presence on His people. This will continue to happen, no matter how events transpire in the real future. What a joy that is!

I am thankful that the H.S. put my pen to paper once again and dictated the course of the text. In allowing Him to do the writing without plan or platform, the results are credited to Him as well. I have just been the stylus holder.

I wish to thank my family for their ever-present support. My children Carrie, Colleen, Michael, and John. My husband Richard, who sees me disappearing to write a few more chapters of the saga and encourages me. To Jean Hannan, who astutely has assisted with editing and clarification of the text. And to the God who sees all and continues to renew our minds so that we can know Him better.

May your journey with the Spirit bring you personal joy in knowing the God who saves, our Lord Jesus Christ.

Chapter 1

Mack Gersham

November 2036

But when the Father sends the Advocate as my representative—that is, the Holy Spirit—he will teach you everything and will remind you of everything I have told you. ~ John 14:26

At 2:00 a.m., Baltimore seemed lifeless. The scene was reminiscent of black-and-white movies portraying the wreckage of crumbled structures after a nuclear explosion. Mack pulled his felt coat collar up while waiting impatiently for the Zorro ride share to arrive.

The driver had been none too anxious to take on a rider at this late juncture, but Mack convinced him that between the safe destination and double fare, it was worth the gamble. A buck was hard to come by in this survival economy, and Mack was paying with genuine American dollars; no coupons. That sealed the deal for the driver.

A dark compact electric car sidled up to the bus stop and the window was lowered.

Mack identified himself to the driver. "I'm Mack Hamilton." He figured it was safer to use the Hamilton last name so as not to create any suspicion from the driver in case he was curious as to why Mack picked this destination.

"Hop in back. I have the destination you gave me earlier. Suburbs. Still the same?"

The Zorro driver figured Mack was ex-military from his tone and the slight limp. He certainly looked like he was making his way better than the scores of former soldiers in the homeless encampment down by the harbor.

Mack stepped in and the Zorro driver accelerated to the top speed allowed by the vehicle—barely 60 if the vehicle was fully charged. That was ten over the limit, but at this time of night, no one cared.

This part of the journey from Whitsville, Virginias, to Baltimore had already been choreographed by Mack in the past few days. Mack's prearranged appointment with a contact from the the Army Intelligence Unit at the Pentagon in D.C. guaranteed issuance of new ID credentials. His updated persona was that of a stern-faced individual who looked the part of a no-nonsense security detail. It would do for a few weeks until he morphed into another individual useful to the resistance. To be on the safe side, he also had donned a set of silicone fingerprints which were untraceable at the moment just in case someone was trying to tail him. Sooner or later, the Federated Forces would figure out the puzzle of Mack Gersham's connection to the Blues Militia. Good research would reveal he was the one still holding the encrypted computer drives detailing the military equipment procurements that had been pilfered from military requisition sites and then sent to safe stash locations for use with the Blues Resistance.

His first goal after returning to the Federated States from the rebel zone was to gain a new identity, but an ID card would not pass muster. Mack chuckled to himself as he thought of the spy movies where deception was achieved by a well-crafted rubberized face mask replicating one of the cast of bad guys. Now he was scheduled for face surgery which would be much more convincing. The face scar received in the drone strike that killed his brother Walt and his young friend Danny, who bunked with Ricardo, would have to be eliminated. Other details were pending.

The goal of this plastic surgery was to create a person who would be accepted in the government database without raising questions as to his identity. Dr. Simon Hamilton, who was doing the surgery in his home, was already prepping for the challenge. Mack would need to convince the government facial recognition database if he was to pursue his mission and be of further use to the Blues.

A few moments later, the Zorro driver cut into his thoughts. "Been awhile since I've come out to the suburbs. Most people here still have cars and drive themselves even though cars are so damned expensive. You live here?"

"No, visiting a relative. Can't afford a car either. Usually get around on the public system." Mack cut off the conversation by gazing out the window. The driver took the hint that he was not the chatty type. Most people weren't anymore. Best to keep a low profile.

Mack marveled at the tranquility of the suburbs they sped through. His mind immediately crafted an image of Mercedes Singleton sitting on her worn couch in Whitsville the night he left months ago. An incredulous look was on her face as she struggled with the revelation that Mack had been posing as his twin brother Walt, who had been killed by a drone strike from the Federated Forces led by General Lu. He had also revealed that he had been working for the Blues Militia, battling General Sturgis Lu, the chief of staff, who was secretively forming a partnership with the One Nation Alliance. This alliance would mean the end of America and the beginning of a one world government.

Replaying those last moments together, Mack could kick himself for pulling Mercedes into this twisted world of espionage. He asked her to find Arun David Polysoing, head of the CLF, the Christian Liberation

Front, who was protesting the leadership of the country and fighting against the abhorrent treatment of Christians in internment camps in the U.S. His own sister, Olivia, a dear friend of Mercedes, had been killed in front of her eyes by the warden of the camp where they were confined the previous year.

What was I thinking? he thought angrily. *Mercedes has no place in this sordid business. Most of us are probably going to be dead before the end of the year.*

Then he refocused his thinking, knowing that reflecting on his memories of Mercedes would not help either of them. She had willingly agreed to do her part. When she was finished, she could become anonymous in the Blues zone. He would do his best to see that she stayed away from harm in Lu's wicked world.

In thirty minutes, the Zorro driver pulled into a tree-lined neighborhood with substantial homes nestled on manicured lawns. It was surreal to exchange the stark weary city structures for some hint of life and color. Mack gazed at the stately homes on the right side of the street. They appeared as a fantasy to his real-world view.

Although the government had crammed families from the lower and middle classes into shared housing after the catastrophic volcanic explosion in Wyoming and the deluge of the Drakee virus, these elites had escaped the stringent enforcement of dual family residences by employing maids and groundkeepers who supposedly resided with them in their homes. The government felt it had done a fair job of addressing the housing crisis when millions of people were forced to migrate to metropolitan centers for services and shelter. Most of this entry level support staff, however, ended up taking public transportation back to their crowded homes in the city at night and the rules were skirted by these suburbanites. They used to be hard-working, white-collared professionals, stiving to outdo others in their social circles. Now most of the wealthy were government officials who came to power with the current administration. This was their gift for being willing accomplices to a strict government that required all to feel the pain. Conditions were miserable for those stuck in the city, but not for those who inhabited the suburbs as though nothing had changed.

The Zorro driver slowed to the legal speed and checked his location on the in-car screen. "Should be coming up, buddy. Guess you are familiar with this neighborhood?"

"Yeah," shared Mack. "Been here a few times. There's the gate. I need to put in the passcode to get in. You can drop me off at the driveway approach. Their security cameras will pick me up."

Climbing out of the cramped car, Mack grabbed his backpack and handed the driver enough bills to cover the earlier agreed-upon fare. *Geez*, thought Mack. *At least I should have crumpled them up to make them look more nondescript.* They were genuine; part of the Blues cache of siphoned supplies, but he wanted things to appear normal.

The driver counted the bills and smiled at the generous tip. He gave Mack a thumbs up. He was not complaining. Cold cash was a hot commodity and this trip was worth every penny. "Call me anytime," he proclaimed as he hastily passed Mack a simple business card with his phone number and first name. While Mack was keying in the code for the security gate, the Zorro driver floored the accelerator to return to the dreary city.

After the car turned the corner, Mack swiftly changed directions, crossing the street and walking into a densely thicketed woods. This silent tract of blackened trees had been parceled off at the inception of the neighborhood development plan as a location for communication resources for this and surrounding homes.

General Marcus Hamilton, whose home was across the street, had been instrumental in the early planning stages by obtaining government approval for this land set-aside, designating the small tract's use as a site to enhance satellite and tower communication systems. The general had realized that there were enemies within the military hierarchy and had spent years building a team and intelligence network to foil their advances. Unfortunately, he and his aide, Lt. Col. Shamir Wells had been killed in an assasination by top military brass when they failed to divulge their network of patriots.

The neighbors appreciated the expansive green space and accepted the small communication tower that rose slightly above the tree line. Buried in the thick woods sat a solitary cement-block building, not completely hidden, but overgrown and seemingly abandoned years before. If anyone had been interested, they would have surmised it was an old communication switch station. Mack knew otherwise.

Hamilton had requisitioned its construction while he was building his own home across the street. The general had known early in his military career that dubious forces were pulling the strings. This foresight led him to construct a command center far from the glare of military inspections. In the past two years, small teams of IT network companies had paid visits to enhance its internal systems. Now it contained satellite compatible computer banks and supplies for living off the grid. The few windows opened to the back, and over the years it had attracted scant attention from the neighbors.

Mack remembered General Hamilton's instructions to come to this location if their plans went askew. This would be a safe house while their next action was reformulated. *The man thought of everything,* mused Mack as he turned on his LED penlight and pressed in the keyed entry code. *General, we're still on your team. We haven't thrown in the towel yet.*

Mack smiled. *Well, I do have another team that I've pledged myself to, but I think you would approve. We're going to need their expertise to see the Blues achieve the goals we set from the beginning. Right now it just feels like a convoluted labyrinth with no escape plan.* Mack was trying to stay positive, but a feeling of doom pushed its insidious tentacles into his thoughts.

In the brief interview upon returning to Washington, Mack had been informed that Lu and his team of military and government schemers had moved forward with their plan to take over the executive branch and tastefully reshape the government to fit their goals of uniting with The One Nation Alliance. This slowly developing organization, mostly secretive in nature, was gaining momentum on the world stage as a practical solution to world peace through one world government. Lu, of course, was instrumental in shaping the emerging behemoth to fit his needs. Those would be power and control of much of the world's population under the guise of peace, planet preservation, and prosperity for all.

The goals sounded lofty and pristine. Peace would be the panacea of the world. But a closer inspection of the means to peace was coertion, corruption, and control. Peace was not the gift of a great God, not the kind of peace a believer sought. This type of peace was crafted through authoritarian control and was touted by people who promised that all would be free to live their lives as they desired.

It was a big lie. Deception by the enemy.

I'm depending on you, God. I don't think we can do this without you.

The lights on the code box flashed green and the faded gray security locks covered in cobwebs released. Mack stepped into the musty room, closing the door softly.

"Home sweet home, for the time being." Setting down his weathered backpack, he switched on a covered lamp and began the task of powering up the pilfered computer system. Heavy on his mind was a need to talk to God. It sounded odd to talk to God that way, but he just let the words and sounds tumble off his lips without thinking. They somehow brought comfort.

You are not alone, Mack, was the response.

"Right," he whispered.

Chapter 2

Santaya Woodring

2008 – 2032
A Look Back

But there is a spirit within people, the breath of the Almighty within them, that makes them intelligent. ~ Job 32:8

It seemed like a total deviation from her former career with the African Assistance Association to consider an employment move to the civilian branch of the U.S. Army Division of Counterintelligence unit. But not for Santaya.

Since the death of Shamir Todotin, her Kenyan lover who had been killed by marauding revolutionary forces in the Republic of the Congo, she was obsessed with the necessity of advanced information. Many days, Santaya still woke up with a hunger for her former lover and the son who she had named after him. If they had only had better technology and prior warning that the Congolese guerrilla group was about to strike with a vengeance against their upstart technology college, perhaps Shamir would still be alive and their dream for bettering the lives of the Congolese would have advanced. *I partly blame myself,* thought Santaya, realizing that she had not taken the earlier warnings of a rebel attack more seriously. She had willingly clung to her Western worldview that people cannot be that filled with enough vengeance to kill innocent civilians. *I need to be less ignorant and more observant. It begins with surveillance and espionage. I want to know what is happening beneath the counterfeit peaceful surface.*

A college friend from Wellington had joined the Army Civilian Intelligence Corp, a branch affiliated with the FBI, after graduation. It had seemed an odd occupation for a progressive-leaning person.

"I just cannot picture you working for the Army, Anita," Santaya replied after Anita had accepted her position during graduation week.

"Oh, you have an old-fashioned view of the military. They aren't obsessed with guns and war anymore. Can't you see we are finally getting to the place where civilized people have better things to do than grab someone else's territory or supplies, or worse, assassinate a world leader? We are all interconnected, and eventually, ignorant behavior like this will see the perpetrators punished and then forgotten," shared Anita, covering the talking points of her new employer. "The modern military is working to forge world peace. We will work to make sure all members of society have a chance to share in equal prosperity. Basically, we are doing the same thing you are planning to do in Africa."

Santaya wanted to believe the new theology of the military, but her experience in the Republic of the Congo still had her wary of human nature. *Would we ever be able to conquer hatred, power, and control at the hands of evil people?* She was not a believer.

Yet, Santaya was drawn by the hope resonating from this doctrine. She yearned for what was most likely impossible as she applied to the Army Division of Counterintelligence.

"Hey, Anita, it's Santaya. I'm here in D.C. for a few days. Can we do lunch?" spoke Santaya into her message board on her phone. Almost immediately, her phone rang.

"What a surprise," gushed Anita. "I want to see you in the worst kind of way. I heard about the attack on your school in Africa from some of our friends. I tried to get in touch with you, but it was impossible to reach your compound. Today works for me for lunch. How about Smitty's Pub on Fourth Street?' she rambled on hurriedly.

"Great. See you at one?"

"One it is."

Lunch was filled with the touching story of Shamir and the flourishing technical college in Congo, yet for some reason, Santaya changed Shamir's name in her recall of events. She was wise enough to know that there were always ways to track information, especially for a price, and she wanted her child, born in Africa, to have a private life, safe with his adoptive parents who were serving as medical missionaries. For that reason, Santaya ignored his existence.

Santaya also listened to Anita's take on working for the Army Counterintelligence Unit. The work appealed to her. She was yearning for stability and purpose after her world had collapsed. Perhaps this could shore up her faith in mankind again.

"Do you think I would qualify for an entry level position in your department?" she quizzed Anita. I filed an application with human resources about a month ago. I can't believe I might be working for the military, but as you said, they have a new way of looking at the world with an objective of peace and prosperity. Not bad."

Anita responded, "After lunch I'll check in with HR. There seem to be transitions on a regular basis with employees. Often our people matriculate to government contractor companies. That's where the money is!"

That evening Anita called to inform Santaya of her discussion with HR.

"They gave me a call today after I stopped in. I have you scheduled for an interview tomorrow at one p.m., if you agree. They have all your personal files from your work with the African Assistance project. Let's just say they were impressed with the resume. It is as though they were anticipating your appearance. By the way, there are multiple opportunities available. Surprising in this tight job market."

What am I doing? mused Santaya early the next morning as she tried to straighten her hair over her temples. *Is this a good move to foster my goals?* She sighed, flagging a Zorro driver for a ride to the Pentagon.

Colonel James DePew met her in the Human Resources department at one o'clock. He discussed the two openings in their department. The new hire would be reviewing foreign documents siphoned from internet sources and revolutionary websites to decipher if trouble was fomenting somewhere in the world.

"We try to do our due diligence in ferreting out troubling locales before they become full-scale revolutions. If we get on the hot spots quickly, we can take action before it hits the world stage. There are clandestine units from our group all over the world. We are starting to see trouble here in the States too. That would be part of your responsibility as well. Our goal is to promote world peace so eventually respect and cohesion become the watchwords for our diverse planet," shared the Colonel.

Santaya nodded her head and assented to taking the offered position. DePew had earlier in the morning read her resume and contacted her references at AAA. He knew she was a strong, qualified visionary with a practical side to her principles. She would fit in with the drive to diversify the Army leadership and would do well if she decided to make this a career.

Excited about the offer, Santaya phoned Anita. "I got the job!"

"Great. Hey, there's an apartment vacant near me in Alexandria that is affordable. Housing is so hard to find, especially because the federal government keeps growing! I'll pick up the rental contract this afternoon from the landlord and get it to you at your hotel. Welcome to the Army!"

* * * * *

A few years later, Santaya was invited along with Anita and some other acquaintances to participate in Mayor Silvia Brown's reelection campaign for Alexandria's mayoral race. Santaya was enamored by the politics of the campaign and made several suggestions for creative marketing strategies. Although the mayor had had two successful campaigns, she faced opposition from others who promised to more successfully remediate the problems of their city. Santaya's new approach of coaxing voters to consider voting again for Brown caught the attention of the mayor.

At the post-election celebration party, where delicate finger foods were plentiful and alcohol flowed in abundance, the mayor personally spoke to Santaya. "I will be scheduling a one-on-one visit with you in the next month, if that is agreeable with you. I imagine you will have other creative approaches to some of our most pressing needs to share. Am I right?"

Santaya smiled and said, "Yes."

"Lucky you," whispered Anita. "You are on your way in Washington. Here it's all about who you know."

That meeting solidified Santaya's yearning to help the lost and hurting in the local community. Alexandria was struggling with an exploding homeless population, skyrocketing crime, and endless drug addiction fatalities. She realized that quicker change would come from the inside of government, perhaps by sitting on city council, so she began to explore the possibility of running for one of the open council seats in the next election.

She chose her good friend from the Army Counterintelligence Office, Marcus DeAngelo, as her campaign supervisor. He had been an active-duty officer for thirty years. Upon retirement, he realized sitting around in a comfy armchair was not his cup of tea.

"Hey, Santaya. The numbers look good for the election. We've got great PR going with the local news *Spotlight* episode this week. You looked really relaxed in the interview. The mayor's endorsement is a big deal too."

"I'm not getting overconfident," said Santaya hesitantly. But she knew her chances were good. After the vote count on that November evening in 2010, she got a call from Mayor Brown.

"Welcome to the team, Santaya. We're going to go places. I need someone with your eloquence to convey support for our ongoing agenda concerning crime in our city. Our constituents are frustrated with what appears to them to be the right messaging but the lack of results. Can you meet me tomorrow at five p.m. for some collaboration time to share ideas?"

"Thank you, Madam Mayor. I'll be there as soon as I'm finished at work. We can certainly come up with a robust program targeting these crime sprees. I'll dig into the issues of gun ownership, accessibility to firearms, gang life and family structure. We need some honest dialogue on the causes of crime if we want to find a cure. My, I'm sounding like a doctor!" she joked. They both laughed.

"I have a few honorary doctorates I can give you," chuckled the mayor.

When she hung up, the mayor ruminated about her young councilperson. *She certainly is not the typical politician. She is driven to solve pressing problems. Most likely this city will eat her up. There is little room for character here.*

* * * * *

In 2014, Mayor Brown appointed Santaya her Deputy Mayor for Health and Human Services, reporting directly to the mayor's office. Sadly, Santaya turned in her resignation notice of her governmental position to her boss. The Army Counterintelligence position had allowed her to see the necessity of good espionage work to keep the world inclined toward peaceful solutions. Santaya approached the quality-of-life issues in the city as though she was running a marathon. They would be conquered, but only with endurance, good planning, and patience. By far, her leading accomplishment was in the area of homelessness. The city attacked the problem by assessing the mental health of each homeless client and then requiring them to either complete remediation measures or vacate the city. When the homeless camps realized that she meant business, some bolted. The others decided to cooperate. Those success stories made it to the press, and Santaya etched a place for herself in the minds of the voters. Successful clients were then provided free housing and services that would hopefully progress to complete independence and the ability to again join the fabric of regular society.

* * * * *

With the announcement that Mayor Brown was retiring, Santaya began to consider the challenge of running for her position. There would be stiff opposition from other qualified candidates, but something deep down pushed her to throw her hat into the ring. She was convinced that she could continue to refine the programs that were slowly bringing change for the betterment of Alexandria.

In the fall of 2019, while her campaign was organizing, her manager, Marcus DeAngelo, hired an up-and-coming legal firm, Stuart, Willard, and Davis to represent them. Santaya had her initial meeting with DeShaun Davis just before the campaign kicked off with a dinner for the movers and shakers in Washington, D.C.

"Ms. Woodring, Mr. Davis is here to discuss issues pertaining to your campaign and to finalize some campaign documents," stated Shirley Smythe as she stuck her head into Santaya's office.

"Good. Send him in. I'm anxious to meet him."

Standing up from her desk, Santaya gazed directly at DeShaun Davis as he confidently strode up to shake her hand. He was quite tall and walked with purpose. His black hair complimented his grey eyes and athletetic build. "I was anxious to meet you too. I've heard good things about you, Ms. Woodring," he said with a pleasant smile which had the effect of relaxing Santaya. "Our firm is extremely pleased to be representing you in this campaign. We know we have a winner."

Santaya was impressed with his natural confidence. They spent the hour talking about the campaign and the role the law office would take in supporting her work. Mr. Davis provided an additional list of power players who would be of great benefit to her campaign to become mayor. "As you know, it's all about who you know," he quipped.

"I would like to schedule luncheons with some of our clients, get to know them on a personal basis and press them for a contribution. I'll talk to your assistant, Ms. Smythe, to begin setting them up, if that is all right with you."

While Santaya was not a newcomer to the political realm, this immersion into a high-powered campaign was an intense experience. What was new was her unexpected attraction to Mr. DeShaun Davis. He welcomed her attention and continued to visit the campaign office weekly, even though it was not necessary. Eventually he asked her out privately to dinner.

"Santaya, I don't know if you have any social or private attachments that I am not aware of, but if I could be so bold, would you mind mixing business and pleasure and accept an offer for a quiet dinner at my apartment?"

The dinner invitation was accepted and the rest became history. Soon after she was elected mayor, she announced her engagement and the upcoming marriage. The wedding was too public an affair for her, but DeShaun reveled in the attention and the media frenzy. He actually did the majority of the planning for the event. They even had a whole page spread in the magazine *Who's Who*.

"How did that magazine get permission to print our wedding photographs?" demanded Santaya huffily as she sat on the couch looking at the glossy photos.

"I was contacted by one of the editors right before the ceremony and signed off on it. I figured you'd like us touted as a fairy tale couple, as well as getting more favorable press as the newly sworn-in mayor of Alexandria. It gives you national exposure."

"Oh, DeShaun, couldn't you have cleared it with me first? I feel like my privacy is being violated. Everything in the campaign was open to the public eye. I wanted my ceremony to be an intimate affair with just a few friends and family."

"Santaya, you are a public figure now. We both are. Get used to it. We'll still have our private time at home," he chortled as he nuzzled her neck. Santaya faintly smiled. She was deeply in love, but DeShaun was different from her. She treasured her privacy. It was going to take work to make that happen.

* * * * *

The office of mayor fit perfectly with Santaya's set of administrative skills. She had made such a name for herself that, in 2028, the current president of the opposing party made a quick decision to offer her the cabinet position of Health and Human Services. He did not just do this because of her skill set. He figured that this was a move favored by the voters.

They were tired of the divisiveness of parties. Reaching across the aisle was the sign of an open-minded and equitable leader. All ideas were to be considered. Little did he realize that in the next general election, he had just chosen the person who would head the opposing party ticket for president of the United States.

Chapter 3

Mack Gersham

January 2037

Don't you realize that your body is the temple of the Holy Spirit, who lives in you and was given to you by God? You do not belong to yourself.~ 1 Corinthians 6:19

Misery was another word for Washington D.C. in January. Mack had impatiently endured a series of cosmetic surgeries that lasted two months to reconfigure his face, and now he had to persist through the grueling rehabilitation.

Before arriving at the "safe house," he had contacted Ed Derkovick and Simon Hamilton, the son of General Marcus Hamilton and a staff surgeon with Walter Reed Hospital specializing in plastic surgery. Ed was General Marcus Hamilton's primary military operative in the Pentagon before the general had been assassinated. He continued in that role as the intelligence lead for the Blues Militia. His longevity and durability had made him a trusted confidant, but his ability to smell a rat in voluminous internet transactions was uncanny.

Long ago he had figured out that something was amiss with Chief of Staff General Lu's strange correspondence with foreign leaders revolving around frivolous concerns. Aware of the constant flow of missives, he began a secret file, making this his personal and private business. Knowing Lu's power and prowess, Ed wished to stay under the radar. Yet having top security clearance allowed him to monitor the flurry of documents. When he was sure he had the fish snagged on the line, Derkovick called his old friend General Marcus Hamilton and paid a visit to him at his office on the other side of the Pentagon. Although these two were in constant contact from 2034, Hamilton was never seen in public with Derkoich. The assassination of General Hamilton sent Derkovich into overdrive to make sure the subversive monitoring was concealed. Ed knew that somehow Lu was connected to Hamilton's death. He was not sure whether he was to be the next victim or if he had managed to stay incognito in his contribution to the Blues.

"Simon," mumbled Mack, coming out from under his anesthesia. "Got some decent results?"

"Well," said Dr. Hamilton, "I've been trying to build up that nose of yours to give it some character, like my father's."

"What?" croaked Mack. He knew the General's nose had been large and quite distinctive. And not very attractive.

Simon Hamilton chuckled. "Not really. Just working to pattern your nose after our alias. It is much more generic than yours. No offense."

"Yeah. Getting it broken a few times playing football did that. A poor coal country boy certainly would not get it straightened."

"I also gave another go at that facial scar. I'm pretty pleased with the results. But it is going to take a few weeks for the swelling to subside and the discoloration to disappear. Right now you look like a heavy weight fighter slugging it out on *Sports Plus*."

Mack queried, "Will this face pass for our alias?"

"Sure of it," the doctor replied. "I've done this work before at Walter Reed, so I'm familiar with how the facial recognition scans operate. I've managed to alter enough of your facial points to bypass the scanners identifying you as Mack Gersham."

"So how is my alias coming along?"

"Derkovich is on it. He's diligently working to not only have you look like identical twins, but also crafting the story explaining your reappearance in the intelligence world."

The set-up of the safe house years before by Hamilton had been a godsend. When Mack made his preliminary contact with Dr. Hamilton, Mack had floated the idea of his performing plastic surgery with the hope that he could continue the work of the Blues Militia unobserved. The doctor thought it was a viable suggestion and floated the idea past Derkovich. It had been done in the past, more than the American citizen would ever know.

Simon Hamilton had been aware of his father's suspicions of Lu on an unofficial basis. At first he thought his father had been overly zealous in analyzing Lu's goals for power and prestige. But after General Hamilton's assassination, Simon sat down with his mother, and she shared what had been developing in the intrigue surrounding Lu's activities.

Dr. Hamilton was shocked that patriots like his father were now the enemy in the military. His mother also informed him of a select group of former military members who had formed an organization labeled the Blues Militia crafted by none other than his father. She was privy to a few names and shared them with her son Simon. When Mack made his first call to Dr. Simon Hamilton, he had used the untraceable phone provided with the Blues supplies and the number that his father General Marcus Hamilton had made sure he memorize. Dr. Hamilton was not only curious but forthright in his commitment to ferret out the enemies within.

"You can head back to your 'retreat' across the street in a few days," shared the doctor. "Just have to make sure the swelling has decreased and we avoid infection. Can you shower over there? You've had all the amenities here at our house."

"Of course." Mack smiled. "Your father was a genius at being thorough. He had the foresight to consider the need for a place to disappear. The funny part is that I am right under their noses and they can't sniff me out. Let's hope it stays that way."

"You've got someone looking out for you."

Mack stared at the doctor. "You're right. I'm relying on the Man Upstairs lots more now. Somehow I have a peace about it. We can use all the help we can get."

Dr. Hamilton didn't say anything more on the subject, but Mack bantered the question around in his mind as to whether he should have mentioned God. He decided what he did was acceptable. He was not going to hide his trust in God. So far in his fledgling state of faith, Mack had found a deep satisfaction permeating his heart during the repetitive facial reconfiguration surgeries. It had all fallen into place. It could not have been a coincidence, and he silently thanked God for His provision.

Dear God, you have been with me though these deep waters. I know you are here. I feel your presence. Keep before me your will. Thank you. This is Mack, by the way.

"Doc, you have any idea who killed your father and Lt. Col. Wells?" Mack paused and assessed Dr. Hamilton's reaction. "Did you know I was there the night of the assassination?"

Dr. Simon Hamilton looked up and grabbed Mack's hand. "I have waited for what seems a lifetime, even though it has only been six months, to hear any iota of information on what happened that night. General Lu sent his lackies over here, touting the link to the Christian Liberation Front, but I could tell something was not adding up with their story. The CLF would have no reason to target my father. He had inside information about their organization and knew they were in Lu's bullseye. Are you comfortable telling me the details?"

"Sure," said Mack, yawning. "But I am awful groggy from those pain meds. Can I share the rest with you after a nap?"

Dr. Hamilton stared into Mack's eyes. "I am in no hurry. I have yearned for the truth every minute since Dad was killed that day. When the neighborhood patrol found my dad assassinated in the car out on the street, I was the first one on the scene, noticing his body covered in blood from a single shot to the head. It was a frontal shot straight into his skull. It could not have been made while he was sitting in a car, as they reported. No corresponding blood splatters from the shot, just some shoddy blood smears on the windows. Real amateurs."

Chapter 4

President Santaya Woodring

February 2037

*But as for me, I am filled with power— with the Spirit of the Lord.
I am filled with justice and strength to boldly declare
Israel's sin and rebellion. ~ Micah 3:8*

Santaya willed herself to open her eyes when her alarm unforgivingly blared at 5:00 a.m. She groggily recalled the phone call the prior evening from DeShaun telling her that he felt quite sick and that it would be best for her to delay her return.

"Honey, it would probably be best if you didn't come home tonight. Anyway, you had said you'd like to stay at Andrews for the Honor Guard Ceremony tomorrow. It'll be a good look for a newly elected president. I'll catch up with you in the morning. I'll call the doctor at Walter Reed if I still feel this crappy when I get up. Probably the dregs of Drakee virus again."

"All right, DeShaun. Get a good night's sleep. Love you." The phone cut off.

Andrew's Air Force Base had been the chosen location for this year's Honor Guard Ceremony for those who had fallen in the line of duty the preceding year. This remembrance ceremony rotated every year to different locations connected to the five branches of the military. Santaya had a deep desire to attend, but her aides had encouraged her to skip the ceremony and send the secretary of state, who usually filled in as the official executive branch representative.

Secretary of State Jeremy Cataberrus had volunteered to step in. He was a team player. She liked him because he was not as superficial as most of the members of her cabinet. She knew he would be there this morning, but if she made an unscheduled appearance, it would hopefully be a pleasant surprise for those attending. Sacrifice and valor were not in vogue at this current time in society. Many American citizens felt that those lost in the line of duty were simply doing what they had signed up for. The possibility of death was just a part of the job. No big deal. Santaya felt otherwise. She knew their sacrifice was instrumental in pushing back on the evil influences of the world. Evil did not back down to simple threats and smoothly phrased words. If there was no force behind those threats and words, they would mean nothing in a world staggering to keep afloat.

The phone conversation with her husband had sealed the change of plans. If he was ill, she would stay away. Her presidential campaign for reelection had sapped her strength. Running for a second term proved to be as hard as the first. Exhaustion had set in after all the rallies, town halls, and debates. She was tired of the constant need to smile, the noise and the food shoved in her face. Her body was screaming for a rest! There would be none. Coming up was the State of the Union speech.

Last evening, while lying in a surprisingly comfortable bed at the base, she also contemplated meeting a couple she had met briefly many years ago in Africa.

Terrance and Maxine Wells had accepted the invitation to participate in the Honor Ceremony for their son, Lt. Col. Shamir Wells. They had endured the daily heartbreak of remembering how their only son had lost his life, stolen by a group of CLF assassins. Their grief was difficult to bear. Being at this ceremony would remind them of the sacrifice Shamir had willingly pledged to accept as he chose to defend his country against the enemy both foreign and domestic.

Although supportive of his decision to join the military, they found it difficult to match the call to live a Christian life with a militaristic call to arms. They had always hoped he would show the love of Christ by joining their medical practice and displaying Christ in a more acceptable way. But Shamir had comforted them, explaining that this was the path God had directed him to follow. They simply could not connect that with their theology.

"Shamir," said his mother softly. "You might need to kill people. The Army is never far away from the chaos and destruction of wars and uprisings. Your life will be in the balance. I can't stand to think of you dying for unknown people in some godforsaken land. In most of these conflicts, it's hard to know who is fighting on the side of 'right.'"

"I know that, Mom," said Shamir confidently. "But that is not a good enough reason to give up on those who are in these areas of trouble all around the world. You and Dad did the same thing many years ago in Africa. You reached out to help those less fortunate with medical care when you were missionaries for our church. There was a threat to life in the Congo too. It's not much different."

"I was not getting shot at," quipped his mother.

"No. I will try to keep myself from danger. But remember, Mom, God is with me and will never forsake me. You know He has a plan for my life too. This just seems to be for some reason, what He has always called me to do. Pray for me, will you?"

President Woodring's staff filled in the secretary of state concerning her unexpected appearance at Andrews at their 8:00 a.m. breakfast. Near the end of the meal, Santaya strolled in to say hello while grabbing a glass of juice and conversing with a few of her aides. She was thankful that her executive assistant, Shirley Smythe, ran interference for her when the lonely media representative from *News Now* pressed in to ask questions.

By 9:00 a.m., the dignitaries had been seated in the hangar at Andrews and the guests were escorted to their assigned seats. Santaya had managed to catch the names of Terry and Maxine on two of the seats in the second row, and mentally made a note to attempt to keep her interaction with them generic and unattached. She would go into play-acting mode again. Her skills had been honed to perfection in the campaign.

Thankfully, General Lu had passed the ceremonial responsibilities to one of his two-star generals, General Brandon James. Ironically, he was the man chosen as a replacement for General Marcus Hamilton. There was no comparison. General James was a lackey for Lu; surly and distant. He wanted to have this distasteful business over as quickly as possible. The guests could not help but pick up on this vibe during the concise welcome speech.

General James was also dismayed with President Woodring's unexpected attendance. He almost had to force a smile in her presence. Santaya was not at all surprised that James held her in such disdain. She was an antagonist to their plans. They knew it. But they were not sure she knew it.

After the Ceremony of Recognition and Remembrance where each family group received a folded flag and a plaque, the announcement was offered that those in attendance were most welcome to share a few words with the president. They were also asked to keep their remarks brief.

An aide from Andrews Air Force staff introduced each family party, briefly sharing the rank of the fallen soldier and his/her military assignment. Santaya quickly noticed that the Wells had joined the guest line. Occasionally she would glance in their direction as they neared her station. When they moved in front of her and the aide announced them as parents of Lt. Col. Shamir Wells, she could barely keep her composure.

Santaya mumbled the standard, "We are so thankful for your son's sacrifice to his country." To this she added, "You must be proud of the good man he had become. I am sure you are wonderful parents and blessed with him for so many years."

Leaning in, Maxine Wells whispered, "We are all proud of our son. He could not have been killed by the CLF. He was part of their organization."

Steadying her gaze, Santaya leaned back, thanking them for attending. As they moved off, she turned brusquely to her assistant and whispered, "Shirley, find a private room for the parents of Shamir Wells to meet with me. Keep this confidential, especially from General James."

She was determined to learn more about Shamir. Perhaps the conversation would provide the leads she needed to identify the actual perpetrators of her son's assassination. For a moment, Santaya revelled in the memory of the love child she had bore to Shamir Todotten in the Republic of Congo years before. Not a day expired where she did not conjure up the faces of those two men, father and son, who had been lost to her forever.

Chapter 5

Ricardo Medina

February 2037

So if you sinful people know how to give good gifts to your children, how much more will your heavenly Father give the Holy Spirit to those who ask him. ~ Luke 11:13

Just before dawn, Ricardo pressed the code into the keypad, produced a fingerprint accepted by the security lock and stumbled into the secluded cement block building. Several computers were blinking colorful combinations of lights, but otherwise, a deep quiet suffused the room.

With an almost imperceptible grunt, he dumped a black bulky body bag unceremoniously on the floor as he closed the door with his foot. Dripping in sweat and breathing heavily, he turned and caught sight of Mack Gersham too late.

"Well, look who came for breakfast," quipped Mack, sporting a military high-grade pistol in his hand and a large bandage over his nose. Ricardo unzipped the bag and dumped out the body of a middle-aged man in Army fatigues. He looked vaguely familiar. It was obvious he was dead. Dark red blood was plastered on his forehead and Mack could detect a small caliber hole in his skull, meant to do the most damage at close range. "You in the bounty hunting business now?" mocked Mack.

"Listen," puffed Ricardo. "The Feds are on their way. They'll be here in ten minutes or less. They've had this place flagged for the past two weeks and have been monitoring your communications – the few that have gone out. Get out of here and destroy whatever you can't carry. Does the name Ed Derkovich ring a bell? He's being rounded up right now and then will be interrogated at Lu's headquarters. He said to tell you, *Blue Danube*. I left you a car down the next street, Dalks Drive, by the stop sign. It's been converted for radar clearance. Note on the front seat as to where to meet me for the next safe house."

Mack froze, stupefied and skeptical. He lowered the gun pointed at Ricardo and tucked it in his waistband. He nodded as Ricardo sprinted out the front door and into the deep foliage. Springing into action, Mack punched the hard drives out of all the computers and dumped them into his military backpack. Then he lunged for a small container strapped to the back of the steel door. Snapping it open, he had no time to review the directions. His memory would have to serve as his direction guide. Softly he removed the explosive device and pulled the release pin. Tossing it into the center of the room, he knew he had 30 seconds to get as much distance as possible between him and the bomb. It should be enough time to get clear of the debris field.

As he tore down the shadows of the street, his brain whirled with questions. Amidst the difficult breathing, he had an uncanny awareness of another companion on the run with him. Questions raced through his mind. *Was Ricardo telling the truth? How could Ed Derkovich trust a man who was hired to capture Blues Militia? Who was the dead man? How did Ricardo know the password?* Then Mack asked the Spirit a question. *Are you behind all this? Are you saving me for something?* In his head, he heard the answer. Yes.

After the tremendous explosion, an immense fireball leapt into the sky and was seen above the treetops. The retort nearly knocked Mack down. However, the noise and fury were so intense, that no one noticed his quick escape in the government sedan. Looking at the paper left by Ricardo on the front seat, he was thankful that the instructions were written in a simple cypher. The safe house was not far from the government campus of cabinet buildings in downtown Washington D.C.

Mack slowed the car to the speed limit and blended in with the flow of early employees arriving for work. He was passed by a bevy of emergency vehicles, sirens blaring, and lights screaming of panic in the predawn darkness. Checking his rearview mirror, he was relieved to see no one following him. Then he realized that his bandage was still taped to his face. Tearing away the adhesive he glanced at a face he did not recognize. It took his breath away.

"Good job, Dr. Hamilton. Hope you are in the clear from this chaos as well. Jesus, please protect his identity and his family." Mack worried about the doctor's safety. Then his mind shifted to Ed. The Blues needed him. He was the lynchpin to the organization now that General Hamilton was gone. *Had all been lost?*

Mack began to grieve for what might be the end of their mission. He slowly coasted to a stop near Ricardo's house, which would be the safe venue for the time being. He was jumpy and not sure whether to stash his paraphernalia in some outbuilding in the area or take it with him. Most likely the car would soon be tracked. He could not believe that two townhomes down the street, there was a garage door open with no homeowner in sight. *They must have left for work in a hurry. Maybe the sirens distracted them.* Mack slid his car inside the open garage and rolled out the bottom of the door after pushing the control on the back wall before it closed.

Slowly he maneuvered himself through the back yards of a few row houses as he scoured them for clues. Nothing seemed amiss, so Mack walked briskly to the sidewalk in front of Ricardo's townhouse. He slipped up the steps and into the old brownstone as the rays of dawn lit the dusty windowpanes. The door had been unlocked, so he silently closed it and pulled the dead bolt back. Then he noticed the protective grates covering the windows and realized that this apartment had been abandoned for years. Dust and cobwebs clung to every stray object in the room. Time had passed by this empty tomb.

Mack smiled. *Maybe it's my tomb.* He sat down on a couch disintegrating before his eyes and waited for Ricardo to arrive. Hours ticked by and Mack wondered if he should stay in this location. His mind checked off the different scenarios as to the role of Ricardo in all this ruckus.

Perhaps Ricardo was still working for Lu and determined to annihilate the Blues. Perhaps he had turned on the general. He certainly had good reason after Danny's death at the hands of the Federal Ops force. Then again, he could have snapped and gone rogue. Or perhaps he was a double agent, the most dangerous of the possibilities. They never ended up fooling the system in the end. Maybe he was spending these hours relishing the trap he had set for Mack, paying him back for his deception in Whitsville. Worse yet, could Ricardo be setting a snare for Mercedes? Mack could be the bait.

Mack began to be angry with himself. *Settle down,* he ordered the thoughts in his mind. A voice also concurred with him. Mack breathed easier and tried to be analytical. *What was happening with Ed?* He closed his eyes and said a prayer for protection and supernatural intervention. "Oh Lord, we're in trouble. We need your help."

Mack heard a tiny knock on the door. He stood up, tucked his gun in his pants and quietly pulled back the rusted dead bolt.

Chapter 6

Santaya Woodring

February 2037

But you are not controlled by your sinful nature. You are controlled by the Spirit if you have the Spirit of God living in you. ~ Romans 8:9

While Santaya was sharing a few intimate moments with the Wellses, parents of Shamir, her aide, Shirley Smythe silently stepped in.

"President Woodring…"

"Really, do you have to interrupt us?" she chided impatiently.

"It is an emergency, Madam President. Your husband has been taken to Walter Reed Hospital. They are not sure of the medical diagnosis, only that he is extremely ill. Your helicopter is en route and will arrive shortly. Your extra staff will return via your personal limousine if that is agreeable to you," stated her executive assistant.

Santaya stood and hugged the Wellses. She knew that there was an eternal bond between them. "Hopefully we will be in each other's thoughts at this difficult time. We will always share the memory of Shamir. I do not want to jeopardize your safety or your privacy with any further communication, but I will be seeking information and answers about Shamir, the CLF, and the perpetrators of his assassination. If I discover any definitive information, it will be forwarded to you."

Maxine squeezed her hand. "We are praying for you. Not only for Shamir's sake, but for the country and the danger you are in. Our Lord will prevail."

Santaya let the prayer and Lord talk pass over her. There were more important subjects pressing in. She smiled and then straightened her lip line. These religious people were fine when trying to deal with the lost and needy, but God talk about personal intervention made her squeamish. She never had liked it and was repulsed by people's need to seek something outside of themselves to solve problems. For her, it was a glaring character weakness. But she realized that the Wellses had influenced Shamir with their faith walk.

When she arrived at Walter Reed, an administrator immediately whisked her into a private waiting room outside the examination room. No one except her Secret Service agent was present. He perused the room and then stepped outside the door.

Waiting impatiently, Santaya glanced around the room and zeroed in on the end table nearest her. The most recent publication of *Healthy Homes* sat on the table. When was the last time she had had time to peruse a magazine? As she lifted it, she was startled to see a cell phone like her husband's underneath. It would not be like him to leave it behind. Perhaps he was overly upset with the events or even left it there with the hopes that she would be the one who would intercept it before it was confiscated by someone else. She smiled at this far-fetched thought. Her mind must be terribly weary to conjure up such a conspiracy theory.

What is happening? she allowed herself to wonder. Slowly she covered the phone with a tissue from her purse and turned it over slightly in her hand. It was his. A message was waiting for him. She was startled to see that there was nothing but an encrypted message pages long as she scrolled through the screen. *DeShaun, is there something I do not know about you. Are you who I think you are?* She tried to push back further thoughts of betrayal and loss. No, she would not dwell on those ugly possibilities.

Dropping the phone in her purse, she rummaged through her acquaintances to decide who could be trusted to crack the code. There were several back in her old office of the Army Intelligence Bureau. Her favorite had been Ed Derkovich.

The examining room door opened with force and a flustered nurse rushed out. She blurted, "Come with me," without fanfare or protocol, and motioned quickly for the president to follow her.

"You need to step into another room," she stated hurriedly. "The doctor and I must scrub up before we meet with you privately. Your husband is being sent to a secure, self-contained unit. The doctor has asked me to inform you that your husband has been poisoned."

Santaya felt faint and grabbed the doorknob of the cramped room she had been ushered into.

"I will be back in a few minutes. I need to have my exposure assessed. Then we will check you as well. The doctor did not feel comfortable meeting you because he has had the most exposure to what we surmise is quite lethal. Your Secret Service agent will remain outside the door."

The nurse slammed the door and whispered instructions to the agent on duty. Then she headed for the emergency exit stairwell. She knew time was of the essence in sterilizing herself from any contagion emanating from the toxic poison.

Within half an hour, Santaya roused herself guiltily from a short cat nap as the door opened and the chief of staff of Walter Reed, Dave Trufello, stepped in and closed the door. She had not intended to fall asleep, but her exhaustion had pushed her to the limit.

"How is DeShaun?" Santaya whispered. "What did the nurse mean when she said he was poisoned?"

"Madam President, his health is grave. We have been able to determine that he has had extensive exposure to a poisonous chemical agent termed Novichok. It was developed by the Soviet Union decades ago to eliminate political rivals. Our best guess right now is that the target was most likely you and not him. Only a slight exposure to this agent can lead to death. Someone with access to your family has targeted you. Unfortunately, DeShaun seems to be the victim."

"Oh my God," mumbled the president.

"We need to assess your exposure, although it has probably only been minimal. Perhaps just some residue in the waiting room. Your staff tells me you were not in the White House last evening."

"I was supposed to return last night, but at the last minute I decided to stay at Andrews for their service honoring our fallen military. DeShaun said he was feeling ill and I should stay away until he was diagnosed. I made the change so unexpectedly that I think most of my staff were not aware that I would not be coming back until today. I consider myself lucky, but poor DeShaun. Can I visit him soon?" requested Santaya.

"I am afraid not. It will be nip and tuck for him, honestly. This nerve agent has a devastating affect on the nervous system. He is starting to convulse unfortunately. We have already requested a crew come in who are former medical personnel during the war in the Middle East. They dealt with many victims of nerve agents and are familiar with the protocols of chemical warfare. They are already assessing his future care as we speak."

The president dropped her head. Her mind was reeling again. An attempted plot on her life, most likely. And her husband was the innocent bystander. *I have lost my lover Shamir, our precious child Shamir named for his father, and likely DeShaun. Oh God, I can't take this,* she thought to herself. She rested her head in her palms and tears dripped down her face.

"Would you like to notify family or your security detail?" asked the administrator with perfunctory precision.

"Yes, my assistant Shirley Smythe. She should be back in D.C. by now. Is the White House safe? I think she returned to her office. And I need to let DeShaun's sisters know he is hospitalized. For now, we will just say he is quite ill with a mutation of the Drakee virus. It is best that we do not panic our citizens into thinking that my life is in jeopardy."

"The team is here to assess your exposure, Madam President," said Dave Trufello as he saw the team briskly walking down the corridor. "Hopefully this will give us some comfort that you have been spared."

"I need to set up a conference with my vice president, cabinet members, and a few aides in an hour," Santaya said, returning to her focused administrative mode. "Do you have a media room that is secure where I can conference with them?"

"Yes," said Mr. Trufello hesitantly. "However, if you have a high exposure to Novichok, you will be quarantined immediately. Perhaps you need to consider alerting the vice president to the possibility of being sworn in, if need be."

"I understand," said Santaya slowly. She looked at the team, anonymous in their hooded and gowned protective gear. "Let's go," she ordered. "I have work to do."

Chapter 7

Mercedes Singleton

February 2037

Teach me to do your will, for you are my God. May your gracious Spirit lead me forward on a firm footing. ~ Psalm 143:10

With each passing day, Mercedes's impatience multiplied. She had diligently worked to get life choreographed in Whitsville so that her absence would not be felt so strongly when she left to find Olivia's brother. But nothing seemed to go according to plan. She still had not heard a word from Mack or one of the Blues Militia agents.

A bright spot in her life was the status of the hospital and school. There were only three patients in the medical wing, all slowly fading with each passing day. Mercedes was able to relinquish her medical charges to Sue Ann, her aide. The only service they could provide was end-of-life care without the drugs.

Mercedes had tried several times to contact Senator Jeremy Roker, hoping to appeal to his primal nature, as she sought a position in his offices located in the capital. He had mentioned the possibility of his hiring her a year earlier while she was still living with David Kim, the world-famous cosmetic surgeon. Roker made sure his staff was filled with what he called "lookers," and Mercedes fit the bill. She knew she could immediately get rehired at Baltimore National Hospital, but the thought of its chaotic environment depressed her. She had savored the freedom of the last several months in Whitsville of making medical decisions based on common sense and best medical practice, rather than jumping through hoops to appease different ideological groups pressuring for upgraded care based on their position, gender identity, or race. There were such mind-boggling protocols in place to deal with certain individuals that medical care took a second shelf.

As for her father Virgil Singleton, Mercedes had convinced one of the church widows, Eileen Pendleton, to visit him daily while she was working at the hospital. They had established a comfortable comradery, and Eileen was thankful for an enterprise that made her feel useful again. Her husband had owned the hardware store until his death. Since then, she had led a solitary life after her only son was killed in the Middle East conflict.

When Mercedes stopped in at the hospital, Sue Ann shared that the weekly mail had arrived with the last bus passing through.

"I'm still hoping for some useful medications," sighed Mercedes. Her disappointed face showed the fact that contraband meds were now next to impossible to receive from her former suppliers. The penalty for getting caught was just too steep.

However, there was a packet of papers from Senator Roker's office. As she tore open the envelope, a personal letter topped the packet of forms.

My dear Mercedes,

How could I forget you? I always remember a pretty face, but more importantly a strong intellect. I will say that I was surprised that you did not go with Doctor David Kim to his current practice in

California. He is an amazing doctor and is forging new protocols for facial reconstruction. My daughter, who is working with his team, speaks highly of his work. We have been able to send additional government funds for his most recent research project. I imagine you might hear from him occasionally.

You had mentioned in your personal letter and the phone message left at our office that you are seeking employment connected to your medical expertise in skilled care for the elderly.

Today is your lucky day. I have a position that has opened at our Washington D.C. site. My Director of Senior Care has transferred to our Atlanta affiliate and we need an immediate replacement. As you know, this office has been diligently reworking our earlier legislation concerning the Fed Care Elder Care program offered by our government to all qualifying seniors. We have realized that after two years of service, there have been quite a few suggestions to reformulate the program to better assist our consumers. The legislative committees for health care have been quite vocal in making improvements quickly for our stake holders.

Knowing your skills in public relations, I believe I can count on you to make the roll-out of these changes palatable to the public. We need to be realistic in the expectations seniors hold for their medical care. The price tag has just grown to astronomic levels compared to the value received by their fellow citizens.

I have sent your resume to the Secretary of Health and Human Services, explaining to him the unfortunate episode concerning the Central Station Rehabilitation Camp. I clarified how you were exonerated from committing crimes against the government and freed a year ago. Unfortunately, at times there are mistakes made by government agencies.

The position is yours if you so desire. Please look over the requirements of this placement.

Affectionately yours,
Senator Jeremy Roker

Mercedes could imagine the spittle flying from Senator Roker's mouth as he dictated this letter to his executive assistant. Thankfully, he had wholeheartedly accepted the government explanation concerning her time in the Central Station Rehabilitation Camp where she had been sent as a religious subversive. Even the Department of Homeland Security under General Hamilton that had issued her pardon had characterized it as a miscarriage of justice.

She was now aware of the fact that Mack Gersham had been instrumental in getting this pardon generated through the auspices of the Homeland Security division. He must have been given vast powers to facilitate such an order. Mercedes knew that Mack had saved her life by providing an order for early release. She would forever be in his debt for such a miracle. But she was sick knowing that many of her acquaintances at the camp were languishing near death for simply choosing to continue to publicly worship their God.

Senator Roker included hotel information where current government hires were temporarily housed, as well as a suggested start date and salary.

She was breathless at both entries. "Two weeks before the position starts!" she huffed.

Yet a voice in her mind calmed her spirit. *I am calling you, Mercedes, to take up your position in My plan. I need you to submit to this call on your life. I will be with you through every step. I've got this.*

How strange, thought Mercedes. She marveled that God the Spirit was in the talking business yet again. *It can't be any clearer than this,* she mused. *I guess with God all things are possible.*

Mercedes spoke a private prayer, checked out of the hospital, and headed home to talk to her father.

"Dad, I have some news to share with you," she started, as she sat next to him on the couch. "I've been offered a job in Senator Roker's office collaborating with Health and Human Services in D.C. to revamp the Fed Care Elder Care medical program. It's a godsend, right up my alley, but I am concerned about leaving you here alone. Will you consider coming with me to D.C.? I'll be able to care for you, and we can qualify for shared housing. I'm really struggling to decide what to do."

Her father took her hand and gazed into her lovely violet eyes. "Mercedes, I know there's more to the story than what you have shared. Mind if you tell me what is going on? I could tell by your troubled spirit ever since Walt left that you have been missing him and perhaps even Ricardo?"

He smiled slightly at the mention of the two men. In his mind, he was sure that she cared for both.

"Oh, Dad, you know you mean Mack, not Walt. That charade is our secret, but it is a good secret," she said with a slight blush to her cheeks.

Pastor Singleton chuckled. "I'm old and senile, but not that far gone. Most of us knew who he was once he showed up impersonating his brother. I haven't asked any questions because I am sure somehow he is connected to the Blues Militia. Do you know where he went? Is he alive? Is he in D.C.? I do not want you involved in this craziness."

"Pops, I do not want you to know things that can only get you in trouble, so I am not going to answer. I will say that I have been left in the dark too with most of the important details. But there is one crucial piece of information you should be made aware of. The Holy Spirit has convinced me that what I am doing is part of His plan for leading our cause forward. That sounds strange – God intervening in our business- but He seems to want me to do my small part. I think He is concerned about His followers and the intense suffering at the hands of our current government. I can vouch for this in my former time spent at that inhumane rehabilitation camp for Christians."

Virgil thought about her comments.

"Suffering is part of the Christian life. I think it's going to get worse. Maybe I am being a pessimist. So, what do you think you can do to help the Chosen?" he asked with a twinkle in his eye.

It was difficult for the pastor to consider the prospect that his daughter would be called into a dangerous plot to assist the persecuted. "Titus I could see would be called into the fray. Thank God he has been spared so far," he said, speaking of his son, Mercedes's brother. "But you, dear Mercedes. I just don't know if I can manage to keep my mind focused while worrying about your safety. There are too many wicked people out there who care nothing about the innocent people surrounding them. They are like animals, ripping apart and devouring their fellow human beings for a few bucks, or for power or a government position. May God bring them to their deserved end," he shouted.

Mercedes was shocked by her father's wrath. She rarely saw this side of his temperament.

"Dad, we worried about Titus when he was called to assist the Christians attempting to flee China, and God protected him. Even if He hadn't, we all knew that the danger he was called to was the place God desired. It's strange that I now find myself in a similar position. I don't like it, Dad. I'm scared. But I know I need to go. Lives are on the line, especially those of our brothers and sisters in Christ. They need rescuing. Not a day goes by that I don't think of my friends at the Central Station Rehabilitation Camp. Their lives are being sacrificed by the government under false pretenses!"

"But what can you do?" moaned her father.

"I don't know. Be available, I guess. I will have someone watching out for me besides the Holy Spirit."

She winked at her father. Enough said. Virgil knew the future had to be played out. Where God was concerned, he would not be a stumbling block. He took her hand in his and she could feel the steady pulse.

"Your mother would be so proud. I will ask Eileen to come and help me with meals and laundry. In fact, I can learn to do them myself!" He laughed.

Mercedes chuckled. "Please don't, Dad. You're like me. We can't cook a lick. I'm sure she will help. We have so much food in the basement canned by Walt. He was such a gift to us."

Mercedes started to cry. "I must leave in two weeks. Do you think there's time to get everything in order?"

Virgil kissed her cheek and straightened up. "We Singletons are tough people. Stay the course. God will cover us with His mighty arm. We're in good hands. Pray with me. I will ask God to cover you with His protective embrace."

At the end of the prayer, Mercedes felt relief and power. She did feel the presence of the Holy Spirit covering her with His call. She knew that she must trust in Him and hold to His promise from now on. Things would most likely get dicey. She started to make a mental list for packing and then paused. *Holy Spirit, please cover my dad. He is a man of the Spirit too. May you comfort his soul and speak to him your peace each and every day. I need to know you have him in the palm of your hand as well. Amen.*

Chapter 8

Ricardo Medina

February 2037

And I will give you a new heart, and I will put a new spirit in you. I will take out your stony, stubborn heart and give you a tender, responsive heart. And I will put my Spirit in you so that you will follow my decrees and be careful to obey my regulations. ~ Ezekiel 36:26-27

Deep in thought, Ricardo tucked the small orange Testament into the far corner of his top desk drawer. Although he rarely used this desk, it seemed like a safe space to keep this childhood treasure.

When he was in the fourth grade, permission had been granted by his mother to attend Religious Release Hour across the street from his school. Ricardo had objected, wishing to stay back in study hall and goof off with his friends. But his mother insisted on his attendance.

The bright spot of the faith program was an ancient man who told stories of World War II. He shared how his small Bible had saved his life. Each week, Mr. Earl, as they called him, would pull out the tiny Bible with the bullet hole drilled through the pages and pass it around so the children could put their small fingers in the puncture wound.

Then Mr. Earl would have them look at the back pages of their own Testaments to discuss nuggets from God which could help them lead better lives. Ricardo as well as the others focused in on the conversations. Dutifully, when class was over, he took his own Testament home.

Over the years, he carried it from place to place, not because of the gold within, but because Mr. Earl had planted a seed in his heart. When Ricardo left for the Middle East War, he made sure to carry the orange pocket Gideon Testament in his uniform. Now this same book made him remember the words of Mr. Earl, but also of Danny.

Ricardo could not erase his memory of Danny, the young teen who had come to live with him in their rebuilt shed in Whitsville, Virginias. Danny had become the brother he never had, someone to joke with, teach about the finer things of life and to share personal reminiscences on the occasions when his guard was down. Their months together as bunkmates were the happiest in Ricardo's life. For some reason, he felt valued and whole. Danny had fallen under Mercedes Singleton's religious spell, as she taught him to read not only adventure stories, but also the Bible. She had even given Danny the Bible she had been gifted when she was confirmed. Ricardo could forgive him for that. Most men would do anything to interact with the lovely Mercedes. But Danny took it seriously, and he shared his faith with Ricardo many evenings in their bunkhouse.

Ricardo did not like Danny's devout faith and tried to steer him into more secular interests, but Danny stood strong—that is, until he was murdered by the Fed Ops team that targeted him as a Blues Militia member and blew him up during a drone strike while he was out scouring the countryside with his pal, Walt Gersham.

Ricardo was caught up in the memory of seeing Danny's lifeless and mutilated body that autumn day. He had sobbed uncontrollably. In his grief, he had wailed in front of the men from Whitsville who had run to the site of destruction. It was the one time in Ricardo's life that he had not controlled his powerful emotions. Today, he ruminated on the verses he had just read from Romans, "All have sinned and come short of the glory of God." *Got that right,* he smirked thinking of his past actions including the most recent murder of one of his cohorts.

He shook his head at his desk, as though to shake the memory out, and told himself to get back on target.

Ricardo's team was now in overdrive, ferreting out the Pentagon connections to the Blues Militia. General Lu had appointed a one-star general, Austin Green, as the lead for the new team. He was a crusader; get your business done quickly and cleanly. He was a good friend of the secretary of state, Jeremy Cataberrus. They golfed together every chance possible. This also gave him an opportunity to catch up with the internal operations of the executive department during a friendly round.

When Ricardo had returned to Washington D.C., tailing Mack Gersham who was pretending to be his twin brother, Walt, he had gone directly to headquarters in the suburbs. Their office was an ample home, divided into two sectors. One side handled military claims as a bona fide business and provided apartments for traveling officers on business ventures to D.C.

This business provided legitimacy for what was happening in the remainder of the building. Lu's protracted investment in the One Nation Alliance found its headquarters here. Anyone monitoring the traffic would begin to craft a list of Who's Who in skewed allegiances.

Upon his arrival, Ricardo shared his information on Walt Gersham whom he had been tailing, as well as his suspicion of Blues activity in the southern territory around Whitsville. Ricardo surmised Walt would be making contacts in the D.C. area and asked to stay on assignment in an attempt to intercept his activities and thus, his compatriots. His current theory shared with the hierarchy of the Federated

Operations Forces was that Walt was a messenger, a replacement for his brother Mack who had been killed by their forces. He was now a currier from the Blues units to their D.C. headquarters. Ricardo made the request to continue tracking Walt with a GPS device he had planted in the unsuspecting Walt's travel gear. What Ricardo did not share was that something about the Gersham brothers was just not adding up. He hoped his intense scrutiny of Walt's activities would allay his feelings that something was amiss.

Although it was a long shot, the Fed Ops acknowledged that this could be an effective tool in setting the trap for the Blues management team. In addition, Ricardo appeared to have a favored association with General Lu who had granted him a security clearance well above his rank. Lu always had his reasons. Maybe, some thought, Ricardo was being primed to do some of the required "dirty work" as a hit squad member. They had discovered that soldiers returning from the Middle East War were perfect candidates for assassination teams.

Ricardo was given an apartment in the complex for a week and set up a computer tracking system to monitor Walt through the agency's centralized IT location. The first few days were crucial, as Ricardo traced calls from Walt to the Pentagon. He realized Walt was smart. They were not really calls, just signals to the recipient that he was in the area. Most likely he was using secure devices to further the conversation.

These calls abruptly stopped by the end of his first week, so Ricardo began to methodically track the inside mole in the Pentagon through other internet avenues. It was intensive work which Ricardo had mastered in the service.

A week later, Ricardo was assigned lodging in a military housing hotel not far from the White House. This was strategically placed by Lu with the argument that additional forces might be needed should there be any disturbance at the White House or the Capitol campus. It was also just a block from the closeted computer lab where Lu based his secluded revolutionaries.

After a few weeks of air silence, Ricardo picked up some phone chatter near General Hamilton's former residence in the D.C. suburbs. Ricardo was slowly assembling a probable scenario including a cast of characters, yet he purposefully released only part of his intelligence to his reporting officer. This he did for a purpose; the memory of his blood-brother Danny and his underlying desire to destroy Lu.

Events had taken a strange turn. Danny's intervention into Ricardo's life had given him a reason other than himself for living. He had loved that kid. He loved the checkers and chess matches, the jokes and private times. Danny still held a large portion of Ricardo's heart. Ricardo had decided to honor his memory by destroying the man who had taken him away from him, General Sturgis Lu, Ricardo's anonymous birth father. Revenge would be sweet.

As Ricardo had followed Walt back to D.C., he had hatched the plan. Perhaps he could be successful being a double agent, working for Lu's subversive band while infiltrating the Blue's hierarchy and making demands in exchange for information and action. Danny would have liked to know he was working for the Blues.

Ricardo knew he was good at subterfuge. His intake interview when he arrived in D.C. convinced the Fed Ops that he was one of them. He also dropped several hints that he courted Lu's favor, which were confirmed by personnel files. He felt he had bleak odds that he could carry this off, but a small voice within encouraged him to stay the course.

Ricardo realized he had something of substance to live for. Never in his life had he felt grounded in a cause, a relationship or a quest. Here he found himself reveling in the knowledge that he could make a difference for something greater and better than himself.

Ed Derkovich was the lynchpin to Ricardo's success. He was good, better than most computer junkies Ricardo had trained with. He had thrown Ricardo off his trail on several occasions. Ricardo was persistent and just lucky when he decided to track Derkovich's government issued car to the tiny edifice opposite Simon Hamilton's house one evening. Mack was not around, but Derkovich had silently accessed the building and remained inside for several hours. Ricardo then set up a camouflaged computer skimmer near the building to track outgoing messages. In this way, he found a portal into the bowels of Derkovich's dealings with the Blues. And it led to Ricardo's first face-to-face encounter with the master mind of the Blues Militia himself.

It was a brief encounter, but encouraged Ricardo in his mission to be a mole inside the Fed Ops organization. Ed Derkovich revealed that Walt had died in the drone strike in Whitsville, and that Mack had come back to the town weeks later impersonating his twin brother. These were the incidents that had troubled Ricardo and now things made sense. He did not know why the government database listed Walt's DNA sample as Mack's, but figured there would be an explanation from Mack.

Up to this point, Ricardo thought he was a lone wolf running the tracking investigation within the Pentagon, but General Green trusted no one and had put a tail on Ricardo. Ricardo was now aware that not only did he have to continue as though nothing was out of order, but that he had to divert the culprit hired by Green. He knew that some of his operation had been compromised. The question was *how much*.

Returning to the office, Ricardo prepared a memo for his reporting officer, specifying his suspicions that Ed Derkovich was their man. He attached a few incriminating memos Derkovich had sent to superior officers that seemed of a suspicious nature. Then he sent Derkovich a coded message pretending to be Walt, alerting him to the Fed Op surveillance.

Knowing that Lu's team had no patience, Ricardo figured a trap was in process for catching Derkovick and Mack in the next few days. When he discovered the raid was to be carried out the following morning, Ricardo went into overdrive. Being a double agent left him with lots of loose strings to tie up.

First would be to warn Simon Hamilton. Those plans had been developed earlier by Derkovich and had been set into motion.

Keeping Mack from being arrested would be more difficult. He would need a body to substitute for one that would hopefully find an escape route at the last minute. Ricardo closed his eyes. *I need some help here,* he whispered to himself as a variety of ideas ground through his brain.

Settle down, Ricardo, he chided himself. *You can do this.* But how could he delay the 7:00 a.m. raid?

He realized he needed a higher authority to take control. It was impossible to accomplish. Danny's cause was in jeopardy. "Danny's God, if you are listening, I need help now."

Ricardo reprogrammed his agenda and started sending out computer missives in code. He most likely would get reeled in with the trap he had coordinated with the Fed Ops. Playing both sides was deadly. He really did not care that much. All he could hear was Danny's voice.

Chapter 9

President Woodring

February 2037

Peter replied, "Each of you must repent of your sins and turn to God and be baptized in the name of Jesus Christ for the forgiveness of your sins. Then you will receive the gift of the Holy Spirit." ~ Acts 2:38

The tests showed that Santaya had only minimal exposure to the deadly Novichok agent. There was residue on her fingers from picking up DeShaun's cell phone. The fact that she had unexpectedly decided to stay at Andrews Air Force base for the evening had likely saved her life.

But she was livid. "This time I am going to fight back," she whispered. "And if I have to get down and dirty, so be it." She knew the adversarial force she was up against. It would call for providential covering in the next several weeks to keep her sanity. And it was crucial that she form a group who had her trust and who could provide a safe environment. If she kept her steps small enough, perhaps she could organize without being noticed.

"How am I going to set a trap for Lu?" she mused. She opened her private door in the hospital. "Get me Shirley Smythe immediately," she ordered the Secret Service detail.

"She's in the building. We had her stationed down the hall in another waiting room while you were being assessed," the agent answered. He messaged through his voice intercom that Ms. Smythe was to join the president.

When Shirley walked into the room and the president hurriedly closed the door, she had a quizzical look on her face. "Santaya, what is the matter?"

"Shirley, what I tell you needs to stay here. Thankfully we are in a room that most likely is free of surveillance, but just in case, I am going to play some soft music to cover our conversation," she said in a low voice.

"DeShaun has been poisoned with a nerve agent called Novichok. His chances of survival are minimal. They were targeting me. I would have been with him last evening but decided at the last minute to attend the Honors Ceremony at Andrews. I had my reasons."

"Now," continued Santaya, "There is much more to share. I've left you in the dark up to now to spare your safety, but I am desperate for a confidante and I need help. Are you willing to be dragged into this assassination mess? You might be targeted as well."

Shirley reached out her hand and touched Santaya's shoulder. "We have been dear friends for ages. God told me that I would be needed to guide you in His safety through the deep waters. I have pledged to do so as long as you need me. We are in a battle with dark and evil players. I'm all in. Do you have an idea who poisoned DeShaun?"

Through tears of dismay, the president said, "Yes. It is General Lu or someone connected to his delegation attempting to destabilize my administration."

Shirley's face showed no surprise. Her mouth was clenched as her eyes narrowed. "I knew that man was a bad one. Every time I see him, the hair on my arms stands up. He's a devil in disguise."

"Well, we need to watch our step. The first thing we must do is roll out the events that explain DeShaun's poisoning. A media team needs to be assembled and our position is that all signs point to some radical group trying to influence the government or retaliate against the changes we have forced. It's an attention-seeking plot to hold me accountable. It's not fair to blame the innocent, but for now it will have to do."

"Anyway, let's create an inner circle media team that we can trust with our PR. It's time the country starts to follow my lead. I will refocus on compassion and community. A new campaign will start emphasizing our need to unite. Courage is needed in times of crisis. And I need to lead through this crisis by displaying confidence in our government. When the news breaks tonight, I will be the symbol of courage," Santaya said, straightening her back and chuckling.

"OK," followed up Shirley. "I will contact the liaison for the secondary news outlets. And of course, we can count on the government programming to be in our corner."

"Don't be so sure. Have you listened to their criticism of my administration lately and their positive spin on Lu's recent trip to Asia? We need someone new at the helm. Fire the government hacks. Make sure Bob Nelson knows that I am not satisfied, and if he does not have a new lead team by Friday, he's fired too. Feel him out to see where he stands. Better yet, get him in here. We need to have our American citizens behind us, or we're sunk. And I must stay a step ahead of Lu. Now get General Lu on the phone. Tell him what has happened and let me know his reaction."

Fifteen minutes later, Shirley returned with some disturbing news. "General Lu said he already heard about DeShaun. He is arresting suspects culled from his sources. One of them is Ed Derkovich, your friend at the Pentagon. I guess he met with DeShaun early last evening."

"You must be kidding. I was just going to call Ed myself to have him track those tied to the poisoning. Lu is going to squeeze him. Get Lu on the phone."

Shirley handed Santaya her government issued cell phone. "Hello, General Lu. This is President Santaya Woodring, calling from Walter Reed Army Hospital… Yes, I am feeling well. I was barely exposed to the nerve agent… Excuse me. What did you say? … Oh, you've got several suspects already in custody? Why are you taking the lead in this? I am directing the FBI to organize a task force for the purpose of ferreting out the snake who tried to kill my husband. I can't imagine who would wish him dead. He never seemed to have any enemies other than political ones… No, the FBI will take the lead on this. Send what you have on Derkovich to them. I want him in their custody immediately. Do you understand? That's an order. We are sending a car. Where should they retrieve him?"

Santaya put the phone down. "Here's the address for Derkovich. As you can see, I'm playing this event from the vantage point that DeShaun is the target. We'll spin that to the media. Lu thinks I'm plain stupid. He's not happy with the FBI taking the lead role, but it does follow protocol. This will certainly rile him up. Failure for him is not an option. But this scenario will, thank God, give us some breathing room. He'll have to back off while the FBI is poking their noses into everyone's business. We need to accelerate our investigation into his organization. But how can we penetrate it? Maybe Derkovich will have some answers."

The next phone call was to Myrna White-Fergeson, the FBI director. "Hello, Myrna. This is Santaya Woodring. I need you to meet me right now at Walter Reed. Bring Ed Derkovich with you. He can be found at…" Santaya relayed the address provided by Lu.

"Ed's with the Army Intelligence Division at the Pentagon. Lu picked him up as a subject under suspicion because he and DeShaun had a brief meal together yesterday. DeShaun has been poisoned. He is struggling to live. We will be holding a press conference soon and I need you here to answer questions. DeShaun is alive but having trouble breathing caused by a nerve agent, the old methods of Russia. I need you to review his locations and human interactions yesterday to determine the players involved in this gutsy crime and to access the safety of staying at the White House."

Santaya paused as she listened to a few questions from the FBI Director.

"Yes, I need to break here and see if I can visit DeShaun before the broadcast. He's in quarantine, of course. I've contracted only a small amount of the toxic agent. My exposure was minimal. Please keep this under wraps. There's more to the story. See you in half an hour."

As Santaya opened the door of the waiting room again, she directed the Secret Service agent to find the doctor. She wanted to visit DeShaun. Slowly thoughts of Lu and her well-being evaporated. Focusing on her husband, she started to cry. Tears poured out as self-control evaporated. "I must stay strong," she chided herself. But again, the tears came.

She could hear Shirley faintly praying in the background. This time it did not irritate her. In fact, it gave her hope.

Chapter 10

Mercedes Singleton

February 2037

I pray that your hearts will be flooded with light so that you can understand the confident hope he has given to those he called— his holy people who are his rich and glorious inheritance. I also pray that you will understand the incredible greatness of God's power for us who believe him. ~ Ephesians 1:18-19

The mobile internet van pulled up to Mercedes's home in Whitsville and the IT specialist knocked quietly on the door. Gazing around at the manicured lawn, he could not fail to notice that somehow things here were quieter and cleaner. He was pondering their lack of water and electricity when Mercedes answered the door.

"Mercedes Singleton?"

"Yes." She nodded.

"I was sent by Senator Roker to retrieve some paperwork sent to you for employment with his office."

"I was expecting you," she replied. "Please come in."

"I really would rather get this processed quickly in my van. I need to get on the road by one p.m. to arrive in Atlanta by this evening." The driver looked a bit frightened about staying in the Middle Region; he had heard stories that likened these people to vampires or vigilantes. "I have the documents required by the Department of Health and Human Services. Most of the required documents had been forwarded, but there are two additional items."

Mercedes opened the folder passed to her and removed two papers. The first was an official letter verifying her full pardon pertaining to her arrest under the Religious Liberty Act. The pardon stated that the arrest and detention had been the result of a faulty intake system.

Inwardly she chuckled. *The government never takes responsibility for the mistakes it makes. It has no empathy or compassion, but simply is propelled by power.*

The second item was a personal statement requiring her signature, stating that she would not seek reparations due to the wrongful imprisonment indictment. Fat chance, thought Mercedes. *There is no way I could get reimbursed for such a travesty. The government is broke. Anyway, any reimbursement would only mean more money diverted from the current rehabilitation camps, leaving them even more destitute.* Her mind flashed to a scene where she was scrounging on her hands and knees for a few missed carrots in the field before returning to camp, in an attempt to subdue the hunger pains.

Mercedes hurriedly signed the final forms he handed her. Before he took off, he stated briskly, "Your paperwork is complete. Looks like your start date is February twenty-seventh. Your files say you are to pick up your credentials and pass at the Department of Homeland Security on the twentieth. You have been assigned temporary housing by Senator Roker. Do you have the address and keypad access code?"

"Yes, that came in the mail last week." She passed him the signed papers.

"You guys still get mail?"

"It comes once a week to the post office. We have volunteers who sort and deliver. As you know, the government has withdrawn from the Middle Region all goods and services."

The tech just looked at her. He was not interested. "Here is an envelope from the senator himself," he said with a smirk, passing Mercedes a smaller yellow envelope.

Opening the business envelope, a prepaid government credit card peeked out. Mercedes was confused and noticed the handwritten note tucked in next to it.

Mercedes, my office staff must appear professional and tailored. Please use this prepaid card to purchase appropriate business apparel for your position as Manager of Health Care for Elder Care. We are thrilled that you will be part of our team. Please also add formal wear to your purchase for our next outing with the Baltimore and D.C. Arts Council. I expect you to grace me with your company. My wife is currently in care at the Morningside Center for memory loss. She suffers from acute dementia. I look forward to working with you daily.

Sincerely,
Senator Roker

Anger was building in Mercedes's soul as she finished the personal missive which culminated with directions in a postscript directing her to his favorite clothing establishment.

How dare you think that you can hire me as an escort, she angrily thought.

The IT worker ignored the proceedings. "I'll be on my way. Welcome back to the free world."

Less than half an hour after he arrived, the scruffy technician was on his way down the crumbling highway. He left worried that his electric van would lose charge long before he reached civilization again.

Mercedes stared at the credit card. She heard a voice intruding in her thoughts.

I have this situation under control. Trust me. Roker is harmless.

Her hands unclenched and she dropped the card into the envelope.

So, you got this, Holy Spirit? You didn't have it so well when the warden was raping me in the rehabilitation camp. She paused. *I'm sorry. You rescued me there. I know what I am getting into here. I have chosen this path. Please protect me from this pawing monster. I'm still fragile. I don't think I can act my way out of it.*

Trust me, came the voice emphatically.

Turning, Mercedes walked hesitantly into the house. There were only two weeks to get her father situated. She could do it.

The weeks flew by. Before she knew it, the bus was pulling into Whitsville, panting its way up the hill. Mercedes was misty eyed. After one last blown kiss to her father, she settled into the hard plastic seat and considered what was in store for her in the future.

Although she had not heard from Mack, she knew the Blues were still counting on her to complete her part of the mission. She was just a piece in the larger puzzle. At some time, she would rendezvous with Mack. She faithfully held this hope, although she had little to show for it. In the past week, a cryptic note had arrived stating that lengthy preparations had postponed further operations. She knew it was from him.

Using her new employment with Senator Roker's office as a cover was a blessing. It would give her the opportunity to get to Baltimore to contact Olivia's brother, Arun. She had made that promise not only to Mack, but to Oliva herself before she was murdered by the warden at Central Station Rehabilitation Camp. Mercedes knew that was one promise she would never forfeit.

As for her new position, she held hope that her skills could be helpful in recrafting the ElderCare bill which had been sent back to committee for further revisions. The senior population, quickly becoming a minority, had seen their benefits shrink with each passing decade. The current economic crisis had not helped in providing the necessary assistance. The bill had been crafted to marginalize the care of seniors by incrementally decreasing benefits with each additional year of life. It was reasoned that everyone had to do their part to sacrifice for the system to survive. Certainly, seniors should be leading the charge.

Mercedes, however, was troubled as she read through the voluminous bill while still in Whitsville. Some of the details in small print would bankrupt thousands of elderly who had meticulously gathered their savings for a dignified retirement. This money would now go to the government, rather than their living expenses. When their savings were gone, the government would step in with end-of-life care.

Spirit, chanted Mercedes, *this is a travesty. It is troubling that the country I love has come to the place where it considers the elderly as excess baggage. How have we gotten to this place? Why don't we treasure their lives as a life well lived? They have value, even if the young see them as a burden. Help us to set our minds in tandem with yours.*

She heard no reply. Her stomach rumbled with concern. There was trouble ahead. She could feel it.

The president had just issued an executive order to curb government spending by ten percent for each government division. The Treasury was approaching a default on its debt and could not pay the monthly stipend to its creditors, the largest being China. The United States of America was teetering on bankruptcy through overspending, an insane fixation with climate control and a loss of economic activity due to the Drakee virus and the military conflicts of the last twenty years. The retraction in spending would affect all areas of government except defense spending. Mercedes could not figure that part out. *Who carried enough power to make sure the military-industrial complex was left unscathed?* She had no idea.

Chapter 11

Mack Gersham

February 2037

I pray that God, the source of hope, will fill you completely with joy and peace because you trust in him. Then you will overflow with confident hope through the power of the Holy Spirit. ~ Romans 15:13

Mack sat in Ricardo's townhouse with trepidation. His mind had run a hundred scenarios during the day trying to zero in on what was the truth concerning Ricardo, but he could not settle on a final reasoned assumption.

He had no idea how Ricardo and the Federal Ops had infiltrated the system developed by Ed Derkovich. Ed was immaculate in his well-crafted plans and covering his tracks, like a chess master always calculating the next move. Mack couldn't bring himself to believe Ricardo was pro-Blues Militia. The best he could figure was that Ricardo had turned mercenary and was playing one side against the other for monetary gain. That would suit him.

Then again, perhaps he was looking for a connection to Mercedes. He certainly could be interested. Most likely, Walt and the local militia had kept him at bay in Whitsville. She must have known he was not trustworthy. Right?

Ricardo knocked quietly on the door and waited for Mack to open up. Upon entering, he briskly turned and slid the deadbolt shut.

"What have you been doing today?" he quizzed. "Keep your gun in your pants. I'm glad it's loaded. We might need to shoot our way out of here." He smiled with a touch of bravado.

Ricardo gazed down the street to see if anything seemed out of place. All appeared ordinary.

The two men stared at each other for a moment. Then Ricardo continued, "It took me all day to clean up the mess at your private hideaway. The general was high as a kite, knowing we had hit a command center for the Blues. He was strutting about and acting like this was his victory, the pompous ass."

After a moment, Ricardo added, "Where are your hard drives?"

"I'd rather keep them in a safe place for now," Mack retorted. "I'm not sure if this is enemy territory. You don't impress me as someone helpful to the Blues, especially when you had the gall to dig up my body in Whitsville."

"Oh, that," shared Ricardo. "I needed information. Glad to know you aren't dead anyway. Ed had to clear up my questions about you and Walt. Somehow your varied identities never quite squared with my suspicions. Was that dead man buried in the tarp your brother Walt? Was he a Blues Militia?"

"No, he never could have managed the Blues code. He was too friendly and too faithful not to let something slip. Much less all the physical limitations he had. But he was my hero."

Ricardo showed no sympathy. "He drove me to distraction. He always seemed to be paying attention to what was transpiring, even when I was convinced he didn't have the brain power. And he never let Mercedes out of his sight around the house. He kept close tabs on me through quizzing Danny. I hated the fact that Danny liked him as much as he liked me."

Ricardo stopped talking. He had not said Danny's name out loud in months. He had thought about him every day. But the exhaustion of the last few days had dropped his guard enough to utter the name of his "kid brother."

Mack immediately recognized his weakness.

"Danny was a good kid. Stinkin' Fed Ops. Guess that might go for you too."

In silence, Ricardo flopped on the couch. A cloud of unruly dust took flight in the slivers of evening light coming through the tattered blinds.

"Nice digs, Ricardo," muttered Mack. "You bring your girlfriends here often?"

Ricardo ignored him. He had taken time in the hectic day to figure out what to do with Mack. Knowing Ed Derkovich was in lockdown at Lu's office didn't help the situation. At least, he thought Ed was still there. No one had heard about him in days. As the mastermind, they were sunk if he cracked. The military had ways of making people talk.

"Your face job is good. I wouldn't have recognized you this morning except for the bandage and your eyes. Simon Hamilton is a master surgeon. He's retrofitted several spies to assume new identities. Those are the ones I know about from Ed himself."

"Somehow, I do not think Ed Derkovich is the kind of patriot who would deal with a black-hearted bastard like yourself. But thanks for the compliment. Do I look like a Hollywood star? I wish I still had my scar as a reminder of you killer Special Ops forces. Did you alert them to Danny and Walt's trek into the mountains?"

Mack chuckled angrily. He had no chips to offer. Ricardo was calling the shots. And he hated it.

"I had nothing to do with that strike. Do you think I would put Danny in danger? I hate the Ops myself for killing the kid. He was the only person I have ever liked. Anyway, back to business. The general is going to find out soon enough that the computer hard drives were removed before the explosion. We'll be lucky if it takes more than a few days to positively identify the DNA of the guy I dumped there. Right now they assume it is someone high up in the logistics of the Blues communication hierarchy. You would have been a good guess if I had not thrown them off your trail by reporting that you were six feet under in Whitsville.

"By the way, how did you manage to get Walt's blood sample submitted as yours when you enlisted? That really worked in your favor. Right now, the Special Ops have no idea you are alive. With that new face, you have officially disappeared."

Without waiting for an answer about the blood sample, Ricardo continued, "We must get you out of here tonight. Turn off the light. No one has been here for years. We might get one of the neighbors suspicious and start snooping around. Wish we had more time to get your alias finalized. Without Ed managing the operation, no telling how we can get your information loaded into the system."

"Just what are you talking about?" asked Mack. "I thought my face was transformed to keep my identity a secret. Are you saying I'm intentionally reconfigured to be someone else?"

"According to Ed, that's the plan. He's got you reappearing as Troy Griffins, one of our undercover agents assigned to the Russian unit at the American Embassy decades ago. Although he was officially part of their staff, there were only a handful of times he was in the embassy itself. When he was there, it was to pass on information to the ambassador.

"Griffins got caught in his own spy games a few years ago and got dropped from American Intelligence in an official capacity. Derkovich is pretty sure that he bit the dust. It would be uncomfortable to have both of you around. Anyway, Derkovich was hacking the system to get you reactivated as an operative assigned to D.C. He's filled in your resume with attention to detail. You're going to have to get to know yourself real fast. The only thing I don't know is whether he finished with your file before Lu trapped him." Conveniently, Ricardo did not mention that he himself had incriminated Derkovick. It was his hope that Ed, being a genius at espionage, would find a way to untangle himself from the accusation.

Mack sat transfixed, mesmerized by the prolonged tale of his new identity. He realized that an operative for the Blues was much more nuanced and secretive than he had previously known.

"Maybe I'm missing something, but how do I know that you are not crafting this whole secret agent tale to entice me to confide in you? After all, Ricardo, your history with me while I was impersonating Walt was as a spy for Lu's Special Ops. How did you get an upgrade in Lu's organization while infiltrating ours? Something is not sitting right."

Ricardo stared at Mack with a twisted smile. "It's about Danny," he said expressively. "I couldn't drop his memory. Something about him kept pressing into my brain every day. I think it was his goodness, his pure spirit. I still hear him at night, talking to God and asking me questions. I can't get rid of him. He would have done what was right in this world, no matter the cost, so I decided to make him proud."

He continued, "When I finally cracked your few cryptic coded messages to Derkovich, I knew I had my foot in the door. Thanks, by the way for the Whitsville connection to the passwords. Made it a lot easier for me."

Mack looked crestfallen. "I don't measure up as an undercover spy. I need to pay more attention to details. I thought you were a chump who knew nothing about internet espionage. Why the heck did the Special Ops send you to remote Whitsville?"

"A sick joke by my father to get me a job and get me out of the way. He knows nothing about me. Wouldn't claim me anyway, even if he was pushed into a corner."

"And your father is…?"

"We'll save that for later. But it came in handy in getting me a hefty promotion in the Ops when I returned from Whitsville. Guess he realized I have a nose like his for smelling out a rat. Sooner or later, he will realize that I am the rat."

"Hey, it's dark," mumbled Ricardo. We got to get going. Say your prayers. I'm going to try to hide you right under their noses until Derkovich gives you the thumbs up…if he can."

"Yeah, Ed. How did you end up in his good graces so quickly?"

"It's amazing what that guy knows. He knows more about you and me than we do. And he's in deep trouble."

"How can we spring him from Lu's clutches?" asked Mack.

"No idea. It will take a miracle. They pulled him in for questioning after he was with the president's husband right before the poisoning incident. Unfortunately, I fingered him as a suspect, thinking his record would be squeaky clean and they would let him off. Doesn't look that way now. I messed this one up royally." Ricardo went into the kitchen for a drink of water.

Mack thought back through the events of the day. He was nudged into an awareness that Ed needed the help of a higher power. "God, Ed Derkovich needs protection from General Lu and his team. Do what you can to keep him protected and safe," he prayed in a whisper.

Now, Mack's mind had raced through some scenarios for God's intervention. Then he checked his ramblings. *For God's sake, he's God!* Mack chided himself.

An unusual peace settled over Mack. Somehow, he knew that God the Spirit was behind the scenes, finding a way.

Ricardo walked silently back into the living room. "I've thought about the plans Derkovick gave me. His capture has thrown a monkey wrench in your move tonight. Best you stay here. I will even give you the couch," he said with a twisted grin.

Chapter 12

Mercedes Singleton

February 2037

But the Holy Spirit produces this kind of fruit in our lives: love, joy, peace, patience, kindness, goodness, faithfulness, gentleness, and self-control. There is no law against these things! ~ Galatians 5:22-23

It was late afternoon when the Zorro driver dropped Mercedes off at the Commodore Hotel in Washington D.C. He was a government contractor, so there was no fee, but he was a bit miffed when she offered no tip.

"I'm sorry," said Mercedes. "I'm short on cash. Give me your Zorro number and I'll forward a tip to your account."

"Don't bother," he said hurriedly and drove away. He could tell she was a defector from the Middle Region. There was something about those people that spoke of self-assuredness and peace. He did not like it. Everyone knew the world was falling apart. Just this week, China had taken a battalion of tanks into neighboring "friendly" Pakistan for joint exercises, their eyes and threatening words targeting India. He would not want to get involved in that war.

Stopping at the front desk, Mercedes registered for her temporary apartment. They were expecting her and handed her a government issued microcomputer pad loaded with pertinent information on neighboring eating establishments, help numbers, and hotel regulations.

The elevator ride up was quick, and she trudged down the hall to her apartment, pressing in her passcode as she pushed the door open. Inside, the furnishings were luxurious. She was taken aback by the attention to detail and the décor. While modern, it still had the hint of warmth. She threw herself on the bed in exhaustion and fell into temporary slumber, awakening a few minutes later with a jerk.

"Good grief! I'm bushed," she chattered aloud to herself. "Thank you, Jesus, for getting me here safely."

Plodding to the desk, she pulled out some stationery and wrote her father a quick note, letting him know she had arrived safely. *This will be the best way to keep in touch with him, and I know he'll be reading and re-reading every word, so I've got to be careful what I share.*

While placing her few clothes in the closet, the hotel clerk rang the room.

"Hello," answered Mercedes.

Her heart dropped when she recognized the voice on the other end. "Hello, Mercedes. I heard from the Commodore staff that you are comfortable in your new surroundings. We are so anxious to see you at my Congressional office tomorrow," said a boisterous Senator Roker. "I am sure you will grace us with your lovely presence as well as your passion for our ElderCare revisions that are pending. Did you get the credit card I sent your way?"

"Oh yes, Senator. Thank you, but there is no need. I can pick up a few professional clothes over the weekend," she said softly.

"Nonsense," he sniffed. "I have an appointment set up for you at Shantelles for ten a.m. Saturday. They know what I am thinking. They are one of the few professional clothiers left. You'll be glad to know they carry a fully stocked line of necessities. Many of their clothes have unfortunately been sold to them from former wealthy clients who have had to hock their wardrobes to stay afloat. Guess those fat cats learned the hard way that equity is not just for the masses. We are in this together. Anyway, you are the beneficiary! And don't forget to pick out a few formal-wear dresses. The Arts Society has a gala event in two weeks, and I want you to be my escort."

"About that invitation…" Mercedes stammered.

"Now, Mercedes, no hesitation please. It was hard enough for me to pull strings and slip you onto my staff as a project manager. As you know, the government stipulations for hiring have practically been frozen with the president's executive order for cuts. I got you in by fudging on the hiring date! You're welcome."

Mercedes paused. "That's fine. I'm just not sure what kind of company I will be for you. I have been away for a long time. I really am not up to speed on many of the events happening in the world."

"That smile of yours and the way you move in your evening wear stills my heart. You truly are an exceptional woman. That will be sufficient for now. You have the skills to make yourself shine. Pay attention to what the attendees think is important. That will give you the key to what you must research by our next outing. See you tomorrow at nine a.m. at the office. Pick up your credentials at eight at the Homeland Security Office. I think these things are covered on your micro pad. You can call me this evening if you have any questions. My cell number is with the recorded welcome I left for you."

The senator hung up.

He won't take no for an answer, sighed Mercedes. She knew fostering a relationship with the senator would be a key part of her contribution to the Blues cause. She was sure that somehow, she would be able to use her position and influence to help their mission, Mack

Gersham, and the persecuted Christians still incarcerated in rehabilitation camps. She was sent here by the Holy Spirit to use her gifts for the cause. "Oh Spirit," she prayed, "lead me in your path for righteousness's sake. Amen."

Chapter 13

Santaya Woodring

March 2037

Humans can reproduce only human life, but the Holy Spirit gives birth to spiritual life. So don't be surprised when I say, "You must be born again." The wind blows wherever it wants. ~ John 3:6-8

The president slipped out of her presidential limosine in the parking garage at Walter Reed and felt the frosty surge of wind slicing through her coat.

Will it ever warm up? she questioned herself. March always seemed to be miserable. Next to her, Shirley Smythe, her assistant and constant companion since DeShaun's poisoning, climbed out the opposite side.

Smythe had spearheaded the media coverage roll-out concerning DeShaun's poisoning. She put a damper on the theory that the poisoning had been targeting the president, yet allowed some conjecture that the president did indeed have enemies both locally and abroad. The news reports struck a healthy balance, allowing President Woodring to continue her executive duties in the White House, while stepping up security. The biggest benefit was the opportunity to place Santaya before the public eye as a sympathetic yet strong figure. She would not be dissuaded from her duties. She assured the public that answers would be forthcoming as the perpetrators were identified. The FBI was intensifying its search for the source of her husband's poisoning.

DeShaun Davis was a miracle. While he had been exposed to a potent dose of the Novichok agent, somehow, he was still alive. The exposure had occurred in his private vehicle. For two weeks he had been placed in an induced coma and his breathing enhanced with a ventilator. The nerve agent had stymied the muscles necessary for breathing.

Each morning the president and Ms. Smythe visited DeShaun at Walter Reed. Although he could not respond, Santaya would spend an hour holding his hand and talking to him about current events, even whispering in his ear tender thoughts and words of hope.

Today, Shirley Smythe stepped in and asked if she could pray for DeShaun. "Santaya, you know I hold a deep faith in my Lord Jesus Christ. He is in the miracle-working business. I have been lifting DeShaun into His presence daily, praying for recovery, strength, and protection. Please do not consider this an intrusion, but I believe in my heart of hearts that DeShaun can be miraculously healed by Jesus. I would like to pray in the Spirit and anoint him with oil, if I have your permission."

Santaya was a bit surprised at the request. "I don't exactly know what you mean, Shirley, but I know your intentions are focused on DeShaun regaining consciousness and health. What can you do that has not already been tried by the medical staff here at Walter Reed?"

"The Great Physician can still help DeShaun," she said quietly. "The Holy Spirit lifts our prayers to Jesus and He answers."

"I trust you," Santaya said, laying a hand on Shirley's petite shoulder. "Do you mind if I listen?"

"Please do."

Shirley poured a small tad of fragrant frankincense oil into the palm of her hand. Its aroma filled the room instantly with life and hope. Then she traced the oil into a cross on DeShaun's forehead and chanted, "In the name of the Father, and the Son, and the Holy Spirit."

Kneeling next to the bed, Shirley took DeShaun's limp hand in hers. She spoke quiet, tender words of life over him. Santaya was mesmerized. She had never heard a prayer like this: intimate, like two friends sharing a confidence, asking questions, speaking an unknown language. Yet Shirley seemed comfortable and content.

When she stood up, she shared, "Jesus knows what he needs. I trust Him. I hope someday you do too. He has DeShaun in His sights. I know because the Holy Spirit spoke words of healing while I prayed."

Shirley blinked back tears.

Santaya did not know what to say. She simply nodded. It made little sense to her.

"We must get back to the White House. Unfortunately, I have meetings all day," the president sighed.

The Secret Service detail called for the limousine and the ladies climbed in. Before they proceeded out of the garage, she tapped the agent on the back.

"Do you think I could walk a few blocks? I need to clear my head."

Although uncomfortable with the idea, he said, "Fine." He relayed the request to the driver to meet them several blocks up the street. The chill winter weather would keep most pedestrians off the streets.

"See you in a few minutes," she called to Shirley as she slammed the door.

While walking the next two blocks, Santaya felt a lightening of her spirit. The doom that had entrapped her mind was beginning to lift. She was musing over the prayer Shirley had shared. It was touching and comforting and personal. She loved that lady and her devotion to God. *Could He possibly be real?* she pondered. Gazing to the buildings on her right, Santaya was surprised to see the church building she had been married in years ago. The memories of the day flooded her mind and produced an internal ache for her beloved DeShaun.

Immediately, a tremendous blast was heard within the next block, followed by a plume of light gray smoke. Her Secret Service agent grabbed her arm and rushed her into the nearest building, calling for assistance.

"What was that?" asked President Woodring.

"From what headquarters is relaying, it's a car bomb, just down the street where we were to catch our limo."

"Oh God, Shirley!" she screamed.

In moments, a less recognizable government automobile pulled up behind the building Santaya had taken refuge in. She was whisked back to 1400 Pennsylvania Avenue before anyone noticed.

"It can't be, it can't be," she moaned.

Her phone rang. "Santaya, it's me, Shirley. What happened?"

"Oh God. I can't believe it is you. Our presidential limo just exploded from what they suppose is a car bomb. I thought you were dead!"

"Well, right after you got out, I decided to talk to the Holy Spirit a bit more, so I asked the driver to let me out too. I guess you didn't notice. I was walking back toward the White House when I heard the blast. Somehow, I knew what it was. Oh Santaya, we have been saved by the Holy Spirit. It is a miracle. Praise God. Thank you, Jesus."

President Woodring was shaken. "Come to my office immediately. I am cancelling all meetings. It is time to take this assassination attempt public, and I need to surround myself with a security team above reproach. Lu wanted a war. Well, he shall have one!" she said emphatically.

Chapter 14

Ricardo Medina

February-March 2037

I can never escape from your Spirit! I can never get away from your presence! If I go up to heaven, you are there; if I go down to the grave, you are there. ~ Psalm 139:7-8

After the urgent conversation with Mack, Ricardo changed his mind and decided to leave Mack in the dilapidated brownstone. If someone had suspicions about Ricardo, this was a better option for Mack. There was no official connection between Ricardo and the ownership of the apartment, and Mack would appear to anyone who saw him as a curiosity since he was in a state of healing from surgery. The staples had not been removed from his nose. "I think a week or two at this place will do," murmured Ricardo. "Just keep the lights out."

"A five-star hotel," said Mack sarcastically.

"I inherited the place from my mother after she died. I hate it. It is full of memories of my mother and father together." He waited a moment. "But the more I thought about it, it was a roof over my head if I ever came back from the war alive. I knew society would be in a shambles by then.

"While I was in the Middle East," Ricardo continued, "a land conglomerate made a bid for my property, saying I was an absentee landlord. I was up to date on my taxes. They were looking for a loophole to confiscate the whole block. They really pissed me off. Their goal was to raze the block and build government housing for the never-ending swarm of immigrants and people from the Middle Region.

"I had learned some tricks of the trade while an IT specialist in the mechanical division of the Army. There was a secret operation that I was privy to, hacking into websites at the behest of my superiors. My training was stellar. Most of our success in the war was due to our ability to effectively track the movements and communications of the warlords and their militias. We kept a step ahead of them. Usually, they found us waiting for them.

"Well, anyway, I used these hacking skills to break into the files of Partnership Properties, the pricks trying to steal my townhouse. I exposed their plans to the public and did enough to tarnish their reputation that the project was pulled.

"I figured I had better update the ownership of the property as well, so I transferred it to a nonprofit which cannot be tracked to me. The transfer is only a piece of paper. The nonprofit has no idea the house is theirs. Now I have a hiding place for our favorite men in blue." Ricardo smiled.

Mack was surprised by the story and the lengths Ricardo had gone to in preserving anonymity for the property. It was almost as if he could portend the future and know that he would need a safe haven.

Of greater surprise to Mack was Ricardo's light-spirited explanation. He had always been so morose.

In the next two weeks, Ricardo snuck in twice with food, medical supplies, and a computer packed with files containing the homework

Mack would need to master. Ed Derkovick had materialized, thanks to the miraculous rescue by the president herself, seeking out information on her husband's poisoning.

"Mack, your alias is finalized," whispered Ricardo, on the second visit to the darkened apartment illuminated only by the faded LED streetlamp. "Have you been studying the files Ed send on Troy Griffins?"

"You think this is going to fly?" questioned Mack. "Griffins seems like an unsavory character. Just the type to get into government espionage, I guess. How are you going to handle my sudden reappearance as Troy?"

"Derkovich thinks there's an eighty percent chance he committed suicide. His family was snuffed out by a One Nation Alliance hit squad. They got his parents and his siblings. No mercy. His last missive said, 'I'm finished.' The official report says he is likely a victim of the KGB. Either one will prove false when you appear again."

"How much are you learning about yourself from the files? You have got to be sure of every minute piece of information on his life. We are working to get you on an inside detail."

"What do you mean by inside?' asked Mack with curiosity.

"Don't think you're special. We need more intelligence at the White House. You have some background in that area. You'll be assigned to the president's staff. Derkovich has made sure of that. He has not left the White House grounds since Lu tried to shake him down for information. He's the new ghost in the West Wing." Ricardo laughed. "Derkovich would scare me. That guy is one strange dude. Anyway, you start in a week."

Mack struggled with the position Ricardo held as a confidante to Ed Derkovich. He had engrained himself into the Blues Militia inner circle, and Mack thought that it was a dubious move by the leadership. He surmised they had to take a chance. He wondered if he could trust him with the same degree of support? Mack could not forget the murders of Walt and Danny at the hands of Ricardo's Special Ops units.

"I gotta go," said Ricardo. "Lots happening at Lu's headquarters. They are trying to ferret out the mole involved in the failed assassination attempt on President Woodring. You heard about the car bomb in her limo?"

"Yeah, picked up the details on the laptop. The sirens around here did not stop."

"Well, she's lucky," shared Ricardo. "After leaving from a visit with her hubby at Walter Reed, she decided to take a walk through downtown, passing by chance, the church she was married in several years ago. Way too repetitive in her daily routine with the hospital visits. Anyway, her bodyguard is Devon Irwin, one of your guys. He let us know the coast was clear once they were out of the car. They had information that the bomb was planted by the driver, who worked for Lu. Lu has become quite impatient with the failure of the Novichok agent, so he decided to accelerate the demise of President Woodring."

Ricardo continued, "Ed came to the rescue again. He had intercepted a transmission from the limo driver which was suspicious. One of the recipients was Lu himself. The plan was to blow up the limo in the White House garage as they pulled in the underground parking station. We were able to duplicate the code for the transmitter used to ignite the car bomb once the president was out, and poof, blasted to smithereens!"

"It was a stroke of luck that Woodring's assistant also exited the car. We couldn't take a chance to make the situation look suspicious. At this point, Lu thinks that the driver just messed up. He's angrier than I have ever seen him. He was going ballistic this afternoon screaming for information."

"Get studying and keep quiet," Ricardo said softly as he let himself out. He'd added a rubber plate to the door latch to muffle the sound.

For a week, Mack memorized, practiced silent calisthenics, and prayed. Every morning he righted his thoughts by staring at the ceiling and thinking of God. "Lord Jesus, I'm in. You know that. I'm in way over my head. Lead me. Let me trust that you've got my back. Give me a clear mind. Have me do what you want me to do. Amen."

It was the early hours of the morning when he was most aware of what lay ahead. A peace settled in. He would call it assurance. It was timely and comforting. It was God.

Chapter 15

Mercedes Singleton

March 2037

And the Holy Spirit helps us in our weakness. For example, we don't know what God wants us to pray for. But the Holy Spirit prays for us with groanings that cannot be expressed in words. ~ Romans 8:26

Procrastinating for as long as she could, Mercedes slipped on the lavender gown, compliments of Senator Roker. He would be arriving by government transport in less than half an hour. A voice inside her head kept asking irritating questions starting with "what if?"

Get control of yourself, Mercedes, she chided the reflection in the mirror. *You've stepped into this with your eyes wide open. You asked for the Lord's protection. He is counting on you to do your part. Show a bit of bravery.*

She twirled two strands of auburn hair and fastened them with a handsome silver clip. *I wonder who had to hawk this to put a warm coat on their kid's back.* She felt some guilt in its glitter.

Briefly she thought about the nouveau riche class of the current decade. They were techy government props who adhered to a totally secular mantra. They came to power with an ideology that trumped reality. Theirs was a world of therapeutic order; everyone must be comfortable with the affirmation of their self-conceived identity. The secular line was to conform to whatever was in vogue.

She would have to watch herself and her cynicism at tonight's charity fundraiser. Practically everyone there would think they were intellectually stimulating and convinced of their "rightness" in the world. *Amazing how pride wears such a disguise,* she sighed.

Her doorbell rang from below. It would be the chauffeur and the senator. Mercedes ran her lipstick over her lips once more, trying to put a protective glaze on herself. Then she forced a smile, grabbed her coat, and walked to the elevator.

Senator Roker had been easier to adjust to in their daily status meetings than she had imagined. He was fluent in the language of government small talk, but he also knew that it was necessary for him to have something to show for his efforts, particularly legislation passed. Older representatives were passé.

The young voters of America were always pushing for change. Their frustration with the speed of completion from start to finish was almost nonexistent. They were his bread-and-butter voters if he kept the change coming. So, he had.

Mercedes stepped into the car through the passenger door opened by the senator for her from the interior. Sliding into the seat, she acknowledged the senator. "Thank you, Senator, for the invite. I am truly looking forward to listening to the vice president tonight updating us on future funding for the arts."

Senator Roker grabbed her arm and pulled her closer. She didn't like the feeling but did not protest. "Listen," he whispered. "You will get lots of stares and comments this evening, being my new escort. But the news on the street is that I am a harmless and impotent old buffoon. Admittedly, I am. I am not a threat to you, but I enjoy the playacting, if you catch my drift. Are you up for the challenge of making it appear that I am a man in his prime, just for the crowd?"

Catching her breath, Mercedes feigned shock. She already knew from her co-workers that sexually, Roker was harmless.

"Why, Senator Roker. You are quite the creative companion." She was going to add another description but decided that leading him on might take her into some other dangerous territory. His hand was groping for her breasts, but she calmly took it and placed it in his lap. "You still have some friskiness, it seems," she said with a contrived grin, "but that will have to wait for another day. I do not want to get all mussed up before we arrive. What would your friends think?"

Roker laughed out loud. "You're quite intelligent, Miss Mercedes. It is a delight to be with you. Here's to the future." He lifted a small champagne glass while handing her one to complement it. They clinked the sides and smiled.

Two can play this game, thought Mercedes. Inside, she was running through a list of conversational starters that might lead to tidbits of information on the Blues, the president, the One Nation Alliance or General Lu. Tonight the room would be filled with political operatives and other favorites of the ruling class. Lips would be loosened, and no one would consider that someone of a different political persuasion would be present.

Walking into the convention center, the senator grabbed her hand. His sweaty palm repulsed her. He loved the spotlight shining on him. The massive revision of the ElderCare bill was swiftly gaining traction. He had already begun a huge PR campaign to paint this legislation as innovative, fair, and progressive.

His young staff had revised the payment structures. What looked like a favorable outcome for seniors was a trap in disguise. This plan would take more of their savings and stymy their voice. Generation

XY looked at the seniors as expendable; the quicker they departed the better.

Mercedes had found her role as manager quite difficult. She worked tirelessly to temper the proposed changes. Most distasteful was the championing of euthanasia, followed by financial reimbursement to designated loved ones of the dispatched. Her staff reasoned that if someone wanted to terminate their life, then let them do it. Society would be the victor and the recipients of the death stipend certainly would not complain.

The dinner plates from the lavish meal were collected by the youth who were supportive of Senator Roker. Then Vice President Bryce Howman rose to an introduction and standing ovation. He was truly one of them. While quiet and unassuming, he was a schemer and had used his contacts to put him in the running for the job when Santaya Woodring's original vice president had met his untimely death in an auto accident. He called himself "the second-in-chief," and he played his cards well.

The vice president spoke for fifteen minutes but somehow mesmerized the crowd with his words, crafting the story that the arts would provide equity for a sorely divided society. He shared how the arts were a healthy equalizer, using examples of low-income schools where students excelled because of the art venues in their curriculum. He failed to mention that their other scores in reading and math showed little improvement.

She had seen some of the art displayed by these students in the vestibule. One yelled out "Pussy Pride"; another "Blood for Votes." All Mercedes could wonder was, where would students with these "gifts" end up in their society? *Probably in a government program teaching other children,* she surmised. But they were solid votes for the cause.

After the speech, Mercedes and the senator wandered through the crowd. He steered her toward the vice president who was having an animated conversation with a well-coiffed gentleman when they arrived. Immediately there was silence as they were aware of the senator but particularly his guest.

"Good evening, Vice President Howman," spoke the senator, watching carefully for their reaction to his presence. Mercedes realized immediately that for some reason the vice president was the dominant person in their circle.

"Nice to see you here again, Al," shared the VP. "I hear your wife is quite ill."

"Yes," the senator replied. "She has been moved to palliative care. A long journey to nowhere I'm afraid. But enough of my cares. This is Mercedes Singleton, now my staff manager handling the revision work for the ElderCare bill. She's an old friend."

The handsome stranger in the group turned to look at her.

"I am Timothy Prescott," he said as he made a modest bow.

She knew the name. Everyone did. He was everywhere in the news. The media darling of the government-sanctioned "church." He became a household name in the past decade as he took to the airwaves with his charismatic message and pleas for hope. Despite many faith leaders facing discrimination and silencing concerning public faith standards of conduct, Prescott was the exception. He was like a fire that burned naturally. The moths that fluttered around him felt that he spoke truth and light. He filled the void of tens of thousands of parishioners who watched his weekly broadcasts or his podcasts. And he never asked for money.

Mercedes had avoided his presence after hearing a few messages. While she had listened, the Holy Spirit had been screaming in her mind, *Don't listen to him. He is telling lies. He belongs to the father of lies.* And she could decipher for some reason the very untruths he was sharing with his adoring audience. Their eyes were only a blank reflection of the darkness he was spewing. It was frightening.

Softly, he laid his hand on her arm in a charming sense of acceptance.

"So nice to meet you." He grinned benignly. "I am thankful you are part of the team that is caring for our senior citizens. They richly deserve the love and appreciation of our people."

When Timothy Prescott touched Mercedes's arm, it was all she could do to stay upright. A force stronger than any she had felt before was coursing through her body. The hair on her arms stood up at attention. Her breath became labored and shallow. The electric jolt that she felt was accompanied by a quick series of mental gyrations trying to figure out what exactly was happening. Then the Truth spoke.

He is from Satan. He is filled with deception and destruction. He drinks from the cup of evil and leads his band to the path of perdition.

"It is so nice to meet you as well," murmured Mercedes, her face now deathly pale. "If you will excuse me," she said, fluttering around in confusion. "I will rejoin you in a moment."

She quickly slid across the polished floor to the ladies' restroom. By the time she arrived, she was breaking out in a sweat. And she felt slimy and sick to her stomach.

What just happened? Mercedes begged for an answer.

"He is part of the enemy force," said the Spirit. "He stalks the church to destroy her from the inside. He is devious and dangerous. Be careful. He knows you do not belong to his company, but he will try to convert you."

Mercedes was confused. *How can such a devious, dangerous man lead the church, Lord? He has the largest Christian faith following in the world!*

"He is here to destroy my work. Satan always wants to destroy from within. Prescott is after what remains of my Church. He is possessed with darkness. You felt it. He knows you are different. Keep away from him. He was instrumental in developing the idea of rehabilitation camps for my people. He is cruel and rotten."

The H.S.

The weight of a hundred fallen angels had landed on Mercedes. Finding Senator Roker, she demurely requested to leave. Her pale face spoke of honesty.

"You look like you have seen a ghost. Good night, my dear. I will call a car for you." Roker was fearful she might be sick with the Drakee virus, so he passed up the opportunity to plant a kiss on her red lips. He waved to the maître de and explained how Mercedes needed to be transported immediately home.

Mercedes ran to the car, choking as she raced. The limousine driver held the door open as she flung herself into the back seat, definitely in an unladylike position. It was all Mercedes could do to catch her breath. Descending on her chest was a heaviness, like an anvil pressing in, pressing out her breath with each successive intake of air. The evil it manifested had chilled her soul.

As she panted, the driver asked, "Miss, would you like me to take you to the hospital? The senator is concerned that there might be something related to the virus that is causing your breathing issues."

Just like him to be afraid of dying after kissing me. "Home," she whispered as she shared her address.

He shook his head, knowing she was in no condition to be on her own, but did as directed.

When they arrived on the rain slickened street, he unfurled an umbrella and escorted her to the door. "We drive for emergencies. Senator Roker said to give you my card if you need me. I'll be listening for any intake calls for a while. And I'll be lifting some words for you too." He looked down at the ground, but she could sense he might be thinking of prayer.

"Thank you. I need it."

Inside, it was unusually warm despite the chilly storm that had blown into Baltimore and D.C. In her distress she flopped into her reclining chair.

Suddenly the weight, the anvil press, pushed in on her chest again. It seemed intent on stopping her heart. Her breathing became labored and shallow.

"Oh God, dear Jesus. Save me from this demonic presence. Send them away to the pits of hell," she screamed.

She knew the Spirit would come.

"Mercedes, send them under my power. Use your authority."

"Yes, in the name of Jesus Christ of Nazareth, I call on all you slithery, seething demons who are present to pay attention. Under the name of the Lord Jesus Christ, and under His authority, I send you to the pit of hell for all time. Be gone."

"Oh, Lord," she muttered. "Thank you."

Rising slowly, Mercedes felt as though she had run a marathon. She slid out of her dress, put on a light nightgown, and dropped into bed.

Chapter 16

Mercedes Singleton

March 2037

"As I began to speak," Peter continued, "the Holy Spirit fell on them, just as he fell on us at the beginning." ~ Acts 11:15

God decided to show Mercedes reality that night. She woke up in a hospital ward. It was a strange place. Much of it was like her home in Whitsville. But it was much larger, with many groups of people in white congregated in small groups. She sidled up to a couple, a man and a woman who seemed a bit distant, but asked them where she was. Before they could answer, a man entered the room and strode to the middle. Those dressed in white all turned and looked at him intently.

Mercedes recognized him. It was her former lover, David. She walked over and gave him a hug. David reached out and touched her thigh, caressing her. Mercedes was shocked that he would touch her sexually in front of all those present. David was surprised that she rejected his advances. "Will you get me those important documents you had promised to give to me?" he said, trying to act as though nothing had occurred between them.

Again, Mercedes was startled. How could he want such precious things? Why would he want them? But she thought to herself, *He is an old friend. I know him. I trust him.* And she went to the closet to retrieve the documents.

As she stepped back into the room, she looked for David. He was nowhere to be seen, but the couple in white was still in their place, so she went over and asked them where he was.

"We told him to go," they said, looking at her with eyes that shone brightly and held power.

Mercedes woke up with a start. She knew exactly what had happened. The Spirit had let her see the spiritual world of angels and demons. Just as the angels had told her of their protection, she saw the creature. The one posing as "David." He was not David at all, but rather a large demon, with a ruddy complexion, a menacing face, and large ears. He wanted to devour her. He was intent on deceiving as well.

And she realized that she had gone to do his bidding. "Thank you, Spirit, for protecting me and sending your angels to take charge. I am so gullible. I went to do that demon's bidding. God have mercy. Please help me to always see with your eyes. I need your help."

Mercedes lay in her bed, replaying the episode that had just transpired. It was as clear as anything that had happened in real life. She knew it was the Spirit leading her into a glimpse of the battle between Satan's helpers and God's army. There would be no way she would ever forget the face of that demon. Its sheer essence was hate. And she knew deception was somewhere just around the corner. It was a wake-up call to pay attention to those she was now mingling with both at work and in the intrigue of searching for Arun David Polysoing, Olivia's brother.

Now is the time to get moving. "Mercedes, pick up the pace," she told herself authoritatively. She sat up, knowing what was next on the agenda and had been delayed for far too long.

Jumping out of bed, she grabbed her computer graphics pad and searched for Mike's Bike Shop in Baltimore.

The web search showed a simple structure, still in business and advertising a few electric bicycles and scooters. She was surprised to see a few ads for the old-fashioned pedal bicycles as well. She surmised that the move to distance bike transportation utilizing batteries to people power was the cause for the shift. They were now deemed harmful to the environment as well. "Not bad," she said as she pondered purchasing a bike. "I think I can still balance one of those things."

Checking to see if there were any sanitary hotels in the area, she spotted two that seemed acceptable and met US government standards, and jotted down their contact information. The plan for a brief jaunt to Baltimore was briskly forming. She would travel to Baltimore the following weekend, on a Friday night, and leave a note in the mailbox at the bike shop. If there was no response, she would try again Saturday morning. She would have to be careful that the mail carrier did not intercept it by accident. Mail was only delivered once a week, so she would take her chances.

Mercedes felt guilty that it had taken her this long to follow up on searching for Olivia's brother, Arun Polysoing. Olivia, her Christian sister who had taught her how to live a strong faith in the Rehabilitation Center, had died under the steel boots of the warden. She was trying to protect a new arrival at the camp from being the next rape victim of this disgusting human.

Olivia had made Mercedes promise that if anything happened to her, her brother could be contacted through the mailbox at the bike shop. Because Olivia's brother, Arun, was now a leader in the CLF, the

Christian Liberation Front, Mercedes was not sure if he would even be around. He was a wanted man.

Now, what do I put in the note? she thought. *I need to be careful that I do not incriminate anyone with my message.* Ruminating on it for a while, she put pencil to paper, scratching out time and again questionable details. It was more difficult than she imagined. *If only I was a spy like Mack, I could use some kind of code.*

"That's it," she laughed. *I'll grab the local Cambodian newspaper still in circulation and paste an 'advertisement' in the current events section. I'll slip the modified page into the mailbox with an ad for a new Mercedes with my phone number. Knowing Arun, he'll put two and two together. If he's even around and if he even sees it.* She was also haunted by the fact that she had not heard from Mack in many weeks.

Mercedes made a phone call to Hotel Horizon for a weekend stay and booked a seat on the speed train leaving D.C. at 4:00 p.m. Friday.

Her imagination rambled off into high gear. *What if someone tailed her? What if the Fed Ops were tracking her communications? Should she work up some kind of disguise?*

Quiet, you silly mind, she lectured herself. *There is absolutely nothing to worry about. After all, the Holy Spirit oversees this plan. I hope He approves.*

Chapter 17

Mack Gersham (Troy Griffins)

March 2037

"Anyone who believes in me may come and drink! For the Scriptures declare, 'Rivers of living water will flow from his heart.'" When he said "living water," he was speaking of the Spirit, who would be given to everyone believing in him. ~ John 7:38-39

After the assassination attempts, President Woodring went on full alert. She thought back to her early days in 2006 building the IT College with Shamir Todotin in Congo. They had been surprised by renegade insurgents determined to kill what they perceived as western influence in their country. Shamir, her lover, and many of the staff as well as villagers were murdered as the terrorists burned the college to the ground.

Santaya said she would never be caught off guard again. But here she was, nursing a husband who was poisoned accidentally while she was the actual target, and by luck, surviving a bomb planted in her presidential limousine. The FBI and its director, Myra White-

Fergeson, had pulled together a task force of hundreds to unravel the network surrounding both crimes.

Some of the leads were dead ends. Others proved enticing. The rare dig unearthed unexpected clues and connections. It was beginning to be obvious that the line between friend and foe was blurry. And Lu was good at covering his tracks. Most of the limo driver connections centered around Middle Eastern terror groups and this became the major focus of the investigation. Santaya knew that part was a distraction. Someone was intentionally leading them off course to keep them from looking at Lu and his gang of One Nation Alliance supporters.

Mack had spent a week and a half memorizing the files on Troy Griffins provided by Ricardo. The assassination attempts had provided the perfect reason for the president shaking up her security team. If there was the least bit of suspicion from those currently working in the executive office, they were reassigned to another detail.

Mack was coming in with three other agents, two men and a woman. They had been vetted by the FBI and the president's personal guard, Devon Irwin. In the process, he found some interesting details pertaining to activities in the military council. It was not a pretty picture.

"Shit," said Irwin to the president that morning. "Things are really messed up. We have our first recruit coming in today. Here's his background."

"Wait a moment," whispered Santaya. She jotted down a message and within minutes, Irwin and the president were headed for the parking garage.

She ditched her coat in the presidential limo with Shirley Smythe. "I found a tracking device in my coat today. This car is cleared," she said with a manufactured laugh. "No bombs today, but I want whoever is trying to track me to be following this car. Go back to Walter Reed and wear my coat, Shirley. Agent Crosby will accompany you.

Pay DeShaun a visit for me. Be careful." She talked to the agent briefly and then got into a compact generic government sedan with Irwin.

"You drive. Head over to Alexandria. We've got a safe house there to rendezvous." Irwin nodded and left the parking garage ten minutes later. Arriving at the home in Alexandria, Santaya got out of the car inside the garage and went inside.

Mack arrived moments later with his Pentagon handler, Caroline Vance, chosen by Derkovich. The group was small and intimate. Vance introduced everyone. Mack was last.

"So, you are a Blues Militia member, former asset for cyber security and procurements for General Marcus Hamilton, and are currently posing as a former Russian intelligence officer, Troy Griffins. Anything else to add to your resume?" joked the president. The group chuckled.

"I like working for the good guys, Madam President," Mack responded. "We've got our work cut out for us and the odds are not in our favor. The anti-American ideology taught in our military academies and schools over the past few decades has poisoned the pot and made for a cadre of enemies within. It's amazing how people do not understand what America will become if we shift to a global commodity with the One Nation Alliance. They think nothing will change. The irony is that the industrial military complex is the one leading the charge with their back-door funding providing the catalyst for this disaster.

"Sorry, I did not mean to get up on my soapbox. I've been penned up for a while. Now that I'm a new man"—Mack smiled—"I can ask forgiveness."

"Mack, Troy," began the president, "I need my team to be one hundred percent reliable. Simon Hamilton gives you his highest recommendation. Thank you for shifting gears and joining our team. We have Hamilton and his family safe. He needs your contacts and requisition cylinders so we can pull in the Blues. But I still have some reservations about working with them. They've done their share of damage during my first term."

"That was because you were on Lu's side," stated Mack boldly. "Until your meeting with General Hamilton, we knew you could not be trusted. This makes for some difficult negotiating with the Blues Militia. Those guys are extremely cautious in whom they trust. I'll do what I can to allay their fears."

"That's why we are hiring you," said Santaya. "Use your skills as a former aide to the ambassador to convince them I am on the right team."

They all laughed.

"Right," said Mack. He knew it would not be easy. Shifting allegiances never was. And there would be defectors or holdouts. They would be the most dangerous.

"Formulate a plan in the next few weeks to reestablish contact. Go slow. I want all the details to be thoroughly vetted before we make a move. Playing this chess game with Lu is making me nervous."

The conversation moved around the room to the other players and Mack listened in. He sat there, feeling uncomfortable in his new face, knowing their coordinated attack had little chance for success. There were just too many variables and too many turncoats.

After an hour, the president called Shirley Smythe and asked her to return to the White House. "We're on our way. A new team is forming. See you soon."

"Now, Troy, I need you to take up residence in D.C. In fact, there are lots of spare rooms in the White House. Let's set you up there for the time being so you're out of the public eye. We're doing another sweep for bugs. Someone is planting them every few days. We're on to it."

"Yes, Madam President."

"Please call me Santaya."

Mack nodded. He knew his former name and personage were dead. His family name gone. His history was erased. His future – well, most likely short-lived.

He was wise enough upon his return to the White House to pray for himself.

"Holy Spirit, affirm what we are doing here is right in your eyes. May our hands and our actions help bring your Kingdom on earth."

Just how will that happen? thought Mack.

Chapter 18

Ricardo Medina

2008-2037

And God confirmed the message by giving signs and wonders and various miracles and gifts of the Holy Spirit whenever he chose. ~ Hebrews 2:4

The sleeves of his tattered coat were pulled over his hands, yet Ricardo could not feel them. It was unbearable with the chilled wind freezing the cement landing to their townhouse. He hated it when the stoic man showed up to visit his mom for a few hours every couple weeks. When he left, she was flushed with joy. But for Ricardo as a diminutive and quiet child, he only felt repulsion for this man who refused to acknowledge his existence. He also pretended that he meant nothing even though he was his son by blood.

After his mother locked him out of the townhouse, he decided to scuttle down a flight to his neighbor's landing, but here the wind continued to whistle through his feeble coat.

Sliding up the stairs again, he stepped gingerly along the abutment next to the entry steps and decided to chance sneaking back into their home. He had done this a few times after dark when he wanted to get away from his mother and watch the older boys down the block have a few smokes.

But sliding through the security bars was not easy. Luckily, the space between the frame and the first bar of the kitchen window was just large enough for his skull. The rest was gravy.

Pulling down the window quickly, he jumped off the counter like a scared cat and cuddled up under the table beneath the floral tablecloth. It was delightfully warm.

The voices in the next room were muffled. Occasionally the general got loud. "My younger son Colin is messed up. I've busted my belt over his ass several times, and he is just as defiant as before. Why won't he listen to me like that bastard outside does for you? He'd freeze to death if you asked him."

Weakly, his mother answered, "His name is Ricardo."

"Well, Colin is totally messed up shit. He smashed our cat's head with a hammer last week. When he came in, he said the cat had run out in the street and been hit by a car. He wasn't crying either. I've had enough tears from the other one, though. I think Colin killed the cat to make his brother cry. Goddamn it, they are both a mess."

Thankfully the tablecloth concealed Ricardo. As much as he hated the general, his son Colin appeared to be a target for hatred too, a chip off the old block. Ricardo had fed a stray cat for a while outside their townhouse. Soon after that he found it dead in the street. He had cried too.

* * * * *

Ricardo and his handball partner Tyrone Keller pushed the door open to the locker room at the Army Health Center Main Campus. The aroma of sweat, chlorine, and mildew wafted through the air.

The H.S.

They bantered with each other about their handball game shots and who had bested the other. These were immediately dampened by the frothing sight of another soldier going ballistic in the locker room.

"F- him," he shouted. "Goddamned cheater. Couldn't play a fair game of handball with anyone."

Ricardo was quick to recognize Colin Lu. He was the spitting image of his father.

"What the hell are you staring at?" yelled Colin, targeting Ricardo.

Everyone in the locker room turned to see the two athletes standing in the doorway.

"Nothing," said Ricardo. He liked the inuendo of the reply.

"You were both on the court too long," sniffed Colin. "My partner and I had to use the last court. You know how crappy and uneven the walls are there. This frickin' place is falling down."

"We were having our last challenge as partners today," chimed in Tyrone, despite Ricardo's signal to stay quiet. "I've been reassigned, so I was determined just once to beat Ricardo in all three matches. No luck. He's too damned good."

Making eye contact with Colin was difficult for Ricardo. He came to the gym often to work off steam from his double-agent lifestyle. He was walking on razor wire and did not need any more entanglement, especially with someone who was his half-brother.

"You that good?" quizzed Colin. "Well, my partner has quit on me, sissy bitch that he is, so how about playing me next week this same time slot?"

Ricardo nodded. Tyrone chimed in, "Good luck. He's tougher than you think."

"We'll see about that. I'm not a good loser."

No one in the locker room dared offend Colin. Son of the chief of staff, he was always deferred to. But Ricardo did not seem the least bit intimidated. Colin felt it and was not sure what to think.

"Maybe he's just a goddamned prick like me," he half smiled.

"What's your name, soldier?"

"Ricardo Medina. Work in cyber security most of the time."

"Well, Mr. Medina, you've got your work cut out for you," Colin stated.

The match the following week was deadly. Both Ricardo and Colin brought their A game. Several of their buddies watched from the observation room upstairs. "I think one of them is going to kill the other," stated an observer.

They were tied one match apiece and the last game hung by a point for the victor. Ricardo knew he could most likely best Colin, but he had other plans. As he lunged for the last ricochet, he purposefully missed and scraped his knees across the floor.

Colin put up his arms like a prize fighter marching around the ring. "Better luck next time," he crowed. Then he reached out his hand and pulled Ricardo to his feet. "Come on, Ricky boy, let's go out for a beer."

"I need one," Ricardo replied stoically.

They hung around Feisty Ladies, a bar full of straight and trans clientele, occasionally watching the entertainment partially disrobe in unusual ways on the stage. The place was so full of smoke from weed and mind-numbing substances that one could hardly see through the haze.

Colin was a talker. In the first hour at the bar, he unloaded on his unhappy home life with his father, mother, and brother. He hated them all. He liked the fact that Ricardo was a listener and seemed attentive during the bitch session.

"Let me get us another beer. This stuff is crap, but better than the Army commissary." Colin laughed. "I'll see if I can round up a couple of girls. You like girls, don't you? There's always a few who will head home with us for an extra book of coupons. Anyway, my family left for the weekend. Want to come back and party? My life is shitty boring."

"I can for the evening. I must report back early tomorrow morning."

"Suit yourself. That soldier crap is not for me. Even though I am officially on the roster as a sergeant major. Let's get going. I'll bring the ladies and the beer with me. You pay our tab on the way out." Colin grabbed Ricardo's phone and typed in the address. "I'll tell the guard at the gate you are an old family friend. He knows not to cross me and to keep it off the roster of guests. I pay him handsomely for his silence."

Ricardo nodded. Although he showed no emotion, his mind was racing. He wanted to run in the opposite direction. If General Lu caught them together, he was history. But this was a gift horse looking at him. He might be able to find a way to infiltrate Lu's house down the road. And he couldn't pass it up. Now was the time to step up his game and work to squeeze some information out of Colin while he was drunk.

Ricardo had to be hopeful that Lu never took the time to peruse the security tapes. The night activities unfortunately involved smoking pot and drinking beer and he was jazzed. But he knew he had his foot in the door and perhaps a venue for bringing down the big cheese. It was worth it.

Chapter 19

Mercedes Singleton

March 2037

The Lord is like a father to his children, tender and compassionate to those who fear him. ~ Psalm 103:13

Pulling the Bible out of the desk drawer, Mercedes took comfort in the words of the psalm. Jesus was preparing events before her. She just needed to follow His lead. She felt an unjustified trust concerning her safety.

"Calm for me," joked Mercedes. "Thank you, Spirit."

She took a Zorro to the train station. The bullet train from Washington D.C. to Baltimore had been running for over ten years. It was part of the Rebuilding America appropriations bill. Touted as a wave of the future for public transportation, it was an attempt to show up the Chinese, but it proved disappointing.

As usual, it was running behind schedule. The spotty engineering and the lack of maintenance had given it a short shelf life. While it still limped along, the top speed of 60 mph was far from the hyped 125 mph target.

There was a stifling silence in the station. When the train arrived, she climbed on and took a seat, observing those around her as she pulled out her phone. This would most likely be a fruitless weekend, but she was back on track following through with a promise.

Staring at her phone screen, her mind imaged the meeting with Arun David Polysoing, Olivia's brother. What would she say? How could she express how much Olivia meant to her family of faith at the Central Station Rehabilitation Camp? How could she explain her freedom from the camp while her friend was murdered by the warden? And what about the actual mission she had accepted from Mack Gersham to make contact on behalf of the Blues Militia. Mercedes breathed a deep sigh which unfortunately was audible.

Mack Gersham had tasked her with contacting Arun, who was an unofficial leader in the Christian Liberation Front in the hopes that they could ally themselves with the Blues Militia.

Mack Gersham. She had thought of him often, and now with nothing else pressing, Mercedes allowed herself to think of their fleeting moments together. She recalled how he pretended to be his murdered twin brother Walt, after the drone attack by the Federated Ops forces. She had been so naïve in not seeing the clues to his actual identity. And she reviewed the night when he had experienced the touch of the Holy Spirit at their last church service together in Whitsville, realizing that he was under new marching orders from a recently found Godhead.

Mostly, she reminisced about the fleeting kiss, completely unexpected. So unexpected that she had not been able to savor the taste of his salty lips, moist with perspiration from climbing the hills to establish contact with his forces. He had promised he would try to keep her safe. And here she was, still waiting for him to personally contact her after months of silence.

Was he still alive? Was she walking into another trap leading back to a rehabilitation camp? She thought about her dream of encountering the deceptive demon. She looked up as the train jerked to a stop.

Before she had time to groan, the train regained some speed and decelerated as it approached Baltimore.

She thought of his eyes, the giveaway that he was Mack and not Walt. That memory was frozen in time.

Glancing up from her phone, she gazed at the people surrounding her. Something felt out of place, but all appeared normal. Most were dressed as government civilian workers like herself.

In her mind she ran through the plan again. Hotel check in. Note left in mailbox. Lunch with a former friend the next day at noon. Wait at the hotel. If no response, return to note drop-off site and deposit duplicate message. *It was the fourth mailbox down at Mike's Bike Shop, right?* she quizzed herself.

"Believe in yourself," stated the Spirit emphatically. He shored up her confidence. Mercedes realized that for this whole coordinated plan of espionage to work, the Holy Spirit would have to take the reins in the background. She would trust Him. Mack had been given his orders. She was to follow hers as well. Doubt was to be left behind. He knew what He was doing. And His goal was to come alongside the persecuted Church. There was no way He could fail. She could, Mack could, and so could Arun. They were human. But she knew He was victorious! She smiled.

Falling into a drowsy nap, she clutched the phone tight just as the train lurched to a stop in Baltimore.

Let the games begin, she thought, refreshed. Grabbing her petite overnight bag, she moved to the back of the car to disembark.

There was that uncomfortable feeling again. *Maybe the Spirit is telling me to watch my step,* she mused.

Walking briskly two blocks to the hotel, she paused a few times to window-shop and get her bearings. She almost ducked into a diner advertising Cambodian and Vietnamese food but decided instead to check into the hotel first.

There was no desk manager any longer, just a security person in the lobby. She inserted her travel pass with chip into the check-in computer. It recorded her information and dropped out a key card with a scrolling message, "Welcome Ms. Singleton. Enjoy your stay."

"Thanks," she told the machine.

The hotel room was adequate and clean. Since the train ride had taken longer than expected, she hurriedly prepared her "Mercedes" advertisement and slid it into her coat pocket.

The walk to Mike's Bike Shop following her GPS in the dark was uneventful. A prayer was whispered for success. Then there were the mailboxes, just as Olivia had shared. Down four was the rusty, flip-top black box, a dinosaur from days past. It appeared not to be in use, but was probably a safer way to transmit information than through cyberspace. Those could be tracked by any computer hacker.

Slipping her note from her pocket, she was thankful for the darkness surrounding her. She lifted the lid and dropped the slim newspaper with the secretive message into the tin box.

Turning, she stepped back onto the sidewalk and turned left to head to the diner she had spotted earlier.

A dark car, parked by the curb, started its engine. "Steady girl," she said. As she walked past, the back door snapped open and a large burly man picked her up and threw her into the back seat.

"Go," he said to the driver, placing a mask filled with chloroform over her mouth. She barely struggled, only getting in a few solid kicks before she succumbed to the sleeping agent. "Oh Jesus, help," she mumbled.

Chapter 20

Mercedes Singleton

March 2037

Then he opened their minds to understand the Scriptures. And he said, "Yes, it was written long ago that the Messiah would suffer and die and rise from the dead on the third day. It was also written that this message would be proclaimed in the authority of his name to all the nations, beginning in Jerusalem: 'There is forgiveness of sins for all who repent.' You are witnesses of all these things. And now I will send the Holy Spirit, just as my Father promised. But stay here in the city until the Holy Spirit comes and fills you with power from heaven"
~ Luke 24:45-49

The darkened room was silently coming into focus. Mercedes imagined she was sitting in some type of contrivance with metal arms and metal foot plates. She tried to focus and will herself to recall what was transpiring.

Whatever had been pressed over her face had only temporary staying power, for she was swiftly waking up. There were people around her whispering and she dared herself to try to see who had kidnapped her.

She was startled when the first face that she saw was Arun David Polysoing, Olivia's brother.

"But I…." Her voice faded away.

"Take heart, Mercedes," Arun leaned in with confidence. "You are among believers." He was smiling more than Mercedes could recollect from their earlier brief meetings.

"Are you a kidnapper?" Mercedes glowered.

"Guess I can add that to my resume. No, just a soldier for God trying to keep you from harm. Do you feel stable enough to get up and sit in this armchair?"

Mercedes glanced around the room. "This looks a bit different than the room I checked into."

Another person dressed as a housekeeper chimed in. "Yes, we were able to get you down here through the service elevator. The night manager is one of us. I moved your personal belongings over here in the dark because your room was bugged. You are a floor down and one over from your original reservation. Someone is still waiting for you to return."

"What do you mean?" asked Mercedes. "Was someone following me? I felt eyes on me on the train."

"Yeah, he's down in the lobby right now. One of Lu's henchmen. They planned to kidnap you tonight and force you to reveal your sources with the Blues Militia. Senator Roker is in on the whole enterprise. Lu is using all his leads to get to the Blues. Your name was linked to Mack Gersham. They think he might have given you the downloaded cylinders with Blues operational information before he was killed in the drone strike."

"It was that traitor, Ricardo Medina," hissed Mercedes. "The last time I spoke to Mack, he was impersonating Walt, his handicapped twin brother. He said nothing of cylinders. He did not want me dragged into this cloak-and-dagger business." Mercedes smiled faintly. Then she froze. Maybe Arun was not an ally anymore. This could be a set up.

Good grief. Have I spilled the beans?

"Just the opposite," shared Arun. "It is Ricado who saved your skin. He recently contacted some of our company and informed us they would be tailing you to Baltimore today."

"But Ricardo is a covert spy for Lu's treasonous plan." There she went again. She had no proof they were in her camp. She did not play their game well. *Oh Lord, show me the Truth. Holy Spirit, reveal your heart,* she spoke in her mind.

Arun kneeled in front of her. "Everyone in this room has a bounty on their head. We have decided to fight for the cause of religious freedom, a foundation of this country. We do it because we love the Lord. He is our boss, our guide, and our director. Willingly we sacrifice our safety to help our brothers and sisters in Christ. Olivia taught me more than you can imagine. I have heard snippets of how she died. I know it occurred because she prioritized someone else's life over her own. She was a saint."

Arun struggled to contain his emotions, but his eyes spoke of love as he held back the tears.

"I need to know more about what happened at the Central Station Rehabilitation Camp. Do you feel well enough to share with me? We're going to take you back to D.C. tonight. The plan is being finalized as we speak."

"But you said that Ricardo helped you out. That is impossible. He's a dirty rat, ready to sell us all out." She wanted to spit his name.

"All things are possible with God," Arun chuckled. "That man has one foot in heaven and the other in hell. Frankly, he probably saved your life tonight. The Holy Spirit must be bending his heart toward Truth. We're all able to be saved by grace, no matter our history."

Mercedes had a difficult time digesting this startling information. The image of Ricardo and his treachery had marinated in her mind for months. It was almost impossible to believe he was an ally. "Still, watch him," said Mercedes distrustfully.

The next hour and a half, Mercedes gave Arun a quick synopsis of her time in the camp prison with Olivia. The pain and suffering reemerged. She was still crushed by Olivia's murder, but as she spoke, the Spirit held her in His arms.

Chapter 21

Ricardo Medina

March 2037

I didn't know he was the one, but when God sent me to baptize with water, he told me, "The one on whom you see the Spirit descend and rest is the one who will baptize with the Holy Spirit." ~ John 1:33

Rising from sleep, he bumped into a form next to him in bed. He did not recognize her. "My God, what did I do?"

Slowly Ricardo's memory clicked in. He had done his due diligence by coming to General Lu's house with his son Colin. Soon after his arrival, he had excused himself to use the restroom, but instead found the controls to the security system and disabled the interior cameras after rewinding the recording enough to erase their entry. He imagined Colin would have done the same thing if he hadn't been so high on meth.

After everyone had gone to bed. Ricardo had also lifted Colin's fingerprints from one of the many beer bottles splayed across the coffee table. He knew what he really needed were Lu's prints.

Where would I find those? he posed. Ricardo pressed the print duplicator stashed in his backpack on the mouse next to the computer in the den, an empty Manhattan glass, and a toothbrush found in the master bedroom.

Come on, old man. Make my day, he laughed to himself.

When he returned to the bedroom, he was glad that his escort was still passed out from the extra drug dose he had slipped into her drink. *She'd never remember last night anyway,* he thought.

Now he splashed some water on his face, jotted a quick note to Colin, reactivated the security system, and ducked down the side sheltered path while calling a Zorro driver for a ride. Knowing he'd be back, he surveyed the property. The plan for readmittance was formed swiftly. He headed back to work.

That evening he got a call from Colin. "Let's do some handball tomorrow."

"Sorry. Working all week. How about you?"

Colin said, "Got some function to go to with my mother Saturday. Some freakin' art auction. Just a bunch of self-serving weirdos thinking they are all that when they paint a few squares and lines. I could do that. Even better. The only perk is coming home with some lovely on the wait staff."

"Your dad going too?" posed Ricardo.

Colin laughed. "That would be the day hell froze over. You've seen him on the news the last few days. He's in China trying to broker a peace deal with India and Pakistan. He thinks he can get concessions out of them before they blow us all up with nukes. They'll never trust the other side. If they were smart, they wouldn't trust my dad either. He's an expert prick."

Saturday evening was thankfully a miserable black night filled with intermittent rain. Ricardo leaned a collapsible ladder over the wall of Lu's mansion. He scaled the wall in seconds, retracting the ladder on the way down. Stealthily pulling himself up a hearty oak tree, he shimmied to the second floor. A small leap placed him on the balcony of the master suite. He slid down the drainpipe and coded in the entry numbers and symbols he had memorized from the earlier visit with Colin.

Colin had fumbled with the entry code the week prior. "Dammit. I can't see the numbers," he said slurring his words. He had already popped a pill, washing it down with beer.

"I'll do it," Ricardo said.

"It's easy. My dad's birthday with a check mark and a star. Surprised he didn't put five stars in it," he said dismissively. "Three-twenty-one-sixty-eight, check, star.

The lock had clicked and Ricardo had opened the door for the party to enter.

Here he was a week later, fumbling to get the numbers sequenced with touch-sensitive gloves. Worked like a charm.

Ricardo came with one objective: to crack into Lu's computer and seek records of the parties who were part of the covert insurrection inside the channels of government. Again, he disabled the security cameras, this time placing a device on the control box that made it appear that all cameras were still operable. Pulling the plastic imprint of fingerprints from his pocket, he thought about how the guys at the lab were geniuses. One touch and he was with power. Now he had to work on a password.

A voice chanted in his head, "He thinks he is Caesar."

Ricardo went with that train of thought. A caesar who could never fail. Unbelievably there it was, "All Hail Caesar!"

"Good one, daddy dearest," Ricardo cooed.

This was the gold mine Ricardo dreamed of. He found emails with scores of encrypted names, lists of travel plans, notes. Any forwarding of documents would be too risky. Ricardo decided to print out several that seemed most relevant, including a few that mentioned the Blues. Maybe he could use them at work to convince his boss that he had something of substance after rearranging the information. For now, he would pass this information to Ed Derkovich ASAP.

Little did Ricardo know that among the missives he gathered was a brief email highlighting the tracking of a suspected Blues operative, a Ms. Mercedes Singleton.

Chapter 22

Mercedes Singleton

March 2037

If you love me, obey my commandments. And I will ask the Father, and he will give you another Advocate, who will never leave you. He is the Holy Spirit, who leads into all truth. The world cannot receive him, because it isn't looking for him and doesn't recognize him.
~ John 14:15-17

Dark drops of rain splattered from the sky as Mercedes and her "kidnappers" exited the hotel through the service elevator. This time she was thankful to be on her feet. She knew she had a role to play once she returned to Washington D.C., one where she pretended nothing had transpired over the weekend.

The first thing she would do Monday when she was safely back at her desk was to call her girlfriend and apologize for failing to meet her at lunch.

As they exited the elevator, two quick bursts of gunfire slammed into their midst. Arun's knees buckled.

"Get him into the car, quick!" whispered the night maid.

Mercedes pulled his torso into the car while Maria bent his knees and rotated him into the back seat. "You know where to go," she directed the driver.

The older sedan swung into the light traffic, cruised around a few city blocks, and headed for the waterfront. Mercedes quickly accessed Arun's condition. It was problematic. He was bleeding profusely from a chest wound.

"Are we going to the hospital?" she frantically quizzed the driver.

"Too risky. They're bound to get him there. I'm sure they are already waiting."

He whisked into a dark alley with a handful of dilapidated metal structures.

This is about as far from a medical facility as I can imagine, Mercedes thought.

Taking a sharp left, they cruised almost to the last building of the dead-end lane.

"We've got help here. Doc Withers is already on his way," said the driver matter-of-factly.

Climbing out of the car, two strong fellows looking like long shoremen from their burly appearance, came out of the dilapidated building, carefully shifted Arun around in the seat, and carried him into the abandoned warehouse. His face was almost without color and he barely grunted as they jostled him with every step.

A small, vacant office sat near the end of the hallway, but they bypassed this logical stop and traipsed across the voluminous room that joined the hallway to a steel door on the other side.

Opening it, Mercedes saw a small cadre of people, silent with a look of sincere concern on their faces. There was also an examination table and large storage bins against the wall marked with labels alerting medical staff of their contents.

A diminutive and distinguished gentleman quickly strode in through the back door. Mercedes recognized him immediately. He had appeared in repetitious government-sponsored health shows on television. There he seemed almost catatonic. Now he was animated as he examined Arun.

Mercedes spoke up. "I am an emergency room nurse practitioner. I've not been practicing officially for a few years, but can I be of assistance?"

Doc Withers looked at her blood-stained dress. "Yes, but what we need right now is seemingly impossible. Arun needs a blood transfusion. We need to get him under. Start the IV and set the drip for five mg. We need to pray for a miracle."

Arun's eyelashes fluttered. He moaned softly. As a few others got him prepared for surgery, Mercedes could not help but see the jagged scar on his abdomen. It certainly had not been repaired by anyone versed in corrective surgery. She hoped this was not some of Doc Withers's earlier work.

"Put on the restraints," said the doc, looking at Mercedes.

"Lord Jesus, here we are again," Doc said. "We need you to stand in the gap against the destroyer. We need some blood and quick. You alone can deliver Arun and save his life. So we ask for this miracle, the blood he needs. Thank you. Amen."

"OK," Doc said. Mercedes could see through the door that more and more people had congregated in the empty warehouse. They stood silent. Some appeared to be praying. Doc broke into her observations. "We need a miracle blood donor, AB negative. Who did God send us?"

The silence was deafening for a moment.

"T-That would be me," stuttered Mercedes.

"Good," said Doc, seemingly satisfied that God had already parted the great sea of the miraculous. "Have a seat. I figured God had this orchestrated already. Get yourself cleaned up as much as possible. I must get that bullet out. Glad he was only hit once."

A few other assistants who appeared to have medical training were ready to help with the surgery. It was as though this was their daily assignment. From the looks of the supplies, they were prepared for a calamitous event.

"Thank you, Jesus," said one of the nurses, a fairly husky African American woman whom everyone seemed to know was in charge of the room. She quickly made eye contact with Mercedes and then Arun. "We couldn't lose him. He is too important to the cause."

Mercedes failed to catch the meaning, but before the surgery began, she stood and quickly walked down the corridor to the restroom. The voluminous warehouse now had hundreds of people standing in silent witness to the risky surgery unfolding on the other side of the wall.

As she returned to the make-shift surgical unit, a droning sound buzzed in her ears. Emerging into the warehouse, she recognized its source; all the people in unison lifting petitions to the Maker with loud whispers, pleas, and prayers. The droning never stopped for the next three hours.

Mercedes provided two pints of blood and watched as the doc transferred them to Arun's arm. She noticed his pale skin start to gain a deeper hue as the blood coursed through his veins.

"We are blessed with your presence, Ms. Singleton," the doc chattered as he sewed Arun up meticulously.

How he knew who she was surprised her.

"Thank you. I've always stayed active, especially during the war, to be a blood donor. It's difficult to find AB negative donors."

"That it is. But Father God was already prepared. On the way here, the Spirit was alerting me to the fact that He was aware of our needs. I heard Him loud and clear. The fact that the bullet passed just an inch from his heart, yet missed the major arteries was…well….." His voice trailed off.

The driver that evening appeared in the doorway.

"Doc, can I talk to Ms. Singleton for a bit?"

"Sure. She's done her work here." He turned to Mercedes. "Thank you. Until we meet again."

Mercedes tagged behind the driver, Lamont Vickers, to the other side of the floor, dodging around the hundreds who were so valiantly praying for Arun. "The miracle is their prayers," she whispered. *Not me, not the doc. They got in touch with the Spirit. He is doing this great work.*

"What happened back there?" asked Mercedes.

"The surgery?" asked Lamont

"Well that, too, but I was asking about the shooting. Was that aimed at me?" questioned Mercedes timidly.

"No, it was for Arun. He's been doing miracles in this city in the underground church. The drug dealers are pouring in to be saved. The Spirit has shaken their hearts and Arun has boldly shown them a life of love and a future of grace. The Driscolli drug cartel is furious that half their dealers have quit to join Jesus. Arun has a bounty on his head. He rarely, if ever, goes out in public. Someone must have spotted him going into the hotel earlier tonight."

"Won't the gunman report seeing Arun to the authorities?"

"No way. First, they want reward money from the cartel. Second, they know they'll be sent to some drug dealer detention camp. As tough as these guys are, those camps are nothing like the old prison system. Every day there are murders by someone who is incarcerated. They are hell on earth. No one cares."

"Listen," he continued, Arun wants to get in touch with you again and talk more about Olivia, but now is out of the question. And we need to get together with some of the Blues operatives. We will make sure you stay in the mix, but it is best to give you very little information for now. General Lu is ready to put us all in front of the firing squad. Thankfully, we are ready."

He gave her a new coat to cover her blood-stained dress. As Mercedes stepped out of the cramped office, she heard a loud murmur. Across the room stood Arun, pale and fragile, but smiling. He touched his heart with his hands and then walked back into the surgery area.

In one accord, the praying turned to praises. The song gained power and amplification. The people undulated to the worshipful words:

Holy, holy, holy Lord
God of Power and Might
Heaven and Earth are full of Your glory
Hosannah, hosannah in the highest
Blessed is He who comes in the name of the Lord
Hosannah, hosannah, in the highest
Blessed is He who comes in the name of the Lord

The chorus rang out again and again. Then the Holy Spirit fell and pressed them all down, some on their knees, some on the floor. The Spirit washed back and forth across the room as the worshippers undulated in His presence. The mighty power of God was so present, no one escaped His breath.

Mercedes had no power to rise as the Spirit washed over her again and again. "O Glory!" she murmured. "The Glory of the Lord."

After some time, she was gingerly lifted by strong hands. "Ms. Singleton. We must be moving. The last train to Washington is leaving in half an hour and you must be on it."

Groggily she nodded and slipped into the natural world again. They glided into a newer model car. "Compliments of the doc," the driver smiled.

Chapter 23

Ricardo Medina

March 2037

May the grace of the Lord Jesus Christ, the love of God, and the fellowship of the Holy Spirit be with you all. ~ 2 Corinthians 13:14

Plopping down in the faux leather commuter train seat, Mercedes let out a sigh of exhaustion. Nothing had gone as planned. She had met Arun and shared some of Olivia's tale, but that had been followed by the assassination attempt on Arun's life. She had no information to take back to a Blues operative other than the fact that Arun was alive.

Ricardo's name had been mentioned. Was he really to be trusted? Where was Mack? Was he still alive? Had Ricardo done something to him?

Mercedes was thankful she had shared with Arun the important events from the camp. She wanted him to know how treasured Olivia had been in her life. Olivia's loss had left a crater in her heart. She was a sister lost way too early. She hoped that her love and honor of Olivia had touched Arun's heart.

But Mercedes was still mesmerized by the falling of the Spirit on the assembly praying and praising their Lord. She closed her eyes and still felt the Presence, the Power, the Glory.

A quiet thud was heard as someone settled into the seat next to hers. Mercedes purposefully kept her eyes closed. She wanted to stay washed in the Spirit.

"It would be a help, Ms. Singleton, if you would continue to keep your eyes closed," said a strangely familiar voice.

Mercedes opened them just a slit. Her breath stilled. *Ricardo Medina in the flesh.*

Her heart clenched.

"It is much safer for us to confer here where there is little danger of our conversation being intercepted. I will try to fill you in on a few details so you can manage things going forward. If that's alright with you, please nod. I'll try to keep my lip movement to a minimum and turn my head towards you to imply I am resting too."

Mercedes slowly nodded. Her white knuckles clenching her purse betrayed her feelings.

"I apologize for frightening you. I know our history is a negative one. With Danny's death, I began to process what I was doing in digging dirt up on the Blues. I did betray Mack's identity, but the FBI verified the dead body in the shallow grave near Mack's old house was indeed Mack. We know otherwise."

He continued, "I tracked Mack back to D.C. While doing that, I devised a plan to honor Danny. I'd become a double agent for the Blues Militia while working for the Federated Ops Forces with Lu himself as my boss. You know Lu is destroying our country. I've found a way to enmesh myself with Mack's former chain of command. Not bragging or anything, but I've saved a few hides in the process. One is Mack Gersham's."

Ricardo paused, stretched and continued. "Listen, we need you to continue your role in Roker's office. You don't know it, but the Fed Ops asked him to hire you, thinking you might be a Blues link to Mack. He was all too amenable to have you aboard. Roker's a pawn, but he thinks he's important. He's careless too. I need you to intercept his emails if possible. Instructions will come soon.

"Anyway, the Fed Ops trailed you to Baltimore through your computer work pad. Luckily, we retrieved your 'Mercedes' flier you dumped in the bike shop mailbox and swept you away before they could connect you to Arun. The CLF is crafting plans to fight back against the repression of religion by the government. They've contacted the Blues and will coordinate to pinch off the menace.

"Enough of that. Your next assignment is to attend the Washington Freedom Gala in two weeks with Senator Roker. President Woodring will be attending to support the honorees this year. This is one of her first public appearances after the car bomb and security will be heavy."

Ricardo had chuckled at the word "freedom." *For whom,* he thought. More rounds of oppressive measures in housing, energy, and medical care all wrapped up with a hypocritical ribbon of compassion were working their way through Congress. He hated the manipulation of the masses. He wondered when they would get sick of the relentless effort to control the mind and start to think for themselves. *Perhaps never.*

"The President has supported the establishment up to this point but has had an epiphany on what is actually transpiring to destroy the country. Two assassination attempts have pushed her to do some soul searching. Thankfully, she was alerted to Lu's plans before Hamilton and his aide were assassinated. That began her journey into intellectually moving to support our cause. We've got some new people in her inner circle who are feeding her truth for once."

He continued, "On the evening of the Gala, you will be approached by one of Woodring's new security detail. We've determined that you will need to establish a permanent liaison with him. Make it look real as much as possible. It will be up to you to carry on this intimate relationship for several weeks. The information you distill from Roker's emails is to be passed on to this agent. Please consider accepting this request for the good of the country. I know this does not appeal to your sense of common decency." Ricardo could not help but to smirk slightly. Mercedes's moral upbringing was a relic of the dark ages. She needed to readjust her code of conduct.

Ricardo moved on with his final intelligence information. "Our Secret Service agent will feed you information that is not true, but Roker will hopefully fall for it now that you have a line to the inner sanctum of the president's office. He will be salivating to pump you for information to pass along to Lu concerning the president. We will make sure it sounds accurate. You need to craft the avenue to feed this false content to him without appearing anxious or willing to disclose the information. I'm sure Roker will enjoy your company as he has in the past, escorting you to his art events. Has he taken advantage of you, the fat bastard?"

Mercedes was silent.

Ricardo put his hand gingerly on Mercedes's leg. "It was a pleasure, Ms. Singleton. I hope I can be of service to you again. If anyone does see me here, you're in the clear. It would be Fed Ops and they know I'm tracking the Blues. It looks legit."

She could hear the slight sneer in his voice, but she steeled herself not to move, even when he touched her. He kept her on edge. She had never liked him. Maybe it was his brokenness she didn't like. She sighed and moved her legs.

Ricardo got up to move forward as the train slowed for the stop at the D.C. terminal.

That was pleasant, he thought. He liked being in control, especially with someone as independent as Mercedes Singleton.

Mercedes was the last to disembark. She was shaken as she flagged down a Zorro driver. In the car she prayed in earnest. *Oh Jesus, Oh Holy Spirit. This is getting complicated. Keep me in your will. Cover those who are fighting for your cause. I need your discernment concerning Ricardo and the assignment with the security guard for the president. I do not want to be forced into sexual servitude again. Oh Lord, I don't know if I can do it. Help me.*

Chapter 24

Santaya Woodring

April 2037

But you, dear friends, must build each other up in your most holy faith, pray in the power of the Holy Spirit, and await the mercy of our Lord Jesus Christ, who will bring you eternal life. In this way, you will keep yourselves safe in God's love. ~ Jude 1:20-21

She should have long ago been asleep, but Santaya could not release her concerns about the potential World War brewing in the Far East. An intelligence meeting that evening had alerted her to satellite images of camouflaged missile launchers slowly maneuvering toward their destination on the Indian border. Here were two world superpowers playing cat and mouse, provoking the other to take the first swipe. General Lu had recently visited a symposium in the area trying to run interference with China to slow their proxy Pakistan's antagonism toward India but had struck out. He did not take defeat well.

Deeper down she felt something else gnawing at her soul—DeShaun. She had just about floated off into an unsettled dream when Shirley Smythe, her executive assistant, called her name. Fighting to regain consciousness, her eyelids fluttered open. She gazed around the bedroom, a bit confused.

"Yes, Shirley."

"DeShaun has taken a turn for the worse. The doctor has requested you come to Walter Reed immediately."

She was so used to turning her brain on and off that it was no problem switching to immediate action as she soundlessly took to the task of washing her face and dressing quickly. *I don't know why I am trying to be quiet. DeShaun is not even here.* Usually she kept the noise to a minimum to spare her husband's sleep.

Shirley touched her arm. "May I come and pray for him?"

"Of course, Shirley," she replied curtly.

In silence they drove to Walter Reed and entered through the employee door where they were whisked upstairs to DeShaun's room. The lights were muted. Nurses recorded the information from the variety of machines that blinked in the night.

Dr. Trufello, alerted that the president had arrived, came into the room and pulled up a chair for her to sit next to DeShaun.

"There is nothing else we can do," he murmured. "The nerves in his respiratory system have been weakened and his heart is failing. I will leave you with him for some private time. Please alert the staff if you need anything. I am sorry we got to the point of exhausting all possible care strategies."

The staff exited and closed the door. Santaya felt helpless, as she had so many years before in the jungle of Congo. She remembered how Shamir, her lover, had placed her in the dense undergrowth to escape the rampaging guerrillas who had come to their village to burn down the new technical school. Again, she felt the same searing helplessness, having nowhere to go, no one to reach out to.

Then she heard quiet words of peace and assurance. Words that took on the essence of life, even hope. Shirley was praising her God

The H.S.

and rejoicing in His presence. She spoke of His power and His desire for events to follow His intent. Santaya turned to see her assistant sincerely pleading for the life of DeShaun before the throne of God.

"Dear Jesus, touch this man. Place your hand on his heart. Breathe the breath of Life into his lungs. Give him time to finish his work for you in this life."

Shirley continued with a low rumble of more words, trilling and tripping over each other as she swayed back and forth in prayer. Santaya moved with her, eyes closed, almost hearing the drumbeat of an uplifting cadence in the flow of the words.

Santaya bent over DeShaun to kiss his dry lips. She begged Shirley's God to open his eyes and come back to her. She laid her head on his chest and felt the slow-moving beat of blood course through his tired body.

"I love you, DeShaun. Please, please, please. I need you now more than ever. Come back to me."

Standing up, Santaya took her tired hands and held his for a moment. "I am not sure what to do," she whispered to Shirley.

"Expect a miracle. The Holy Spirit says one is coming."

Both ladies resumed their seats.

"Thank you," said the president. "Your prayer gave me comfort. You pray with a melody like some voice from beyond."

"That it was," Shirley replied. "God's words for you and DeShaun. He is watching."

This time Santaya did not protest or even reject Shirley's assumptions. She had nothing to offer in this situation. Her theology on the meaning of life stopped with a person's last heartbeat. For her, that was why a life well lived had to be lived now. It was all we had. But she could see that Shirley's timeline was eternal. "Wouldn't that be nice," she said dejectedly.

* * * * *

Both ladies guarded the bed and called for continued life for DeShaun in their own way. The late hour claimed them eventually, as heads began to nod.

Then Shirley sat upright as though jolted with a bolt of electricity. "Good Lord, he's back," she whispered.

She poked Santaya.

"Look!"

DeShaun's eyes were open. His dry lips parted. "I felt you kiss me. Then I went on a trip somewhere. Perfection…. light…voices. Yet I knew you were in the background holding my hands and refusing to let go. Something touched me with a powerful energy. Then I was here and awake. Guess I have fallen asleep at the hospital for a few hours. Did they figure out if I had Drakee or another virus? Maybe that new strain in India? I feel groggy for sure."

"Don't talk so much, dear," said Santaya patting his hands, tears running down her flushed cheeks.

"Shirley, call the doctor in. Let's see if we can keep this under wraps for the next few days."

Santaya could not explain her emotions of peace and acceptance. Here she had witnessed a true miracle, yet she accepted it as fact. There was no other explanation.

Then the voice of something spoke into her mind, a voice that had a cadence like the melodic prayer Shirley had chanted over DeShaun. The voice firmly spoke. "I AM. I AM the beginning and the end. I AM. Heed my voice."

A wave of shivering wracked Santaya as the forceful words drilled the Truth into her mind. For the first time in her life, she would admit to the supernatural presence with the name, I AM.

Chapter 25

Mack Gersham (Troy Griffins)

April 2037

But it was to us that God revealed these things by his Spirit. For his Spirit searches out everything and shows us God's deep secrets. No one can know a person's thoughts except that person's own spirit, and no one can know God's thoughts except God's own Spirit.
~ 1 Corinthians 2:10-11

Being on the inside detail of the president's Secret Service brought its perks. Mack had the freedom to observe the daily flow in the executive office and realize that those in and around power were very different from him. Everyone played a role, some better than others.

He was working to become adept not only at his new job but at his new identity.

He also knew that the Oval Office held no secrets. Although it was swept for listening devices each week, it was common knowledge that somehow more were planted by people who were considered friendly forces.

Mack was briefed in the morning by his boss, Captain Devon Irwin. The agenda for the day would include a security detail for the president as she attended the Washington Freedom Gala.

Knowing her, he guessed she was not thrilled rubbing shoulders for an entire evening with the new elites of the city, but she also knew that a hefty amount of her campaign funds poured into her coffers through this type of work, so she would put on her game face for the chore.

Just a few days prior, Mack had had a stealthy meeting with Ricardo on the National Mall plaza strolling on the side alley. Briefly, Ricardo alerted him to the fact that Mercedes would be attending the Freedom Gala, accompanying Senator Roker. Succinctly, he shared the events that had recently transpired in Baltimore when Mercedes had attempted to contact Olivia's brother, Arun.

Strategically, Ricardo did not cover the supernatural events of the day. His brain chose to sift things of this nature out and into the trash bin. Yet the facts gnawed at his mind.

"Now, Troy," shared Ricardo, "we are getting our alliance with the CLF and the Blues Militia solidified. We are going to need all the players working for the same objective. Arun Polysoing and the Blues management have rendezvoused several times and are formulating a plan to be proactive when the time comes to out General Lu and his pack of traitors. Unfortunately, we have discovered that the list of defectors has grown quite long and has extended its tentacles into all areas of the government. We are walking around land mines all day long. The plan is to set the trap with lightning speed and the full force of our available troops. Our chances, as you know, are slim. The biggest issue is the betrayal by friends."

Mack chuckled at Ricardo's comment. "Do I sense a hint of sarcasm in your voice, Ricardo? It's been difficult for me to believe you are prepared to put everything on the line for us. I must accept in good faith the trust Ed Derkovick has in you. I imagine he knows you better than I do. So, what do you want me to do at the Freedom Gala? Make contact with Mercedes? Fill her in on who I am and what we are trying to accomplish?"

"Just the first part," shared Ricardo. "We can't risk her knowing what is evolving in the movement. She has some idea after her episode in Baltimore, but she is not trained in intelligence work. She can play her role a lot easier if we keep her focused on intelligence-gathering from Roker's office rather than what we are planning to do with the information. I've asked her to get into Roker's files. We will be giving her the tools. We knew he was part of Lu's team from the beginning. She has gained Roker's confidence as a good employee, but he was asked to hire her by Lu's team as a possible contact for the Blues. She needs to watch herself."

He continued, "Roker loves her as his escort to all these charity events. He slobbers over her and paws her incessantly. The devil is married. His wife is in a dementia ward. He doesn't seem to care. I'm not sure Mercedes minds either."

"That's not fair to Mercedes," glowered Mack. "She's not a loose woman. She's playing the part for us. I asked her to do what she could for the cause."

"Well, she has her past," said Ricardo with eyes of steel. "Let her decide how she wants to run the operation. You both hold to God's provision. Why don't you let her trust Him for protection?"

The sarcasm did not escape Mack.

"Goddamned, you're cold," snapped Mack. "We all have a past."

"Figure out how to get her attention on Saturday. It is fine if you are obvious about it. Roker will like Mercedes getting close to one of the President's personal detail, so he can dig for information.

"Play the role of the masculine Casanova. She'll love it."

"You don't know her very well. But I'll gladly accept the assignment. I've been waiting months to see her."

Mack could not refrain from recalling their last encounter in the darkened living room in Whitsville and the kiss he placed on her moist lips. She had often been on his mind, imagining their eventual meeting. He had to admit his attraction to her was powerful. Those fantasies had to be tamed once again.

"I hope you can skillfully reveal your identity without her making a scene. You'll get another set of orders before Saturday by President Woodring herself."

Ricardo turned brusquely and walked away. Mack still did not trust him, and he certainly did not like him.

Chapter 26

Santaya Woodring

April 2037

On the day of Pentecost all the believers were meeting together in one place. Suddenly, there was a sound from heaven like the roaring of a mighty windstorm, and it filled the house where they were sitting. Then, what looked like flames or tongues of fire appeared and settled on each of them. And everyone present was filled with the Holy Spirit and began speaking in other languages, as the Holy Spirit gave them this ability. ~ Acts 2:1-4

Stretching in bed, Santaya tried with all her might to will herself to rise. This was one of the few mornings she did not have to be up at 6:00 a.m., and her body begged for more rest.

But she also knew the day was critical for developing a strategy for trapping Lu and his counterparts in their treasonous plot to hijack the country. That took precedence. She swung her weary legs around and gingerly stood up.

Ringing for her assistant, Shirley, she briskly showered, dressed, and reviewed the agenda for the day.

"We'll need to go to the Breakfast Club at eight." She winked at Shirley, who acknowledged the request.

Just before 8:00 a.m., they stepped into the elevator and got off at the first floor using the back service elevator. Upon exiting, they turned right and continued down a shadowy set of gray cement steps, opened a fire safety door, and stepped into the crowded laundry room of the White House.

Surprisingly, it smelled of coffee and Danish. A few chairs sat in the corner, one filled by an athletic and alert man who stood at attention at their arrival.

"Please sit down, Troy," said Santaya. "Sorry to meet like this, but privacy comes at a premium in the White House. Thank you for filling me in on your background at our last meeting off campus. I know you are a trusted source through your work with the Blues and particularly with General Hamilton. I had no idea Lu was a traitor until the general apprised me of his tactics just before his assassination. It's strange, but when we conversed, I knew he was telling the truth. I had no idea how to counteract Lu's treachery and figured that Hamilton, the Blues, and others would be taking a lead on that. Now I find myself in this partnership as well with Ed Derkovich. We are working on what seems an almost impossible plan with questionable outcomes. How we could ever have come to this juncture so quickly is hard to fathom.

"Up to this point," she continued, "we are lucky to have proceeded with little detection. As you know, we are rallying our friends from the Blues Militia and the CLF, the Christian Liberation Front, to carry this through. Such irony, that two banned entities are the ones who are going to redeem our country from the enemies of the state. And I will admit I fell for their lies and treachery for way too long. Enough of that, though. It's time to fight."

Mack nodded.

"Now, you let me know that you were present the night General Hamilton and his aide Shamir Wells were killed. Am I correct?"

"Yes, Madam President."

"Call me Santaya, please."

Mack nodded.

"Do you know who pulled the trigger?"

Mack replied, "I've replayed that scene so frequently. I couldn't see the triggerman, just the victims. But his voice sounded familiar. It has a distinct tenor. I've been rehashing it in my memory for months. Since I am part of your security detail, I am hoping that my interactions with government and military personnel will give me greater exposure to our possible murderer. He certainly kills without remorse."

"Agent Griffins," Santaya said, staring intently into his eyes, "I understand you are going to be on my detail for the Freedom Gala this Saturday evening. You will be tasked with contacting another of our operatives, an old acquaintance of yours, who might be able to gather information from other sources. If we can put all these bits and pieces together, we might have a more complete picture of what we are up against. I will play along as you strike up a friendship which will lead to a romantic relationship. You need to act your part. I don't think it will be difficult. But it is your duty. If by chance, you hear the voice of our assassin, try to get my attention and brush the hair out of your face. I will be looking for you several times throughout the evening's activities. There will be so many from the Washington power set, we might just get a break and find our man."

"Madam President...I mean Santaya. I was also led astray for years, with my anger, first toward my father and then against the treachery of Lu and his followers. It is justified anger, but a destructive one. When I heard a direction from the Holy Spirit earlier this year, to give up and follow new marching orders from God's Son, I accepted the assignment. Now I know I am on the right team."

He continued, "Believe it or not, I now have more faith in our fellow citizens making the right decisions because God is directing my path. He's got this. Look at what He has done so far to preserve the lives of both you and your husband."

"Well," Santaya said hesitantly, "you could see it that way. I guess it won't hurt to know that your God is on our side. If He orchestrated these miracles, I will forever be indebted to Him."

"He is the God of Truth and justice. Without His authority, we can do nothing. I truly believe."

"Amen," Shirley chirped in.

Santaya nodded, stood up, and started back to her office as Shirley grabbed some coffee and strawberry Danish. Shirley grabbed Mack's hand. "Another seed is planted. Thank you. We're on our way to see the president's husband. Did you hear he had a miraculous recovery in the past few days?" She pointed to the sky.

Chapter 27

Mercedes Singleton

April 2037

Those who are dominated by the sinful nature think about sinful things, but those who are controlled by the Holy Spirit think about things that please the Spirit. So letting your sinful nature control your mind leads to death. But letting the Spirit control your mind leads to life and peace. ~ Romans 8:5-6

"Oh, dear Jesus," Mercedes whispered as she attentively applied her lipstick. "I am shaking." Inwardly she processed what would transpire that evening. *This spy stuff is so frightening. I don't know how Titus, managed to keep his composure. Please help me to keep my eyes on you.*

Mercedes peered at her reflection in the makeup mirror. Grabbing a clip filled with glittering stones, she pressed it into the side of her glossy, auburn hair, holding down a few stray strands that would not cooperate.

Closing her eyes, she prayed for peace and wisdom. The calm of the Holy Spirit fell upon her and spoke in a prayer language of His Presence and assistance in time of need. "Trust in me, Mercedes. This night, you will find my Presence in the extraordinary. Hold onto all you see and hear tonight. I am with you."

Opening her eyes, she glanced at the clock.

Oh, my ride will be here shortly. She grabbed her coat which looked a bit stodgy and made a mental note to upgrade her apparel to appeal to the base instincts of Roker. She knew he was nothing more than an opportunist and a predator in official Washington clothes, gratifying himself in any way he could if it was undetected, or at least not reported by the government media.

That had been easy to stifle several times in his career with a few choice calls to the reporter's management. One scratched the back of the other. Roker often passed them security information that was supposed to remain private. The media moguls used it to their advantage, especially against the minority members in the legislature.

Her cell phone chimed, and Mercedes whisked down the hall, onto the elevator, and out the front door of her apartment complex.

Awaiting her was a sleek limo, much smaller than the earlier ostentatious models, but still luxurious inside. The driver held her hand as she stepped in, revealing a look at her long legs as the dress she wore separated at the fold.

Roker sniffed. "Looking lovely, Mercedes. You can slay anyone with those legs, friend or foe! Am I a friend, Mercedes?"

She could tell the senator was inebriated, far more than usual. "Of course, Senator," she calmly whispered as she pecked his cheek.

"Here. Have a drink, my favorite, a Manhattan." He handed her a glass and she demurely took a sip.

"Oh, my grandfather would drink these," she responded. "Not my father, though. Never touched a drop."

"Your father is a Neanderthal. Teetotaler, preacher man, and supporter of the Blues. Useless and dangerous."

Mercedes sucked in her breath. *Oh, you sly devil,* she thought. *Satan trying to agitate me right from the start. Well, I'm on high alert, you reptile!*

Turning to the senator, Mercedes spoke with a warm purr. "Now, Senator Roker, my father is a good man. He's off in his own world in his head. I've never once seen him have any connection with the Blues. What gives you that idea?"

Roker paused to gather his thoughts. He knew he was spilling privileged information. "I thought I heard that somewhere. Never mind. Come on, down your drink. To your grandfather!" he cheered as he raised his glass shakily.

The Freedom Gala was an event of excess. Mercedes was sickened by the extravagance of the seven courses served. She could see the envy and hunger in the eyes of the servers. What must they be thinking, with all the fine silver, china, and overabundance of delicacies? Midway through the meal, there was a rustle of voices moving in waves through the assemblage. Looking up, Mercedes spied President Woodring and a few of her Secret Service detail belatedly entering the room.

Her mind raced back to Ricardo's directive informing her that she would be contacting one member of this team during the evening. Despite the pressure, she relished the excitement of the unknown. *Play the part,* she chided herself.

After dinner, she excused herself to go to the powder room. Arriving, she glanced at herself in the mirror. *Not bad for a little country girl.* The teal dress hung elegantly from her white shoulders and was styled to accentuate her figure. A bit too tight for her liking, but Roker had chosen it.

Slowly she walked past President Woodring's detail, and accidentally stumbled over a tray stand holding the dessert plates.

A warm hand grabbed hers and steadied her.

"Thank you," she said, looking at the slightly burly Secret Service man holding her hand perhaps a bit too long.

He looked stern, but there appeared to be a hint of mischief dancing in his eyes. Something about him seemed familiar.

"I've been looking forward to this evening," he said.

"As have I."

"Would you care to move down the hall a bit? There are others here watching the president. It will be for just a moment. You can follow me at a distance."

Down at the end of the hall outside the ballroom, the agent stepped into a tight storage room filled with starched tablecloths and miscellaneous paraphernalia. The agent closed the door behind her softly and turned out the light. A faint glow rose from under the door, enough to roughly see the details of the room and its occupants.

"Thank you for coming," he whispered. "My name is Troy Griffins. I am a fairly new recruit to President Woodring's security team. I know you were alerted to the fact that we would rendezvous at this gala. It is a delight to meet you."

He smiled and Mercedes felt uncomfortable. Yet something about him struck her as familiar.

"Somehow, I feel like we've met before," she said. "I understand from a contact that you will be a liaison in the next few months so that I can transfer information back and forth to Roker's office. It seems that we've been tasked with developing, as they call it, a 'romantic relationship.' It's certainly useful as a source for passing on to Roker skewed information which he thinks will be coming from the president's inner circle. Roker of course will pass it on to Lu. Do I have that right?"

"Yes," he said as he grabbed her shoulders and pulled her to him, pressing a kiss on her lips. "We are to be lovers," he said nonchalantly.

Mercedes staggered back a step. She held up her hand to catch her breath. Inside, forces were battling for control. The kiss felt genuine.

But she didn't even know him. He was a stranger, and she would not demean herself sexually unless it was absolutely necessary. There were many scars from her relationship with Dr. David Kim and of course, the repeated rapes of the warden at the rehabilitation camp.

"Don't worry," said Troy with a soft chuckle. "It is fine to play along. And I will take it at your pace. I'm a gentleman and won't force myself on you. Look into my eyes so that you can see that I am serious."

Agent Troy flicked on the light and they both blinked at the sudden illumination. His youthful smirk was gone as he stood there in earnest, staring at her bewilderment.

Mercedes raised her eyes to his. She stared for a protracted series of seconds as her mind jumped to a silly conclusion.

Those eyes look like Mack's but are the wrong color. The speck is there. But look at that nose. Definitely not. Who is he?

Closing her eyes, Mercedes hung her head. "I will do whatever is necessary to save those lives put in danger by the demonic forces in our government. I will gladly suffer for them," she spoke dispassionately.

"I will do everything in my power, Mercedes, to keep you from suffering. I, too, am led by a higher power to assist the persecuted and suffering, particularly those who suffer for their faith. That is a pinky promise from me, and Danny and Walt."

The words shocked Mercedes.

She stood transfixed by the short speech from the supposed stranger. He leaned in and kissed her again. "Mercedes," he whispered.

She pressed into him and voiced with suspicion, "Mack?"

Woodenly, he nodded. "A bit of cutting here, a tuck there. Definitely a new nose and tinted eye implants. Voila! I'm an identical twin to a former government operative in Russia. Low and behold, I have been revived! What do you think?"

Mercedes sputtered, "Well, you are still strong and handsome in a different way."

"Good enough for me. Will you be my accomplice in this dastardly operation?"

"Of course." She grinned.

"Let's practice," he said as he pulled her in for another kiss. "I've dreamed of this for months," he whispered as his warm breath covered her mouth.

Mercedes responded to the embrace. Her mind was flying in a thousand different directions at once. But somehow, in some way, she felt prayers had been answered. Her dreams were coming true.

Silently, the couple mingled into the self-absorbed crowd. Mack occasionally met the eye of President Woodring as she slowly worked the crowd as required by her political position and this event.

Then it was time for the short speaking engagement scheduled on the program. Moving behind the podium, her security detail placed protective shields in the traditional locations and silently exited the stage. Compassionately, President Woodring linked the arts to the best of humanity, connecting the individual's inner yearnings with the opportunity to express oneself.

"We were created with these gifts," she explained.

Mack hoped she would continue, "by the grace of God."

Although she paused, it was to refocus and continue the script. Something to Santaya suddenly felt amiss. She felt as though evil had entered the stage and a shiver ran down her spine.

Following her speech, the National Awards for Art Expression were awarded to American students in attendance. Santaya held the medallions as Marcus Chenyuk, the Association President, passed them out.

At the conclusion of the ceremony, Santaya stayed seated on the stage as Marcus announced the incoming chairman, Mr. Kevin McKay. There was a quiet rumble throughout the room. It seemed an odd choice by the Arts Council. McKay was a retired Army general and married to the FBI director, Myrna White-Ferguson. The president was mystified, as were most in attendance, when he came to the podium to thank the membership for "enhancing" his selection.

"I so appreciate this opportunity to reach the children of America in a more intimate way, through the arts. It is my hope that children all over the world will have access to express themselves freely someday in a similar fashion, unencumbered by the ancient strictures of religion, morality, and nationalism. Art will then know her true place in freedom."

President Woodring caught the slight hand gesture by Mack. While all the eyes were on McKay, she was transfixed that Mack was straightening his hair repetitively. It looked like he had a cowlick that had gone rogue. Recognizing the sign Mack was giving caused Santaya to immediately refocus on Kevin McKay. It was evident that his was the voice Mack had heard when General Hamilton and Shamir Wells were assassinated.

Standing ten feet from her was the murderer of her son, Lt. Col. Shamir Wells and executioner of General Marcus Hamilton, leader of the Blues Militia. Her blood ran cold. She stared at the man who now desired to be champion of America's school children. She surmised this was an avenue to indoctrinate a teen army into his worldview. His comments were sickening.

Santaya grabbed the sides of her chair and struggled to refrain from crying out, "Murderer!" Shaking with anger, she stood and applauded at the end of his rallying speech. But hers were claps of revenge and hatred and icy hot rage. And she had to acknowledge another voice, one more peaceful. "He's mine as well."

Realizing that he was married to the FBI director meant that all she had shared with Myra White-Ferguson was now common knowledge to Lu. Santaya wondered if their cause was lost. But now she knew who had poisoned DeShaun, her husband.

Chapter 28

Mercedes and Mack

April 2037

We are witnesses of these things and so is the Holy Spirit, who is given by God to those who obey him. ~ Acts 5:32

In her wildest dreams, Mercedes had no idea she could experience true love. Yes, she had lived with Dr. David Kim in a relationship based on mutual respect, adventure, and sex. But with Mack, it was different. A few weeks into their stealthy dates and dalliances, Mack asked her to marry him. "Nothing formal, mind you, Mercedes. I would not want you the way I do and feel that God would bless our relationship if we did not follow convention. Please say yes to my proposal. I love you."

"Mack," she responded, tears welling up. "I am so touched. I do love you. I guess I always have in some way since back in Whitsville when you asked for seconds on potatoes. 'Yes' is my answer."

Mack was shocked.

"Where can we find a pastor?" quizzed Mercedes.

"I know who to ask—Shirley Smythe, the president's executive assistant. She let it slip one time while we were talking, about a special message her pastor had shared with her. She knows I am a brother in Christ."

Two days later, they met Reverend LeTron Allison at an intimate park on the outskirts of D.C. He brought along his wife as a witness and Shirley attended as well. He blessed their union, they shared their personal vows with each other, and then with a great flourish, he declared them married in the sight of God. There would be no public record, but in heaven's courts, the wedding bells rang and they committed themselves to a shared relationship chiseled by God's command.

Moving in with Mercedes, the couple observed a new bliss; partners more devoted to each other than themselves. Many late evenings, they shared intimate thoughts, personal stories, damaged egos and wounds. Nothing was judged, just spoken to an equal who cared enough to carry the other's pain.

Mercedes's former partner, Dr. David Kim, had always centered his life around himself, perhaps because of his parents' enmity and eventual divorce. Whatever the reason, he liked Mercedes for her beauty, poise, and availability in the bedroom. Now she found a completion with Mack she had never felt before—peace and deep appreciation.

Their love for each other was recognized by each of them as something different from their earlier sexual relationships. Their love making was not centered on obtaining sexual gratification for themselves. Rather, each of them pressed into their partner with a desire to make them the center of an outward expression of their profound love. The results were mesmerizing and heightened times of intimacy they had never experienced before.

Before they fell asleep each night, Mack would begin a prayer. He would chant a praise to Jesus several times over.

"Good thing you don't try to sing," laughed Mercedes, knowing his lack of ability to find the notes.

The H.S.

Then she would call on the Holy Spirit to surround them, their work, their families, friends, and country. "Holy Spirit, bind Mack and me to each other forever, until you call us to be with you."

One night, Mack seemed troubled after her prayer.

"What is bothering you, Mack?" she posed.

"I need to come clean about something from my past. It's been burdening me for years. I've tried to say it was justified and right, but I don't think it was, and the Spirit has been working in me to clear this up with Him."

"Do you think it needs to be aired, or would you be better just letting it lie dormant? Do I need to hear about your past? Is it about your former marriage? Listen, I have just as much baggage as you and won't cast any stones."

"No, before that, when I was a kid. Back in Whitsville."

"What could be so dramatic, Mack? Borrowing your aunt's car to go joy riding? I know that almost cost us the state championship when the sheriff let you off with a warning instead of throwing your sorry behind in jail for a few days." She chuckled at the memory and tenderly punched him on the arm.

"Oh, you heard about that?"

Mercedes laughed. "Nothing is safe in a small town. You should know that."

"Well, this never came to light and I'm ashamed of it. I have never been able to forgive myself." He turned to Mercedes and gazed into her eyes. "Mercedes, I killed my dad."

"What?" she exhaled in disbelief. Her voice had risen several notes with the revelation. "What are you talking about? He died in a house fire. That's when Walt came to live with us."

"Yeah, I had been out drinking with some buddies the night before. Dad got angry with Walt because I wasn't there to take him to a bar, so he beat Walt up pretty bad. I didn't notice until the next morning. My brother's face was so swollen, his one eye was almost closed. Dad was an animal. He couldn't see how wrong it was to beat up a poor kid who would not defend himself.

"Anyway, I knew I was leaving in a few weeks for boot camp and that Walt would be left alone to take his abuse. Walt always made excuses for Dad's awful behavior. I knew it would just escalate because no one would be there to push back on his anger.

"I asked Walt out for breakfast and ran back into the house to grab a few things I needed, as well as some keepsakes. Dad was sitting in his chair, passed out from several fifths of booze. I lit a fire by his chair with some old rags, grabbed my duffle bag for camp and headed to the café as nonchalantly as if nothing had happened. Walt was on cloud nine and couldn't see the inner turmoil in my heart. While we were eating, the sheriff came in and drove us to the house. I couldn't make myself feel anything when the firemen told me dad was dead. But Walt, he was heartbroken. He always was a better person than I was."

Mack dropped his gaze. "I am so sorry. I've kept this to myself all these years. It would have crushed Walt. I always said Dad deserved it, and he did, but it was wrong to take his life. I'm sorry, Mercedes. I want to rid myself of this egregious sin. Can I ask God to forgive me? Can you forgive me? I know I would handle it differently now that I am a Christian. But I need to pay for Dad's death."

Mercedes was rendered speechless. Slowly she regained her thoughts and took Mack's hands in hers.

"Mack, you need to ask God for forgiveness. Until now, you were not ready to admit your guilt. Now you've grown in your faith and understand that this sin is lying between you and God. And between us too. I have a hard time understanding how you could do something so heinous, but I think that if I was in your shoes, I would have thought of ways to protect my brother as well. Killing your father was not the solution. Can you ask the Holy Spirit to grant you forgiveness?"

Mack got out of bed and fell down on his knees. He was weeping. He didn't care. "Dear Jesus, I killed my father. I am so sorry. I broke your commandment to love my father and not to kill. I sinned and grieved your Spirit. I want to ask for forgiveness. You know I don't deserve it. But I can't go on with this guilt. It has been eating away at me since I became a believer in your grace and love. I need your forgiveness. Please Jesus, heal my soul and punish me as you see fit."

Mercedes knelt down on the cold floor and put her arms around him as he prayed, praying with him quietly in her sincere God talk. She was weeping as well. When he was done praying, she said, "Mack, God forgives us when we are truly sorry and repent. You have done that. He will do with you what He wishes. For now, you need to go on. God is using you in amazing ways to help our Christian brothers and sisters who are trapped in those despicable work camps. You can't turn yourself in! That would blow your cover. You've done the hard part and admitted your guilt. I still love you. This is just such a shock."

For the next several days, Mercedes made sure to affirm Mack's understanding that he was forgiven by God. Man would perhaps in the future demand another accounting. One night she patted him on the thigh. "Hey, lover boy. I miss church. It's been forever. I wish I was back in Dad's church worshipping with some semblance of freedom. When are we ever going to get our right to freedom of religion back in this country? I feel stifled! At least in the Middle Regions they are brave enough to flaunt the restrictions on communal worship. What happened to the church?"

"You've got TV preachers," Mack responded, adding mischievously, "what about Timothy Prescott?"

She punched him softly. "Oh, the minister of the high and mighty, the corrupt and evil? He makes my skin crawl every time I see him. Occasionally I see him wandering through the Senate halls visiting his comrades. I try to plead the blood of Jesus over our offices after he leaves. Senator Roker seems to be a favorite of his. Imagine that! Eventually he'll show his Satanic side to the world, but right now people are devouring his easy-to-swallow swill. He's always at the events I attend with Senator Roker. Of all the dangerous people in Washington, I think he is the worst."

"Easy girl," joked Mack. "Worse than General Lu?" he added as he propped himself up to look in her eyes.

"Well, Lu is a physical danger, under evil influences seeking earthly power and control. Prescott, on the other hand, is a spiritual danger. His syrupy portrayal of Jesus as the Messiah of social change is a perversion. His acceptance of evil in mankind using the excuse that this is just how we are made, leaves out the necessary ingredient of our sinfulness and our need for redemption from a Savior who can redeem. Prescott wants to be pals with everyone. Anything goes, and he twists Jesus into some sort of comfortable social worker. We end up affirming the sin and the sinner. I wouldn't be surprised if he thought he was the Messiah."

"Preach it, Mercedes," teased Mack.

"Jesus came to us to bring change because we are so broken. All of us. He wants us restored for His kingdom. Prescott is just making citizens for hell."

"You really hate that guy," kidded Mack.

"No, I hate his deception. I pray for the millions of Christians and agnostics who drink his swill. They look to him instead of the Holy Spirit for answers. He's become their god."

That night, Mercedes had a vivid nightmare featuring Prescott and his followers. Together they were all connected by a rope that was threaded through hooks in their noses. They were forced to pull carts of dead bodies toward a deep chasm. It was filled with a vile, stifling odor which rose and surrounded them. Meanwhile the decomposing bodies chanted, "We trusted you as our salvation. We followed you into perdition. God help us." Their arms and legs flailed about in the cart with no purpose. The vision was bone chilling.

Waking with a frightened start, Mercedes flung her arm toward Mack and felt his rhythmic breathing as his chest moved up and down in his peaceful repose.

Oh Jesus, are we losing the battle? It is so ugly out there. How can we fight for you when so many are alienated? It seems desperate and the end looks like defeat. I am afraid for us. Give us time together to love and live.

She closed her eyes, folded her hands, and snuggled into Mack.

Mercedes, you just saw Prescott's followers. A forever world of torment, lost, hideous. I am making a way to rescue the faithful you left in your camp. Strengthen yourself in my word. Hold on to me when troubles come; and they will. I hold you in my heart.

Again, she felt something she could describe as a "touch" on her body. She felt the power and the healing.

He is here, she thought as she spread out her arms. *I am yours. Give me your strength to muster on. Protect my love, dear Mack. Guide us, Holy Spirit, into your true and chosen path for our lives. Amen.*

Chapter 29

Arun Polysoing

May 2037

But when you are arrested and stand trial, don't worry in advance about what to say. Just say what God tells you at that time, for it is not you who will be speaking, but the Holy Spirit. ~ Mark 13:11

Stepping out from his basement apartment in Baltimore, Arun felt the late spring warmth bathe his shoulders. Instantly he felt God's hand upon him.

Since the attempt on his life, his miraculous surgery and recovery, Arun had continued to transform from an angry, defiant motivator, to a perceptive, willing servant. He had realized that nothing would be successful in assisting his persecuted Christian brothers and sisters in Christ, if God was not in control.

And so, he had stepped back into his rightful position as a servant leader, continuing to minister to his fellowship of the underserved by following God's lead.

"Finally," said the Spirit. "It took all that ruckus to get your attention!"

Arun was listening, seeing supernaturally, called to "Pay Attention" to the obvious guidance from God.

As he read some pocket scriptures sitting on a camp stool in the dilapidated back yard filled with remnants of discarded junk from a family long gone, he heard the Spirit say, "Now the time has come for an alliance. Send your messengers to Arizona to the leader of the First Nations and tell them they must bring their people to Washington. We need all the warriors for Christ, prepared for battle against the brazen enemy. Battle lines are drawn on August 24. The First Nations with their allies must stand in the gap. They have found me afresh in the Spirit and are ready to lead."

Startled, Arun sat for a moment, shaken by the directive. He was aware that for the past decade, Christians by the tens, hundreds, and thousands had fled the decaying cities and the heavy rule of the Federated States to find refuge in the Native reservations of the west. The autonomous rule allowed them to welcome the faithful, their way of life, and their desire for communal worship, free of interference from government restrictions.

These newcomers had also brought prosperity to the First Nations, bringing resources, businesses, and a community willing to step into their guests' homeland with respect for their history. Amazingly, the revival of the Christian faith had been breaking out in these forgotten barren zones for decades. They were called revivals. Yahweh had poured His natural blessings on their territories with ample rain and a startling agricultural bonanza.

Into these former deserts, life in abundance was springing forth.

Faith City had been developed, platted and built by a wealthy construction company owner, Bob Pachandi. He and his wife Phyllis had been called one night to go to the desert and pray. They drove for hours until the Spirit said, "This is the place for my city."

They had met with the native chief and explained their call. Chief Red Raven Bishop had been born again in the Revival of the Desert. He knew the Spirit was making things new. His support convinced his fellow tribesmen to accept the call of God and allow for the movement of the Spirit that would revitalize his people. Permission for the city was given and the miracle began.

Back in Baltimore, Arun met with his elders that evening.

"We need to send you to the First Nations as our representatives from the underground church. Time is of the essence. You should be able to move safely, as so many people continue to migrate from one place to another, seeking employment and shelter. If anyone questions you, simply state you are moving to Faith City. The government has given permission for believers to gather there. They perceive it to be a destination that gets troublemakers segregated in the desert, far from their concerns."

One of the elders spoke up. "How are we going to convince the chief that you have heard from the Spirit? He will have to convince his followers that we need him in Washington in August to fight for our fellow Christians. They are at peace in their reservations and enjoying the full life of the faithful follower. This would bring them into harm's way."

Arun answered, "The Spirit will have to convict their spirits of God's move. We can do nothing without their assistance. But I imagine the Spirit is at this very moment calling to our fellow friends in the desert, making our way smooth and safe to begin the journey."

The elders fell on their knees. Samantha, a prophetess, spoke words from the Spirit to direct this undertaking.

"Oh, valiant ones of God, step into your task for the Lord. Take up the armor of Christ and meet your allies to do battle for the Lord your God. It is good that you follow His ways. It is good that you come before the Lord with your ears and eyes open to His directives. It is good that you lift the banner of Christ to free the suffering..."

She continued, "I will lead you in my steps, old steps, ancient steps. Follow me! My vanguard will lead the way. Do not let your eyes be distracted to the left or to the right. The world does not comprehend my Truth. Listen instead to my voice and you will be content. I will give you springs of living water to refresh your souls. I will determine your victory. I am with you always to the ends of the age."

Samantha and the others shook as though they were buffeted by a mighty windstorm. The Holy Spirit wafted His presence through their minds and bodies, pressing into them His Truth. They shook for joy and praised His name.

A song broke out:

Holy, holy, holy Lord,

God of power and might, All the earth is filled with your glory.

Hosannah, hosannah, in the highest,

Blessed is He who comes in the name of the Lord.

Hours of prophecy and Presence continued for Arun and his team as they listened and prayed. God was orchestrating another season of battle against Satan. They would be wary. They would be prepared. They were sure the First Nations were ready as well.

"Lord, make your Way, our way," praised Arun.

Chapter 30

Ricardo Medina

May 2037

Then he said to me, "This is what the Lord says to Zerubbabel: It is not by force nor by strength, but by my Spirit, says the Lord of Heaven's Armies. Nothing, not even a mighty mountain, will stand in Zerubbabel's way; it will become a level plain before him!"
~ Zechariah 4:6–7

"Damn!" whispered Ricardo under his breath as he barely missed the last powerful ricochet of the handball that whizzed past his face.

His playing partner, Colin Lu, had become a worthy adversary on the handball court at the Army base. They were well matched in strategic aptitude and physical prowess.

"You're killin' me," grunted Ricardo to Colin.

"Guess I got the goods on you today, old man."

"Hey, you're older than me," Ricardo retorted.

Colin flashed a suspicious smile at Ricardo. "How do you know?"

"I'm making a guess from things you've said about your family."

Colin changed the subject. "You look worn out this week. What's the Army got you chasing? Between you and my dad, I would guess the heat has turned up a notch or two. He's been hotter than hell the past couple of nights. So angry, it's useless to have a conversation with him. You should hear him screaming to himself when the doors of the den are closed. Who the heck could make him that angry?"

Ricardo laughed. "Probably the team, including me, who are on the front lines. There are changes being made in personnel every week and we're all jittery. Seems your dad is unsure about his inner circle and who can be trusted. That's the world we live in."

"Shit, I hate the world," Colin returned. "It's a mess. No purpose. Let's go get a beer. Life's simple pleasures. Maybe pick up a lovely lady to chase the blues away too."

"Sure," Ricardo replied. He liked to spend time with Colin at the bars as alcohol loosened his tongue. He hoped that some of the disinformation fed by Mercedes to Senator Roker might show up in the conversation. Perhaps that's what Lu's ramblings were about.

When they got to the bar, the flat-screened televisions were featuring a world soccer match. Much of the world had diverted their attention to the intense competition. It had a way of soothing the soul and making the world appear as though normalcy had returned, when in actuality it was all a ruse. The world was falling apart. Colin and Ricardo gazed at the screens, disinterested.

"I miss baseball," sighed Colin. "Prickin' progressives ruined the game. Alienated the fans with their constant barrage of social causes and identities that neither the fans nor the players cared much about. All we wanted was a diversion to cheer for. It used to be 'America's pastime.' That sure fell out of favor when the idea took hold that the USA was an evil empire. Guess the owner's association bears some blame too for getting caught funneling money to Japan and China to fund competitive world teams. The fans like me said, 'Enough.' They killed America's game; the last gasp of air was breathed at home plate last fall. Adios."

"Don't get so dramatic," chipped in Ricardo. "You do a good job when you are on your soapbox, but baseball was boring. That's no better," he said as he pointed to the TV screens.

As they shifted their gaze, a news flash hit the screen. The anchor announced, "We now interrupt this program to carry an unexpected news conference with President Santaya Woodring."

President Woodring, dressed in her usual attire, walked to the podium at the White House. She was dressed in her traditional suit and appeared alert and composed as she thanked the American citizens and others around the world for keeping her and her husband in their thoughts and prayers.

"It has been an extremely trying time here at the White House. The accidental poisoning of my husband along with the assassination attempt on my life has forced me to live a more sheltered existence. We have enemies within and are working diligently to bring the perpetrators of these heinous acts to justice. We will not shirk from our duty as our work to benefit you continues.

"This broadcast, however, is not about me. It is about you and the direction of our country. As you know, I have been working nonstop in an attempt to broker a peaceful solution between the sparring nations of China, its proxy Pakistan, and India. They are on the brink of conflict and there is still a glimmer of hope that diplomacy will win over conflict. A war, if engaged, would most likely spread. My team and I are determined to do what we can to resolve this peacefully. It has been a trying journey. We need all of you to hold out hope that mankind will prevent this senseless tragedy from escalating. God help us." Santaya accidentally let this phrase slip out. A faint smile touched her lips.

"I have not forgotten you here on the home front. In looking to the players on the foreign stage, I've seen again the precious gifts that you, as citizens, share in our country of individualism and freedom. We were built on the foundations of a Constitutional Republic with rights that most of us cherish, and with the hope that they lead to the fulfillment of our hopes and dreams.

"Our country has suffered this decade through war, a killer virus, and a catastrophic volcanic eruption. We were forced in the bedlam that ensued to encroach on your rights for the good of the country. I believed it was necessary for us to enact strong legislation to control the unrest and chaos. Many did not. In those harrowing times, we had sections of cities burned to the ground, random gangs and militias turning their ire on innocent civilians, kidnappings for ransom, and attempts to disrupt daily services such as water and electricity. We have battled these incendiary forces and have emerged victorious. And we have survived!

"But amidst all this upheaval, we lost sight of the reason we as a government exist. We are here to guard your rights, not take them away.

"The right for religious expression and the freedom of religion has been severely restricted. Public worship is illegal, as you know. Perpetrators have been punished and sent to rehabilitation camps. Most of these people are not guilty of serious threats to our way of life. They do not belong to terrorist groups or other extremist entities. Some of the religious groups were labeled as terrorist perpetrators, I believe, and have been mistakenly categorized.

"It has come to my attention that life in these rehabilitation camps is hell; perpetuated by our ignorance, sponsored by us, and existing in squalor while we turn a blind eye. I am going to show you a five-minute clip of life in one of these camps made by a government doctor assigned there."

The screen shifted to a series of disgusting images, footage of beatings, inhumane torture, and starvation. Those watching could not believe that these were the conditions so many had willingly sanctioned. It was a mirror of the concentration camps of WWII, except for the crematoriums. Unfortunately, those were also a reality.

"I had no idea that our fellow citizens, sentenced to these camps without a trial, have been denied the simplest of human rights and are treated so inhumanely for simply placing their faith in a certain religious structure. We should be ashamed and dismayed. Yes, there are dangerous elements in these communities. We will ferret them out. For now, I will present an executive order that these detainees be given a speedy and fair trial in the next three months, assessing their threat to the country.

"If they are found to be nonviolent, my executive order frees them from serving any additional time. Any jailed unfairly will receive a stipend for the work they were compelled to do at these centers. We will no longer perpetuate terror and rampant cruelty. The Department of Justice, under the able leadership of my new director, Evelyn Soo, will be leading this project. Salteri Worthsire has been relieved of her duties."

She continued, "One additional matter needs our attention. We need to think of the future. Our country is on the cusp of rebounding from the disruptions of disease, war, and climate. It is time to build a strategy to return to our abandoned home territories in the Middle Region where many of you were required to leave to receive government services.

"I have crafted a small team of ten business leaders to assist in drawing up a plan to revitalize twenty small metropolitan areas in locations formerly closed due to our shutdown of areas affected by the volcanic explosion in Yellowstone. It is time to slowly go home. We will work diligently by year's end to begin the process of repatriating you, our treasured citizens, to once again reclaim your communities. This will be done by rebuilding city services, preserving energy consumption, and providing a better quality of life for those of you who have endured the hardships of the past. This will also energize our economy and provide thousands of job opportunities for those seeking valid employment. Hope is on the horizon!

"I am thrilled that your lives are once again going to reflect the rights and privileges assigned to every American citizen. We can do this together. It won't be easy. We will need to sacrifice and pitch in, but in the end, we will find that we are greater together as a body of individuals who truly care for one another. It is up to you to step up and do your share. As President John F. Kennedy so aptly stated, 'Do not ask what your country can do for you, ask what you can do for your country.'

"Take care, brave Americans. Until we meet again."

Santaya Woodring walked back into the White House as the corps of reporters regained their thoughts after the stunning speech. They began to hurl questions to no avail. But they had lots of commentary. They could not remember when they had last heard such a personal speech full of redemption and hope. The video played and replayed on their news outlets for the remainder of the day. It was now time for soul searching and accountability.

Ricardo looked at Colin. "That was some serious shit. That lady has guts!"

"What the hell are we keeping prison camps like this for?" breathed Colin. "Crap, that's disgusting. Those people were walking skeletons."

"Your dad will be reacting shortly to the news, I'm sure," said Ricardo. "I better get back to my post before something hits the fan. There will be a lot of finger-pointing in the next few days."

"Sure, man," said Colin. "Game next week? Same time?"

Ricardo nodded. His mind was racing. He knew Lu would feel threatened that President Woodring was flexing her muscles by reinstituting First Amendment rights. Lu wanted the citizenry to stay captive to fear and proposed a tightening of control rather than loosening the reins. As a bonus for the president, she offered the American citizen hope that many of their former homes and communities would one day be habitable again after an era of forced migration to the metropolitan centers. Many of the citizenry tonight would undoubtably hold some sort of primal hope in their hearts.

Woodring was being publicly savvy. She had endeared herself in the hearts of the hurting and the lost. "Smart lady," he mumbled. "But not smart enough."

Chapter 31

Mack Gersham

May 2037

As soon as they heard this, they were baptized in the name of the Lord Jesus. Then when Paul laid his hands on them, the Holy Spirit came on them, and they spoke in other tongues and prophesied. ~ Acts 19: 5-6

Mercedes was bursting with excitement, waiting for Mack to return from work. He had called stating that he'd be home later than usual that evening. He would fill her in when he got home.

After Santaya's press conference, Shirley Smythe, the president's executive assistant, asked Mack to come with her for a visit to a very special location within the White House. Her words confused him.

"You are one of us. Follow me. Better clock out first," she said in business-like fashion.

Shirley hugged Santaya who looked weary. "Madam President, God has spoken through your words today. Thank you for giving those who live in America hope and purpose."

Then she realized that perhaps she was being too familiar, especially in the White House hallway.

"I'm sorry. I was so overcome by your words," whispered Shirley.

"I appreciate your kindness. And just a private word for you." President Woodring leaned over and whispered in her ear. "I am on my way to pick up DeShaun. He's been cleared to return home. I want to keep this under the radar." She smiled thinly.

Shirley squeezed her hand.

Mack returned from completing his daily report and stood at attention next to Shirley.

"This way, young man," she directed him down the hall.

They wandered through a labyrinth of corridors. Arriving at a private meeting room deep in the bowels of the White House, she knocked on the door. Slowly it opened.

The room was darkened, but not silent. Speaking quietly, singing softly, joyous noises emanated from the small gathering.

"This is our worship service," quipped Shirley with a huge smile. "And we are in a celebrating mood! Halleluiah."

Shirley could not contain herself. She silently closed the door, trapping Mack. He observed from the back wall a group of Jesus Christ followers participating in illegal behavior, but hopefully such worship wouldn't be flaunting the law for long.

The presence of the Holy Spirit was wafting through the room. It poured itself over Mack and he fell unintentionally but softly to the floor, moaning and singing. In his mind, he knew God was with him, covering him with acceptance and joy. Mack held out his arms to receive the forgiveness he cried for, and the Spirit accepted his pleas. The Spirit coursed through his body, shaking his mind, body, and soul with a cleansing power.

"Dear Jesus," he chanted over and over. "Lord, touch me again," he asked. And the Spirit sent another wave of Presence over his prostrate body. All his mind could comprehend was the amazing presence of God in the moment. A change of being, like a new birth, a new dosage

The H.S.

of blood filled his body and mind. "Oh Lord," he said softly. "I feel my wounds closing, covered, complete, cleansed."

Mack was in the process of letting the Holy Spirit reshape his identity. Then he dropped into a deep trance.

Chapter 32

Ricardo Medina

June 2037

One day as these men were worshiping the Lord and fasting, the Holy Spirit said, "Appoint Barnabas and Saul for the special work to which I have called them." ~ Acts 13:2

Ricardo was nursing his beer, sweat droplets still forming despite a cool shower after a prolonged handball match with Colin Lu.

Colin was uncharacteristically quiet. In a whisper he muttered, "All hell is breaking loose. Warn your friends at the White House to keep vigilant. A coup is brewing."

Transfixed, Ricardo managed to reply, "Who told you that?"

"Derk."

"Derkovich?"

"Yeah, best man in town. He decided now is the time to warn you to cover any tracks that might possibly be exposed. My dad is angry. By the way, good job breaking into the family computer and pilfering some of those emails to give us an idea of who else is involved in the plot. Dad figured his missives weren't safe a couple months ago and changed the password. For the life of me, I could not figure out the new one and couldn't get back in."

"How long have you been a mole in your own household?" asked Ricardo nonchalantly.

"A year or so. Derkovich approached me with proof the bastard was selling out the USA to those nut jobs at the One Nation Alliance. They want to be the next world dictator. They've done a good job messaging and convincing a large swath of the world that they can achieve world peace and control the climate changes, all the while allowing for the individual to flourish. Bullshit. Nothing but communists with pretty faces. Indoctrination leads to domination."

Ricardo was silent. Inside his mind was a raging battle, questioning how much he should share with Colin. He trusted Ed Derkovich, but Colin Lu? That was another matter.

"Do you know about us?" posed Ricardo.

"Us? About our handball expertise?" scoffed Colin.

"No, us—you and me." Ricardo smiled. He had one-upped the general's son and for a millisecond, it felt good. "We're half-brothers. Your dad and my mom were lovers. For years. Nice to say, 'hi bro' to you now and mean it."

Colin's face contorted in anger. "That Goddamned son of a bitch. Cheating on my mom again. No offense, but he has made her life miserable. This news will kill her. I'm surprised he didn't snuff you out years ago."

"He probably thought I was nothing. Anyway, I ignored him all my life because I hated his guts. He let my mom rot in a putrid care center when she was dying of cancer and did nothing to find her better treatment. When I got back from the war, I couldn't find a job and finally turned to him. He sent me to the Virginias to sniff out the Blues Militia. While there, the Fed Ops killed the kid I was bunking with.

For some reason, they thought he was a Blues Milita. Blew him to bits with a drone strike."

He continued, "I came back here to get revenge. Danny was the best person I ever knew. Your dad, I mean our dad, is responsible for his death. I want to kill him someday with my bare hands."

Ricardo was seething with rage. Colin glanced at him. "You got some of Dad in you, for sure. Calm down, brother. We'll work on this problem together. Best we just go on as handball partners and leave the dirty stuff to the experts."

Colin paused. "Do you think you could kill him?" he posed.

"No problem. He discarded my mom like trash. Me too. He deserves anything he gets."

Colin gave a half-smile and nodded.

Chapter 33

Santaya Woodring-Davis

July 2037

Above all, you must realize that no prophecy in Scripture ever came from the prophet's own understanding, or from human initiative. No, those prophets were moved by the Holy Spirit, and they spoke from God. ~ 2 Peter 1:20-21

The president called a meeting of her support team early the next morning. Richardo had passed a coded message to Mack concerning Colin's warning.

Carefully the small team of comrades, the president, Shirley, the security detail, and two cabinet members who were part of the Christian worshippers gathered before office hours. One was the new head of the Secret Service. The other was head of Health and Human Services. They spent an hour brainstorming exactly how they thought Lu would craft a coup.

"Do you think it will be another assassination attempt?" asked the president.

"No," said the Secret Service chief. "He'll be more creative, and an assassination brings too much compassion from the masses. Lu hates that."

Mack's mind raced. He was mentally pouring through all the pilfered emails Mercedes had managed to download from Roker's computer. Was there a clue in them?

"I've been perusing Roker's emails," Mack said. "I could spend the afternoon looking deeper into the contents. Maybe there's a code or something. He'll certainly want his team of Benedict Arnolds to be ready to guard his back after he unleashes whatever he has planned."

He continued, "It's good to see you again, Ed. Have you picked up anything? I know you've had to lie low these last several weeks. You are a wanted man. You vanished well!"

Ed Derkovich looked crestfallen. "I just don't know where to look. He finally figured out my game and has deleted my files from my secret Pentagon computer system. I'm like a ship without a sail. It's obvious a storm is brewing. We do have others who are keeping tabs on his emails and contacts. There was a message from the One Nation Alliance again today."

The president cleared her throat. "I took this job to help preserve what I thought was our uniqueness and our common rights. I never thought our enemies would come from within. I always thought they were on the other side of the aisle. They are deeper than that. They have tried to kill me and poisoned my husband. They have also killed souls near and dear to me."

Her voice weakened. "What we need to do is get the American people back on board. Reunite the sides against the true enemy. Bring us together with continued reform, less restrictions, and more dialogue, a healthy democracy. We need to get the facts out to the public. For too long we've restricted their access to the espionage occurring in D.C. Our only salvation is to be big and brash. Accuse Lu of treason.

Fast track executive orders to reestablish the freedom of the press, speech, religion. The whole First Amendment. It is time!"

There was silence. Everyone nodded. "Lord," whispered Shirley, "we need your hedge of protection. The enemy is going to be on fire. It's time." She closed her eyes in prayer.

Devon Irwin, the security chief, questioned how the president planned to take these actions without the approval of the Congress. "They'll try to stop you," he stated. "Lu has too many friends in high places, as we well know. Releasing their reins of power is beyond acceptable!"

"I know I'm stepping on their toes. But most of our friends are the voters out there." She motioned out the window, covered in a gold tapestry window covering with a modern simple cut. "They are the only ones who can save us. They need to step up. If we can get them on board, perhaps we'll have a chance to counter Lu. We need the preemptive strike."

"We know we have the Blues Militia and the CLF on our side."

The president was shaken. "Are they really friends? Maybe the Blues, but the CLF? I thought they were covertly assassins." Santaya recalled her conversation with the couple who had raised her son from infancy. She knew the CLF was not responsible for the heinous acts perpetrated against General Hamilton and his aide. But she would continue with the prevailing diatribe for the time being.

"No," said Mack hesitantly. "General Hamilton coordinated the Blues Militia. Trust me on this. They are prepared to immediately step in to protect this office. The CLF have new leadership and they are our friends. Mercedes has met with their leader, Arun Polysoing, and he has pledged his fealty."

"So I've been told," sighed the president. "It seems they were falsely targeted with the death of Hamilton and his aide. Sick business. We need to punish the killer, don't we, Troy?"

Everyone looked at Mack. How would he know the back story of those assassinations? The eyes that stared at him had many questions. He most likely knew much more than had been shared. After all, he was instrumental in diverting vast swaths of military paraphernalia to depots now used by the Blues resistance while working with General Hamilton.

"All right," began the president, taking charge. "Let's get a statement put together laying out our position. We need public dialogue groups and solid leaders who support the return to constitutional rights. A slogan too."

"Mercedes can help," volunteered Mack. "She's wrapped up her work with the ElderCare Senior Health Initiative revisions. She's a genius in marketing. What about the communication systems? How are we going to entice the broadcasting companies to break ranks with Lu?"

"We've got our government station. And we can do it the old way—an airdrop of pamphlets in the metro areas before they know what hits them. We need a team who can jam the government computer systems long enough to get our message out to the public. They will try to blow us out of the water with their familiar charges of disinformation or conspiracy theory. We've only got one shot at this."

"I'm on it," said Ed Derkovich. "I might be down, but I still have some tricks up my sleeve. I should be able to manage that for a day or two. We will put the Pentagon in a tizzy, though." He could picture Lu's contorted face.

"All right," said the president. "Shirley, will you say a prayer? We need the Lord to help us in the firestorm that's coming."

No one registered surprise at the request, but all present had seen the slow advancement of the president's newfound faith, once DeShaun had returned to the White House. She knew a higher power had saved his life and she had become a seeker.

Shirley asked for a newfound awareness of God the Spirit to guide their paths. They were few in number and needed supernatural protection. "Dear God," begged Shirley as she continued, "Our work is impossible without you."

Chapter 34

Mack Gersham

July 2037

One day when the crowds were being baptized, Jesus himself was baptized. As he was praying, the heavens opened, and the Holy Spirit, in bodily form, descended on him like a dove. And a voice from heaven said, "You are my dearly loved Son, and you bring me great joy."
~ Luke 3:21-22

When Mack returned to the apartment around dusk, he asked Mercedes to go for a walk with him.

She looked at him bewilderingly, knowing the risk of encountering either local drug dealers or black-market gang members. While he checked his gun holstered under his arm, she nodded yes.

Wrapping themselves in dark windbreakers, the pair marched quietly down the alley and then turned toward the river walk skirting the Jefferson Memorial, more carefully monitored by law enforcement.

"I need to talk to you about our meeting in the Oval Office today," said Mack straightforwardly. "We have information that the president and her team will soon be targeted by Lu in his bid to remove her from office. He will take over the reins of government. We aren't sure how or when, but it is necessary to be prepared. Potentially, our lives are in danger as well. This is no longer a simple game of cat and mouse. That rat is ready to pounce. He has the benefit of knowing the game plan. We can only just react.

"I need you to be safe." He gazed at her stomach a moment and smiled. "And the little person too. How we've been blessed. Anyway, if something happens, I will try to notify you. Your job will be to get out of this city safely and back to Whitsville. If that's not good enough, find the Blues. They can shelter you indefinitely."

Mercedes paused and grabbed his hand. "Mack, I would never leave you. You know that. It took us too long to find each other and God wants us here to support each other and the cause of freedom."

"Mercedes, we have more to think about than ourselves," he spoke hurriedly. "I'm not asking you to hide forever, just until it's safe. Lu and his gang, including Roker, are close to setting the trap. If I'm caught in it, I need to know you are safe. Otherwise, you'll be interrogated inhumanely, and most likely, we would never see our baby alive. Chances are they have also figured out that you have pilfered Roker's emails as well, so you are at risk of arrest for your own actions. Promise me that if the time comes to flee to safety, you will go."

Mercedes turned and looked Mack in the eyes in the dark shadows of the evening, but said nothing.

He continued, "I've put in a requisition for a government car for the next month. I'll retrofit it with a rotating license plate, so that it can't be tracked. Use it to drive to Whitsville during the day. Try to go in the early morning if possible. It's dangerous in the dark on the remote roads farther out. You know about the carjackings. Get to your dad's house. I've sent him instructions through a friend."

The look Mercedes gave Mack was heartbreaking. Holding her stomach with the palm of her left hand, she questioned, "Is it that bad,

Mack? Has the enemy been unleashed? How are you going to escape the carnage?"

"Yes, it is a time of extreme danger. Our enemy has no mercy. Since they think I am Troy Griffins, it really makes things dicey for me. He played with fire too many times and got all parties angry with him. He double-crossed the Russians and from what I am finding out, he also tripped up Lu as well. Lu had some secret dealings with the Russians during the Middle East war. That guy was cavorting with the enemy long before joining the One Nation Alliance in secrecy. He's been selling our secrets for decades. Lu knows that Troy Griffins can provide proof of his covert actions aimed at enlarging his offshore bank accounts. He has millions stashed in these foreign accounts but is still looking for the haul that Troy Griffins promised to forward to him. Griffins stiffed him from some very lucrative proceeds that were promised to come his way."

"If I send you a text or note saying, 'All is well,' leave immediately, Mercedes."

In her mind, Mercedes could hear the words of the song, *All Is Well with My Soul,* racing through her brain. "But, Mack, I can't survive without you. Can't you just sneak out with me?"

"Sooner or later, someone is going to figure out who I really am. Plus, I'm on the president's inner team providing her security. We will always be prime targets to get to her. It's too late to disappear and I have a duty to perform. I guess I knew this a few years ago when I pledged my allegiance to General Hamilton. He was sticking up for the American people. There aren't many survivors. It is the right thing to do."

"Oh, Mack," Mercedes cried as she buried her tear-stained face into his stiff coat of well-worn wool. "I can't bear to live apart from you."

"Don't worry. I will always be with you. You know the promise for us believers in Jesus Christ. In the end, we will be with Him in glory.

But right now, I am not giving up. I plan to come get you when this sordid episode is over. Stay strong for us. The Blues are already aware that you might need their assistance."

Mercedes continued her muffled cry. He caressed her soft auburn hair and lifted up her chin, letting a few lost-in-the-moment tears form in his sad eyes as well.

"You've got work to do starting this evening. The president needs a new PR campaign pronto. It will be a roll-out of the return to our First Amendment rights. A new slogan and an effort to unite us in our common needs for peace, safety, and hope. The naysayers will scream against it, but the rest of us, I believe, will be on board. People want change. They are tired of the heavy-handed restrictions and want to breathe again as free citizens. We need to capture that desire. We must try while we still have a country."

"Yes," she beamed. "I understand. But you need to promise me you will do everything in your power to stay out of danger."

"I'll do my best. That's a promise." Mack smiled and dried her tears.

That evening Mercedes sat down with a notepad and pencil. Trying anything on her computer pad could pose the possibility of discovery from Lu or his team. Everything had the capability of being hacked in the world of the internet, AI and smart devices. Mercedes succinctly stated the goals for beginning anew with the "Right to Rights" campaign. The First Amendment was listed point by point with the clear expectation that the public would again have the benefit of securing these freedoms.

When she was finished with her one-page presentation, she liked the results. *Now who can format this document into a public service announcement to be presented by the president?* she mused.

Immediately, she thought of Shirley Smythe's daughter, Cassandra, who had recently graduated from an exclusive Ivy League college with a degree in advertising. *Perfect*, she thought. *Trustworthy, a strong*

Christian, faithful to the cause. Mercedes would have Mack deliver the outline to Shirley Smythe at work in the morning. Shirley could easily pass it on to Cassandra at home so she could begin to professionally format it, if it met with the president's approval. Time was of the essence. They were pushing for a three-day window.

Mercedes attached a note to Cassandra. "Don't worry about the product. Just let the Lord's presence through the Holy Spirit lead you to develop the approved ideas into a graphic the president will use on Thursday or Friday. We trust He will fill you with all wisdom. Godspeed."

Chapter 35

Mercedes Singleton

August 2037

The Spirit of the Sovereign Lord is upon me, for the Lord has anointed me to bring good news to the poor. He has sent me to comfort the brokenhearted and to proclaim that captives will be released and prisoners will be freed. ~ Isaiah 61:1

The marathon running in her mind was exhausting for Mercedes. She was struggling with the frightening warning shared by Mack. Most likely, the temperature of the conflict would accelerate dramatically with the president's upcoming press conference. In her thoughts, she was deeply worried for Mack's safety and that of the child within her. That was a miracle! She could not believe she was pregnant. It was beyond the realm of possibility after the botched abortion at the Central Station Rehabilitation Camp. And to think she must have gotten pregnant soon after moving in with Mack.

But God, she thought, is in the miracle business. With Him all things are possible.

Twice she had been able to stealthily participate in Christian worship held in the bowels of the White House. It was like nothing she had experienced in her life.

During the first service, an unearthly peace fell into their midst, rendering the faithful totally silent and completely paralyzed. Into that environment poured the Holy Spirit with private messages of assurance for each of the worshippers. Fear not was the common thread of the message as they shared their Spirit interpretations when they were finally released from the physical restrictions. All those present knew what those words referenced, while holding onto the faith that their Lord would prevail in the events that would soon transpire.

Mercedes held the words in her heart as, day to day, she vacillated between anxiety and a recall of the dictate of the Spirit.

The second gathering, a few days earlier on a Friday evening, was totally supernatural. As she had begun to lift her praise to Jesus with Mack by her side, a band of angelic beings began to invade the room, posting themselves in the alcoves of the ceiling, in the corners, and around the perimeter.

Mercedes sat speechless as these warriors in white moved as though a heavenly breath was causing them to slowly sway back and forth. Years before, in Whitsville, one of the church widows had told her that someday she would see angels. But though Mercedes had heard the prophecy, she had let it lie dormant when nothing had occurred.

Now she knew God was in their midst. He was lending His resources for the battle for His people. *The Spirit whispered into her mind,* We have come to encourage God's own. We bring the Lord's armor to strengthen you in body and mind. Stay the course. Walk in the Lord's footsteps.

Some of the angels fluttered enough to draw her attention to them. Two flew near her face and brushed her cheek with a touch of the divine. Heat and power and strength surged through Mercedes as she sucked in her breath. Mack, while touching her forearm with his hand, heard her whimper. He immediately pulled his hand back from the heat that was present.

"Are you all right?" he whispered.

"Angels," she managed to whisper, pointing to the ceiling. "They are here."

Mack could not see, but believed her with all his heart, and nodded at God's gift.

"Of course they would visit the angel in the room," he shared in a whisper, attempting to again hold her hand. This time it was a bit cooler, but still coursed with power.

"Amazing," he began, "God is so good. Our baby is going to be supercharged!"

That night, she and Mack continued to make their escape plans. The ElderCare bill was moving through Congress at a snail's pace. She had resigned from Senator Roker's office a month before, aware that if she stayed any longer, she would be implicated in accessing his emails. The senator was not unhappy. He had moved on to another escort once Mercedes shared with him that she was in a relationship with Mack.

Roker, of course, was aware of her cohabitating with Troy Griffins, a White House security guard. There were eyes and ears everywhere. Roker's imagination would have no problem envisioning Mercedes and Griffins in the most intimate of positions. He had tried crudely for the past few months to gain information from her as to what was happening at the White House, so Mercedes, playing along with the game, pretended not to notice that he was seeking information on the president.

Mercedes would strategically drop disinformation when she was coached by Mack. It was an entertaining game for her, but she also was aware of its intrinsic danger.

Lu and his forces were frustrated that their persistent forays into the Virginias and other non-Federated lands were turning up little in the way of information, and almost nothing with bodies. They were beginning to figure that the information Mercedes had channeled their way was faulty and that she most likely was not a friend in the espionage world.

She was surprised that the Blues still managed to operate in almost total invisibility.

That evening as they prepared to go to bed, Mack pressed in on her troubled thoughts. "Mercedes," he said as he kissed her hand. "You need to leave tomorrow. I have a driver who will take you to Whitsville, but it must be in the morning, early," he said bleakly. "News from Ed is that our time has come. He cleared his workstation out of the White House and has moved to an undisclosed location at the order of the president. From there, he will try to run all our covert operations. Knowing him, he is probably going to be right under Lu's nose. Derkovich was always a step ahead."

"But Mack, I don't want to leave until it is absolutely necessary. Since we found each other, our time has been so short."

She turned to him and pressed into his warm body. Their love and care for each other took over as they made love for perhaps the last time. Mercedes could not keep this thought from her mind. She was so intense with their love making, that Mack chortled, "Perhaps I need to get myself in compromising situations more often!"

Mercedes softly punched his shoulder and then lay her head on his chest. "I could never live without you, Mack. You have completed me in a way I did not think was possible. I love you to the depths of my soul." She kissed his cheek, his neck, his chest. He turned and kissed her tenderly on the lips. "My love," he whispered. When she finally fell asleep in his arms, she only slept in fits and starts.

In the middle of the night, she woke to feel Mack's hand resting on her pregnant belly. Was he perhaps communicating with the child he might never see?

Softly, the tears, warm and salty, rolled down her cheeks. Sniffing, she reached for a tissue and felt Mack's warm breath on her face.

"I will always love you, and our baby. If it is a boy, can you give him the middle name of Walt?"

Silently, she nodded.

"Lord Jesus, we need your protection," Mercedes prayed with passion over and over. The Spirit of God lifted her prayer to heaven and the throne.

When her eyes fluttered open as the sun began to shine muted rays over the dingy D.C. buildings, she felt for Mack. He was gone.

The alarm had been set, and a short note left, reminding her of the portage from D.C. to Whitsville.

Taking the few things of value in a worn backpack, she stepped into the car that had pulled up to the curb at 6:00 a.m. Her driver wore sunglasses and a gray jacket pulled up to his ears. He seemed all business, saying little other than, "Step in, Mrs. Gersham." He then accelerated through the narrow streets which were quickly filling with government transports. Mercedes noticed that there seemed to be an abundance of military-type vehicles.

"Probably just my imagination," she mumbled.

It did not take her long to drift back to sleep, knowing the drive would take all day. When she awoke with a start, the driver was slowing down and pulling into a concealed gravel drive. Exiting the car soundlessly, he moved into a barn-like structure.

Mercedes could see movement and wished she knew what was happening. Sliding out of the car, she tiptoed up the drive to the barn.

Arun David Polysoing stepped out and looked up into the sun, his face heavy with sorrow.

The driver turned quickly to face Mercedes.

"Titus?" she said in disbelief. "Titus!"

There stood her brother whom she hadn't seen in years since he'd left for Nepal. All those years spent assisting Chinese Christians fleeing to freedom had been spent far from the States and his hometown of Whitsville. She recalled his arrest and sentence to a lifetime of servitude in a horrid concentration camp in China. Miraculously, he was rescued by a Chinese national during an explosion of a munitions yard next to the camp. Titus ended up in Nepal, jockeying escapees to safe ports across the world. Now, amazingly, he was back in the States.

"Oh, Titus," she said crying. "You are a sight for sore eyes."

"So are you, sis. And look at that baby bump! I couldn't resist the invitation to rescue the damsel in distress when I heard it was none other than my dear sister!"

He hugged her with his big bear hug.

"Take it easy, Titus. I can hardly breath," she laughed.

Chapter 36

President Santaya Woodring

August 2037

Now he is exalted to the place of highest honor in heaven, at God's right hand. And the Father, as he had promised, gave him the Holy Spirit to pour out upon us, just as you see and hear today. ~ Acts 2:33

"I'm sorry," Titus said as he gazed at her.

"For what?" asked Mercedes. "You are free. You are safe. You are a miracle!" She hugged him again.

"Hey kid, I can't breathe," he joked. His phone buzzed.

"It's Washington D.C.," he mumbled, looking at Arun and away from Mercedes. "All hell has broken loose."

* * * * *

President Woodring had begun her normal Monday staff meeting when Shirley Smythe barged into the meeting room. Mack was on detail down the hall.

"Madam President, we are under siege. General Lu has just entered the building with a large patrol of soldiers. He demands to speak to you immediately. The Capitol Police have put up no resistance. They seem to have joined his forces. What do you want us to do?"

"Show him in," the president responded coolly. Her heart was frozen in her throat. Just yesterday her husband DeShaun had warned that Lu was plotting an overthrow of the Federal Government; a temporary taking of power, as he described it, until order could be restored.

Lu's military forces strode down the hall, sweeping into each nook and cranny of the White House in SWAT formation. There was a bit of sporadic gunfire from her security detail led by Devon Irwin. Mack raced toward the sound but was dropped by a stun gun by two soldiers from behind. Trying to contact his supervisor over his telecom device, the cordless microphone was swiftly yanked off by Lu's henchmen. Mack was clapped in handcuffs.

General Lu strode into the Oval Office as though he owned the place. He walked up to Santaya's desk with a smirk.

"What is this all about, General Lu?" she spoke, raising her voice. "This is America."

"Madam President, you are under arrest for treason against the United States of America. You have sold military files to the One Nation Alliance in an attempt to shore up your campaign coffers. Other charges are pending. Please come with me."

Lu moved toward the president as the television crew he had hand-picked panned into her startled face.

"You Goddamned liar," she hissed. "You are the…"

Lu had reached her chair and grabbed her face, covering her mouth. "Get that camera out of here," he screamed as the picture continued to be broadcast to millions of screens around the world.

"You are an embarrassment to your country," the president said as she stood up, straightened her back, and faced the camera crew in the hall still catching glimpses of the action.

"What country?" Lu laughed maliciously. "You are finished. Same thing for your husband. I've returned him to Walter Reed. He's sick again." His evil glare was hard to take. Santaya almost fainted. "This place has a brighter future under my watch."

He spoke to the military detail standing near the president. "Lock her up in solitary at Andrews. We have work to do. Get those pimple-faced legislators up here on the first jet out of Atlanta to speak to the public. Explain the evidence and why we have not replaced her with the vice president. You know he is implicated as well; same with the speaker. We'll bury them all."

The president was escorted down the hall, past Mack who was prone on the floor. Lu hovered over him. "My dear Mr. Griffins. Such a surprise that we would meet again. I've been waiting for this day. I believe you have some information you will wish to share with me. You must have forgotten all these years that I am still waiting for a delivery. At this point, the charge of treason pertains to you also. Firing squad for you." He laughed and walked down the hall, riding the elevator to the ground floor and stepping out the door as though he had just conquered the world.

Lu stood on the portico porch and asked for the camera to be turned on again. He briefly stated the evidence he had which implicated the president. He promised that like all Americans, she would have a fair trial. Others would be brought to justice as well. There were people in the Pentagon and the House of Representatives as well as the cabinet who had assisted President Woodring in her treasonous assault on the sovereignty of America. All would see justice served.

Lu exited the grounds in his chauffeured military vehicle. He had failed to give further instructions to the camera crew. Seeing the opportunity, they turned and headed back into the White House, now a scene of chaos as troopers tore through files and artifacts, taking trophies for themselves and stuffing important papers into their jackets.

The cameras caught footage of soldiers dragging Mack and a bloodied Devon Irwin out of the building.

The announcer chattered on. "It seems that Troy Griffins, a former envoy to the Russian delegation with dubious ties to the Kremlin but now employed by the president, is being implicated in this affair as well. He is not only complicit in the president's dealings with the ONA, but also a bribery scandal with the Russians a decade ago where he sold top secret codes during the Middle East War. Surely, he will face swift justice from General Lu, who has no tolerance for those who seek to destroy our country from within for personal gain."

Mercedes was listening to the reporter on Arun's satellite phone. Her face blanched at the news.

The news of the president's arrest sent the world into a communication firestorm. By six o'clock that evening, the government press corps was holding a news conference. Out trotted General Lu with his succinct accusations, again reassuring the citizens of America that this was done to preserve the nation, to save democracy.

"What proof do you have?" asked a reporter from the *Post*.

Lu turned and pointed to a shy teenager escorted by none other than televangelist Timothy Prescott.

Mercedes's skin crawled. She recognized them both. It was Shirley Smythe's daughter, implicating not only the president but her mother.

Timothy Prescott spoke. "Cassandra Smythe came to me to share some of the accusations you heard today. She is a patriot. She trusts me as a devoted confidant, and I encouraged her to do the right thing. Once I heard the information, I surmised that the general would like to be made aware of the seditious nature of the executive branch." He droned on about "…integrity, love of country and the necessity to preserve our democracy."

Mercedes felt sick to her stomach. Shirley Smythe worshipped that girl. *That man is Satan incarnate.* She spoke aloud, "He is a deceiver and child of the devil. He is using Shirley's daughter to disseminate lies. Little does she know that she will be discarded when she is no longer any use to them. I bet they offered her immunity... probably convinced her to save her own skin and turn on her mother and the president. They are full of lies."

Silent tears rolled down her face as Titus again held her. This time she slumped into his rigid frame.

"I am so sorry, Mercedes. Satan has always been full of deceit. Look at his boldness, using a so-called Christian pastor to attempt to convince the American people of Santaya's sins."

"I talked to Cassandra just days ago about the president's new campaign to roll out a program to return our First Amendment rights," Mercedes confessed. "In fact, I am the one who suggested she help us. It was delayed several days while we made sure that everything was substantiated and that we had enough information to proceed. Part of the campaign was to expose Lu for his underhanded dealings with the One Nation Alliance. We were going to bury him and his cohorts. Now it looks like they have returned the favor. They are charging the president with what they themselves have done! I know that from what Mack has shared."

She bit her lip. Mack was supposed to be dead.

"Explain," said Arun.

As Mercedes gave an abridged version of the last six months, Arun and Titus stood transfixed. Arun knew from his contacts that President Woodring would be charged for the very crimes that Lu had committed. He was a stealthy snake. But he had not been aware of the reassigned identity to Mack who was posing as Troy Griffins. Ricardo had not shared that detail. He wondered why.

"This is very bad," Arun mused. "Lu will not want him to spill the beans on his former dealings with the Russians. You see, when Troy

Griffins was assigned to the Ambassador's Office in Russia, he was involved in a nefarious game of making the most of his position.

"Griffins was not only meeting the Russian envoy in back-door meetings, he was also dealing with a three-star general on the field in the war by the name of General Sturgis Lu. Lu was promised diamonds and bonds from certain international companies if he would provide inside information on tank and drone technology used by the American alliance. Lu gave the information to Griffins. It led to the death of several thousand allied troops. We couldn't jam the radar of their drones which had been disseminated to our enemies in the conflict. Griffins, who was supposed to deliver the bonds and diamonds, disappeared. He still has the booty. Only a few of the diamonds have turned up on the black market, and that was a year or so after the incident. Everyone figured he got snuffed out by someone either in the Russian delegation or Lu's people."

"How do you know all this inside information?' queried Titus. "You sound like you were there yourself."

"No," said Arun hesitantly, "but there is a gentleman in my faith community who came to me one day wanting to share something of his past. He is a broken man, feeling responsible for the deaths of his extended family. You see, they were all killed in a home invasion while he was out on assignment for the government. He shared how he had compromised his position for personal gain, and that his family became the victims of his avarice. He could not forgive himself."

Arun continued, "He is now a very sick man, close to death. Cancer is eating him up. But worse than cancer is the guilt in his mind. He cannot find freedom from what he did to his loved ones. It is a sad story."

"Do you mean to tell me that Troy Griffins, the real Troy Griffins, is still alive?" asked Titus. "Does anyone else know his real identity?"

"I can't imagine," said Arun. "He always conceals his identity in some way. In fact, the several times we have conversed, I didn't know it was the same person who came to talk penance. He is a master of disguise."

"What is going to happen to Mack?" Mercedes interrupted. "Oh God, please protect Mack." She collapsed on the ground at their feet. Moving swiftly, Titus lifted her with tender hands.

"We need to get moving now," said Arun. "I'm going back to Baltimore. We are planning to rendezvous with the Native Nations team according to the direction of the Holy Spirit. God help us figure out these next steps and keep His people walking into His Truth. I pray they are not swayed by this campaign of lies against the faithful."

The men shook hands and said a short prayer for each other.

Arun began, "Lord, pour your favor over our body of brothers and sisters in Christ. Lord we are dismayed that the events of the day have allowed those who follow Satan to disrupt our government. But you, Lord, you will prevail in this situation."

Titus continued, "Dear Spirit, move among your followers and strengthen them in their resolve to hear and see the Truth of this gross abuse of power. Speak your Truth to them so they know that what they hear on the airwaves is nothing but fabricated lies. You alone will prevail. You alone deserve the glory. Teach us to walk assuredly in your path, knowing that we work for you and your kingdom. In the name of the Father, and the Son and you the Holy Spirit, Amen."

Titus placed Mercedes in the back seat of the car, trying to make her comfortable.

"I'll get her to Whitsville and then return to join you," he shared with Arun. "We need a miracle."

They both left, assured that God would prevail.

Chapter 37

The Native Nations

August 2037

The church then had peace throughout Judea, Galilee, and Samaria, and it became stronger as the believers lived in the fear of the Lord. And with the encouragement of the Holy Spirit, it also grew in numbers. ~ Acts 9:31

Laboriously, the caravan of buses, dilapidated cars, and ancient box trucks plodded into Washington D.C. It had been a miracle that they and their human cargo had been able to complete the journey. Along the thousands of miles they traversed, there was a perpetual need for fuel, food, and lodging.

Yet, it seemed whenever they were about to be stymied on their quest, someone always showed up with tanks of gasoline, a temporary dinner tent or comfortable accommodations to get a sufficient night's sleep.

Few had noticed this unlikely band of travelers. The world was caught up in the explosive events surrounding the coup in the American executive branch. News broadcasters were not sure who to cheer for in the coup by Lu and his government cronies. They promised only temporary military control of the executive branch while the legislative and judicial arms of government studied the case of treason charged against the president and much of her staff as well as some of her loyal supporters.

Some citizens, those brave enough to voice their thoughts on social media, blasted Woodring's administration for her leadership in crafting and promoting legislation which restricted public worship, controlled free speech, and punished those who refused to adhere to the draconian measures. They felt she deserved a taste of her own medicine. It was her administration that had removed the promised rights of the Constitution. If that was her position, who would say that her administration had legitimacy as a democratic government.

Yet others championed her leadership in maintaining order through the reorganization of the Federated States, her strong witness to social justice, and the courage to let the buck stop with her office.

She had shown growth and flexibility, they pointed out. Abuses such as the government rehabilitation camps for religious believers were being shuttered as the reality of this Orwellian experiment had been brought to the attention of the public. She was a fixer and she did not tolerate failure.

On that bright, clear day, August 24, the buses of the Native Nations crawled into D.C. as the sun appeared over the horizon. The two thousand visitors, led by the Native Nations chief, Red Raven Bishop, disembarked, stretched their legs, and moved in steady determination to the Reflecting Pool stretched out on the lawn below the Lincoln Memorial. As they tramped to their posts with conviction, other vehicles arrived. Masses of humanity, many the poorest of the poor, had that Sunday morning pressed into the subway system heading to D.C. Arun Polysoing and his followers were among the throng.

It was time to take a stand.

A few roving reporters, who knew the Native Nations caravan was arriving, set up posts near the National Mall to press for interviews and clarity, but to a person, all conscientiously declined and kept moving toward their assigned posts. The silence of the throng was annoying to the reporters. They loved conflict, violence, anger, and fear that should be emblematic of the rabble. What was the matter with these people? The reporters were at a loss for words, so their stories did not gain much traction in the news world.

The D.C. Police chief was flummoxed. He had seen the collusion of the Capitol Police force with General Lu's military takeover a few weeks earlier, and the almost bloodless abdication of power had infuriated him. Under his watch, he was not about to hand over the reins of the District of Columbia to Lu and his militia. His staff had been aware of the arrival of the crowds and observed their behavior, but they did not interfere with their mission.

The police chief put out a press statement. "I need to announce that the Native Nations are simply expressing their First Amendment rights and have been peaceful in their assemblage. They have also met all requirements for a public gathering on national monument grounds. As long as this assembly adheres to the requirements of the District of Columbia, my staff will encourage their activities as free citizens of the United States of America."

Lu had other thoughts. "Looks like the vermin are gathering for a party," he snorted, gazing from the Oval Office at the moving columns of people. "Protesters are such a formidable class of people," he added sarcastically. "What do they think they can possibly change without force and weapons, power and position? Let them waste their time eating sandwiches and singing 'Kumbaya.' They can rot out there in the mud. A good rainstorm should drive them away."

Though their presence and bravery perturbed him, he knew their influence was negligible. Power at this stage of the game was not in the hands of the populace. It had not been for a long time. That had been a mirage. It was held by the ruling class, whether it be by elections or government agencies. The vestiges of democracy were now in the hands of those who had risen to the peak of the ruling class. This was a tangled matrix of social media barons, government insiders, and secret alliances with power brokers who pulled the strings. Sadly, the regular citizens thought their concerns were being addressed. They were only useful pawns.

* * * * *

As Santaya Woodring sat in her solitary confinement cell at Andrews Air Force Base, she realized just how much she had unwittingly contributed to the debacle before her. "Good God," she moaned. "I was a pawn in their game. I never realized that in empowering the legislature to deprive the citizens of their rights, I was eroding the foundations of our country. I was complicit in destroying what I thought I was preserving."

Inwardly she was seething. "And now I am not allowed due process after I cancelled habeas corpus during the uprisings. How ignorant I have been."

She wondered who in government was troubled by the turn of events. In her confinement, she was not allowed contact with her lawyer or a news agency. The situation seemed helpless. *I never should have allowed Lu into the White House. I let that rat get the cheese without even a fight. How could I have been so ignorant of human nature, knowing that things were brewing in his camp? Couldn't I have been more proactive in bringing in troops to protect the White House?* Mentally, she beat herself up over the myriad of thoughts that began with "could have" or "should have."

The H.S.

On her third evening in jail, she was handed clean clothes, fresh water for a sponge bath, and the typical meal of a military facility. The soldier dropping off the supplies mentioned in a faint whisper for Santaya to be prepared for interviews in the morning from Lu's staff.

As she left, Santaya noticed the glint of a scrap of paper caught in the locked door. She did not reach for it, as she knew she was under surveillance. But later that night, she pulled it from its trap in the darkness and pressed it to the floor where a seam of light escaped under the door frame.

"We are with you. May our God lift you up and give you peace."

It was a penciled chicken scratch, but for Santaya, it was hope and sanity. Memorizing its contents, she lay down on her cot and formed each word on her lips.

"Our God," she whispered. "Please, our God, whoever you are, I need you now. We need you now. I am so sorry to come to you so late and in such desperation. I ask for forgiveness in relying on my own strength. I have none now. I need you and I must trust you will come. Give us a miracle."

One was on the way.

Chapter 38

Ricardo Medina

August 2037

I baptize with water those who repent of their sins and turn to God. But someone is coming soon who is greater than I am—so much greater that I'm not worthy even to be his slave and carry his sandals. He will baptize you with the Holy Spirit and with fire. ~ Matthew 3:11

Chairman Lu had flown to Geneva to inform the One Nation Alliance concerning the current political situation in the United States. So far, he had had little push back from most of the government power brokers, but he was not sure how long that would last.

He was now brash enough to offer the ONA a part in reimaging an America that would be the lead partner in the One Nation Alliance. There were bickering sessions and power struggles breaking out in the organization, so the timing was perfect.

No one liked the fact that a big bully was about to take control of the helm. Lu would crack a few heads into compliance. He was already planning on deposing the current chairman, the president of Austria, and slipping confidently into her role. She was a loser in his book anyway. His contempt for her placating nature was not disguised. The One Nation Alliance needed to operate from a position of strength, not compromise.

Back on the home front, it was day three of the protest movement spearheaded by the First Nations Native American tribes. Loudspeakers had arrived and a podium swiftly erected. The movement was dubbed, "Establish Justice," and it transfixed a nation watching such an unusual sight on public media. The loose organization was headed by the fiery evangelist, Red Raven Bishop. He was eloquent and brave. He took it upon himself each day to explain the tyranny of the current government and its need to be revamped. "America must adhere to her original promise of liberty and justice for all," he shouted. The throngs cheered. People in their homes, apartments, and government projects listened. This was a new message. They felt as though a dark cloud of indecision, doubt, and hopelessness was slowly lifting.

In small increments, the message sank in. They wanted the something more that was spoken of from the platform. Twelve sprawling white tents, like those used in a traveling circus, were meticulously placed around the perimeter of the mall. These were filled with chairs and used during the afternoon sessions for small group Bible study, discussion of faith topics, and prayer circles. Each succeeding day brought more participants to the National Mall. Small private tents began to appear on the outskirts of the spectacle.

That was hope. Red Raven prayed at the end of his fiery speech. The next day, a vibrant rainbow appeared over the Washington Monument after a brief shower. The people rejoiced in the promise. But what happened on day five of the gathering caused even the reporting teams to pause and wonder.

In the morning, a faint cloud began to hover over the assembly. Then it gained size and substance. It descended over the protesters, now numbering in the tens of thousands, and enveloped them in the Presence of God.

Most onlookers were curious, but not sold on the presence of a higher being. They touted a scientific explanation for the persistent atmospheric oddity. But the Presence fell heavily on the chosen. And from that moment, they had a renewed fire in their bones that shook their souls to the core.

God was on the march. The battle lines were drawn. People of faith from all parts of the nation began a private pilgrimage to the sacred sight. They wanted to see and feel the presence of God. Every day of the revival, the Presence, like a heavy fog, enveloped the participants. Watch fires were lit in huge barrels between the main tents and fed with trash and garbage day and night. The fog that settled over the gathering at night took on a fiery glow resembling a smelting furnace.

* * * * *

Ricardo Medina pressed his forehead into his hands. He was fishing for a way to help Mack. Colin Lu sat next to him on the dilapidated chair in his townhouse.

"How was it so easy for General Lu to just walk in like that?" groused Ricardo. "Those sissy cops on the Capitol staff just rolled over. Whose side are they on?"

"I imagine they were already bought out by Lu. Anyway, Woodring herself demanded that there be no bloodshed. She went down without a fight. She's culpable for her current situation," Colin replied.

"She's weak. Always thought she spoke for the people, always looking for compromise and a peaceful resolution. She never could see that the snake was going to devour her because she had nothing to fight with. Her ignorance got us here."

They turned their attention to the small television spouting yet another round of breaking news.

"Today a three-person panel of jurists found the following staff of President Santaya Woodring guilty of treason: Don Masconi, secretary of Health and Human Services; Troy Griffins, Secret Service staff member and former aide to the Russian Ambassador; Shirley Smythe, executive assistant to the president; and Devon Irwin, chief of staff of the Secret Service detail at the White House. He is currently recovering from wounds received in a short gun battle the day the president was arrested. Their guilty verdict necessitates death by firing squad at Andrews Air Force Base this Friday at noon. There will be no appeals process, as the jurists are assured they have seen all incriminating evidence which leads to this judgment. We are awaiting a timeline for justice to be served."

The media staff then rambled on with the press release, highlighting the examples of treason committed by this group of traitors.

Shirley Smyth's daughter was then interviewed. "I had to tell my spiritual advisor, Timothy Prescott, what was happening in the White House. It was hard to believe my mother would be complicit in the events that led up to her arrest. I was shaken when I realized she and the president were planning to remove General Lu from his position as Chief of Staff and appoint a new person in that role that would look the other way from her treasonous activities. As I later learned, the president was doing this because she had sold military secrets to the One Nation Alliance. General Lu is there right now to reassure them that their mission of world peace will not be compromised. That is the desired goal of all peaceful citizens of the world. The One Nation Alliance is the vessel for peace throughout the world. It will bring us together to save the planet. They would never ask for military secrets from our leaders. The president was caught in a trap to benefit herself personally. She and my mother deserve what they get."

She continued, "My mother was led astray by a false god and a false spirit. It tells lies to her and hurts our cause in the One Nation Alliance. My mother is a fool. Thankfully, Pastor Prescott encouraged me to go public and share what had been happening in the Oval Office. That was the center of this treasonous plot."

An anchor for the government news questioned her. "Aren't you saddened and ashamed that your actions have led to your mothers arrest and scheduled execution?"

"No," she answered confidently. "My mother was misled by the president. She deserves the justice she receives."

Ricardo and Colin raptly listened to the news details pertaining to the scheduled execution for Friday.

"That is a hell of a way to go out," Ricardo mumbled. "I never cared for Troy, hmmm Mack, but he served us well as part of the team. He was too much All-American boy for me. And he snatched one heck of a girlfriend from my clutches," he laughed maliciously. "Guess she will be available after Friday. We need some help. Do you think we can find Derkovich?"

Colin paused. "He's been in hiding since just before Woodring's arrest. He knew a few days ahead that something was coming, and he moved from public view after warning the president. He vacated his post at the White House. No one knows where he is."

"God, what a mess," spouted Ricardo. "And what about this protest at the Mall? Peaceful protest, they call it. New name too. 'Establish Justice.' Catchy. I wish they were all armed with AK 47's and turned and fought. We know that won't happen since their guns were confiscated a decade ago by those who knew better. We have no one left to back us up but the Blues Militia who are somewhere hiding in the woods. Great help they are! And where is the CLF? They should have shown up by now. Although I don't have any idea what they could do for us."

There was a soft knock at the door.

Colin pulled out his gun and stood behind the door while Ricardo opened it a crack.

The hooded figure seemed familiar.

"Let me in, now!" he mumbled. "Derk sent me."

Ricardo pulled the door open briefly and grabbed the man by the arm while Colin frisked him for guns and transmission devices. He appeared clean.

"Derk who?" asked Ricardo.

"Derkovich," he replied pulling down his hood. There stood Troy Griffins himself!

Ricardo and Colin were mesmerized for a second. "What the hell … how did you get out?" whispered Colin.

"I'm Troy Griffins," he responded. "The real Troy Griffins, not some knock-off who has been impersonating me for months. He's done a fair job at it from what I hear."

"Damn," said Colin appreciatively. "You're real. Where have you been? Good thing you didn't show up earlier."

"Holed up. Once I saw the government had decided to replace me, I figured they were pretty sure I'd been rubbed out by some of my enemies. I would be a hot commodity to be prancing out in the public's eye. But life has a way of playing all of us for the fool. Realized about a month ago that I was dying of terminal cancer. I found a doctor in the dregs of Baltimore who made the assessment. I've only got a few more weeks to live, so I got in touch with Derkovich and gave him everything I have on the collusion of General Lu and the Russians during the Middle East War. I've got videos and voice recordings of almost all the deals. I know Lu will say it's just AI generated stuff when it gets out, but we can set a pretty good trap for him in real time if we're smart. Plus, I've got the diamonds, and the bonds Lu has been looking for, so I'm sure he won't give up this opportunity to become a rich man so quickly.

"In addition to Lu, I have some definitive details of treason by our most distinguished legislators. Ironic that they are the loudest ones yelling for the demise of Woodring on the charge of treason. That's usually the way it goes in Washington. If you are guilty of something nefarious, accuse your enemy of it before the finger points the opposite way. That's just what Lu is doing to Woodring.

"I came here today at the behest of Derkovich himself. He has concocted a plan. A long shot, but that's all we have. That's life, I guess, or what is left of life. I'd like to go out on the right side of history. For now, let's sleep on it. I'm exhausted."

He stretched out on the couch.

Ricardo and Colin looked at each other.

"Best get some shut eye too," said Colin.

Ricardo moved back to the cramped bedroom. He thought for a moment about this stale room where his mother and the general had conceived him years ago. He hated them both. Then in the darkness, Danny came to his mind. It was as though he was real. He could hear his voice.

"Hey, Ricardo. You are my hero. I always wanted a brother like you. Are you making any progress in the journey? Will I see you again? I love you, man."

Danny faded from the room. "Goddammed head case. That's what I am." But Ricardo could not fall asleep. He pulled out the drawer in the bedstand and reached for the small orange testament he had transferred there from work.

"Tell me, God," he whispered sarcastically. "Is Danny with you?"

"Yes," came a solid voice that almost sounded audible.

Ricardo was shaken. He knew the voice was not his. Surreal. It made no sense. But his heart was aching to know more. For the first time, he opened the Testament and read a few pages in the book of John by the faded light of the streetlight outside. Ricardo could not understand how he was in such turmoil and comfort at the same time.

"Oh God, I want to be with Danny. I miss him. He made me feel real … even worthy."

"Follow me," came the words to Ricardo's mind. "Follow me to life."

Ricardo reached out his hand into the darkened space of the musty bedroom. "Take me," he whispered. "Take me, man called Jesus. Take me to Danny."

Chapter 39

Mercedes Singleton

August 2037

And because you belong to him, the power of the life-giving Spirit has freed you from the power of sin that leads to death. The law of Moses was unable to save us because of the weakness of our sinful nature. So God did what the law could not do. ~ Romans 8:2-3

The ride to Whitsville was flooded with childhood memories and career events, but predominantly, Mercedes thoughts always raced back to Mack. She tried to bear up under the crushing questions prancing in her mind. *What happened to President Woodring's staff? The president's Secret Service detail? Would she be left adrift in this horrid world? Was there a miracle left for Mack? Would she survive Lu's relentless campaign for power?*

Titus tried to keep her distracted by small talk. Their arrival late in the evening at Whitsville and their reunion with their father was touching. They had woken their father from a deep sleep and guided him into the sparse living room where they all settled in on the frumpy couch and chair. Pastor Singleton, though frail and weak, could not stop holding his children, Titus and Mercedes. His tears flowed over his chanting lips, "Thank you, Jesus. Thank you, Jesus. I didn't think I would ever see you again this side of heaven."

And he was enchanted with the news of the baby who was now slightly showing in Mercedes's belly. "Thank you, Lord. A gift in my old age. My life is complete. My world is filled with your joy!"

They spent the dark hours of the evening reminiscing and giving their father a few details concerning the events of their separate lives.

Then Titus broke in solemnly, "I need to leave very early in the morning. You need to know that I have joined the CLF and the protest at the Mall. Mercedes, your friend, Arun Polysiong, has been sent by the Holy Spirit to be a prophet to our people. God has provided a path to restoration for his people here in America. I will fight the fight for Him here in the States. I am sure it is not going to be any easier than my years spent in Nepal. We are under attack all around the world. I'm thankful so many have decided to step up and take a stand with us. While there is not safety in numbers, it thrills me to know God is burning in the hearts of the faithful."

Mercedes was surprised. "I could see God's hand in Arun's life. He is called for such a time as this."

"Yes," Titus continued. "He told me how you saved his life with the blood transfusion. Thanks to you, Dad, both Mercedes and I have AB negative blood. Seems that came into play with an episode in Baltimore. You saved the day, Mercedes, by giving your blood to Arun. I guess you are now part of the movement, as part of you races through Arun's veins."

He smiled. Mercedes whispered, "Keep the rest from Dad. I don't want him worried." Mercedes pulled her father gently to his feet and led him back to his bedroom. "I'll tuck you in dad and share more with you in the morning. It has been a busy day."

Virgil's face brightened. "Oh, how your mother would rejoice. A baby to cherish. Now you two need some rest after that long drive. Let's forget about Washington right now. It's such a blessing you are here."

Mercedes pulled the covers over her father. "See you in the morning. Say your prayers," she kidded affectionately as she bent down and kissed his forehead.

He touched her hand. "Our Jesus sent His Spirit to deliver you safely home. My eyes have seen the hope I have been praying for, God's name be praised."

"Amen," Mercedes whispered as she closed the creaky door.

When Mercedes returned to the living room, Titus continued, "Sadly, I would love to stay here and spend some family time together. But there is so much happening in Washington D.C. and there are events transpiring there that need my attention."

"You are crazy," said Mercedes grabbing his arm. "There is no room for the dissident. No tolerance. Now that Lu has grabbed power, he will squash the resistance under his boots. He will likely push back on the throng at the National Mall."

"Listen," Titus said as he gazed into Mercedes's eyes. "Charges of treason have been filed against the president and her staff. You need to stay strong for Mack and the baby, no matter what happens. This child is your future. We are going to try to exert some pressure on Lu and his legislative cohorts to release President Woodring, but he holds most of the cards. We have very little leverage. But ..." he paused. "God isn't impressed by power or numbers. He is with us and He will prevail. God help us."

"Do you think Mack has a chance to make it out alive?" sobbed Mercedes. "Can someone ask for a stay of execution?"

Titus put his arm around his sister.

"We have friends in high places." He smiled. "Look at me. God helped me escape from the Chinese prison camp. And thankfully, your rehabilitation camp at this very moment is being dismantled and your friends have returned home."

Mercedes turned, surprised at the news. "They are home? How do you know?"

"Simon Hamilton. He deftly downloaded scads of files from the base computers detailing the events in the past few years. Arun has received correspondence concerning the death of his sister Olivia. Although no blame was assigned, the government did send condolences concerning her unfortunate passing. We need to give a shout of praise to the president for her executive order, freeing our enslaved brothers and sisters in Christ. Hopefully, there will be no more deaths like Olivia's at the hands of madmen. We have lost so many persecuted brothers and sisters in Christ."

Mercedes replied angrily, "Most likely Lu will reinstate the policy. He is in collusion with the enemy. And so is that sham of a religious icon, Timothy Prescott. There is utter darkness in D.C. right now."

Titus' countenance clouded.

"What's the matter?" she queried.

"There is more information on the results of the tribunal," he shared looking up from his cell phone. "Mack has been implicated as a purveyor of secret documents. It looks like he has committed treason. Lu is ready to wipe out the threat to his one world order." Then seeing Mercedes's face, he stopped.

"I'll do what I can to help Mack. Don't give up yet, Mercedes. We have friends in unusual places. Can you believe Ricardo Medina is helping us? What a snake of a guy. Coming to Whitsville to spy on the Blues. We all played the part of the fool. Guess Danny touched him so deeply, he decided to play the role of turncoat. If they discover his duplicity, he's a goner."

"And believe it or not, Colin Lu, the general's son, is assisting us too. He and Ricardo are a band of brothers, literally."

"What do you mean?" questioned Mercedes.

"Ricardo is Colin Lu's half-brother. They have formed a team to free Washington and the president from Lu's grab for power."

While the news stunned Mercedes, it did nothing to give her hope. "What can we do?" she cried. She grabbed Titus's phone and read the press release concerning the tribunal's decision.

"It says next Friday," she screamed. "Death by firing squad! Oh Jesus, help Mack," she cried as she slumped back into the couch sobbing hysterically.

Titus prayed over Mercedes. "In your name, dear Jesus, the Christ, our Lord. Take your people, our beloved Mack, the president's staff, and the believers who have been arrested and surround them with your hedge of protection. Touch them with your presence. Give them your assurance of salvation and the peace that passes all understanding. Never leave or forsake them. You promised us that. They are your people. Bless them with your power and might. Amen."

Titus held Mercedes for another hour before she fitfully fell asleep on the couch. His prayers and supplications were lifted on the wings of angels to heaven, where they were presented by the Spirit to the throne of the Father and the Son.

"Thy will be done," Titus whispered as he stealthily closed the front door and returned to his concealed car. He had a long drive back to Washington and would have to take some side roads to avoid the roadblocks.

Chapter 40

Ricard Medina

August 2037

So we have stopped evaluating others from a human point of view. At one time we thought of Christ merely from a human point of view. How differently we know him now! This means that anyone who belongs to Christ has become a new person. The old life is gone; a new life has begun! ~ 2 Corinthians 5:16-17

Ed Derkovich had cooked up a plan that resembled an old gangster movie script: mobster arrested, plans to break him out of prison, guns blazing in the jail break, gangster survives and goes into hiding. Well, perhaps not guns blazing, but there would be explosives.

Near dawn, Titus returned to Washington to be part of the team. It was too risky to allow outsiders to be part of their strike assembly. There was no time to revamp his identity. That could be worried about later. Since he had been outside the country for a few years, there was no updated information on his data file. They were hopeful that he would not be flagged as an insurgent.

When the team met with Ed Derkovich, they were shocked at the scope of the plan. "It's not that complicated," he assured the intimate group as they looked at him in astonishment. "It has a chance. No one is going to expect any type of jail break. The Christian insurgents on the Mall appear peaceful and overt religious militias have not been heard from since the death of Marcus Hamilton. Lu thinks they are cowering in a corner. If we approach this methodically, it will work. The best part is the small number of players. That works to our advantage."

"Really?" stated Ricardo. "You think we can just waltz in with a few teammates and spring President Woodring and Mack Gersham at the same time? They're locked up at Andrews, for Christ's sake."

"Where is your faith?" joked Derkovich. "We have a slim chance of success. It's not much, but something."

They had only a couple of days to iron out the details. The biggest hurdle was getting into the facility reserved for the most dangerous criminals. That would need a clever set of protocols to be welcomed into the bowels of the prison.

Early the following evening, Titus met with his tiny team of three, prepared to do his part. He was leading a band of CLF believers dressed in fire-and-rescue garb. They were hidden in a fire truck "lent" to them by a crew of city firemen who didn't question the requisition by a towing company to pick up the engine for its yearly maintenance check. As they scanned the work order the chief had authorized, they handed over the keys. "Guess the chief is sending the work out to a new company," one of the rescue crew surmised. "Always new government regulations to follow."

Titus and his crew climbed into the fire engine at Tim's garage, where the sign was posted, "Work You Can Trust."

The night before, Titus had managed to add himself as a reserve to the janitorial staff at Andrews, compliments of Ed Derkovich's manipulation of a government database. He unloaded two carts of supplies from their transport and followed the cleaning team down the prison corridor. Thankfully, Derkovich had fitted Titus's fingers with a false set of thumb prints to match his government identity, and he slid in undetected with some of the team who were lazy and sleepy. It didn't hurt that a few were snorting coke on the way in.

"Hey, bud. You new here?" asked a slovenly man with stringy hair. "Name's Harvey."

Titus replied, "Yeah, filling in for Edwards. He's sick. I regularly substitute on different government cleaning teams when they need an extra hand."

"No surprise Edwards is out. He was trippin' really hard last night. Took too many snorts of the good stuff. Doesn't come around much these days. Only left a few for me, but they were free." He reached in his pants pocket and pulled out a bag of high-quality cocaine.

"Haven't seen that stuff for a long time," said Titus.

"Where you been, man? It's been runnin' the street for a year." He looked at Titus suspiciously.

"Yeah, used to deal for a gang. Got knifed a few times." Titus pulled up his shirt and showed the scars on his torso. He smiled to himself, remembering the beatings he took at the Chinese prison camp. Several times, he had been beaten almost senseless.

Harvey nodded. "Comes with the territory. Sure you don't want some?"

"I'll pass," he said, trying to appear as though he really wanted to get high. "I still have to pass the weekly drug test. Part of my shortened sentence with the DA." Titus laughed sarcastically. Harvey joined in. They both knew that drug dealers were usually shown the door after an arrest. The money coming in the back door let them waltz back into the streets.

The public's mindset was, *If you leave us alone, take all the drugs you want.* Sad to say, that theory did not work. Deaths from overdoses were spiraling out of control and so was street crime. The elected DAs were not going to change their behavior either. No one seemed to have answers to the problem.

When they pulled into Andrews Base and had their ID's checked, Titus had moved to the back. As they disembarked, he manned one of the utility carts with supplies while a larger woman with purple hair grabbed the other.

After they were only perfunctorily checked in the cargo dock, the troop moved to an employee cafeteria for reassignment. Most of the team did the same job each night. Titus was to follow up on Edwards's duties: bathrooms, including those for detainees, prisoners, and staff. The foreman of the crew was thrilled that Titus understood the scope of his assignment with one explanation. *They actually sent us someone who hasn't fried his brain,* he thought.

"Travis," the crew chief said to Titus. "I'm waiting on your military escort. He'll assist you in monitoring the internees while you clean their latrine. He's on his way."

Around the corner swung a soldier who seemed very displeased to be assigned toilet watch duty.

"Damn it," he swore under his breath. "I've got the dirty job again. It's crap, literally."

Titus recognized Ricardo. He had heard about him both through his sister Mercedes and Derkovich. Mercedes's description differed from what he observed. Ricardo appeared to be trimmer but more muscular. He carried himself like a soldier. Somehow Derkovich had managed to send Ricardo in for this detail instead of the regular loser. Or perhaps Ricardo had encountered the regular staff and disposed of him in a broom closet. The body wouldn't start smelling for a few days.

Ricardo was aloof but managed to give orders to Titus on the procedure for cleaning and sanitizing each restroom once the prisoner was removed from handcuffs and foot shackles.

"Good thing we only do this thing once a week," he mumbled to Titus. He was thinking *or once ever!*

In each bathroom, Titus removed the lid to the toilet and inserted a small tube that had been hiding in the toilet paper supply he had wheeled in. He joked with Ricardo, "Only two rolls per week. Keep control of the discharge." Ricardo chuckled too.

Inside the tubes, floating in the toilet, were high-powered explosives, strong enough to crumble the cell wall. When they were done with the first wing, they passed through more security checkpoints and continued to a more secluded corridor. Cameras in the rooms and hallways monitored their progress, but nothing seemed amiss.

At the end of the hallway, they encountered armed guards outside two of the locked jail cells.

They barely acknowledged the cleaning staff and escort. Derkovich for good measure had jammed the security cameras and an IT repair crew was on site trying to figure out the issue. One of the IT crew radioed the guards to check the electric switch box at the hall entrance.

While these guards trotted down the hall eager for a change of scenery, Ricardo entered the formerly guarded room. "President Woodring," he spoke slowly. "Wake up. I have some information. You must pay close attention. We're going to attempt a jail break tomorrow morning at four a.m. Here's the plan." He passed her a small notebook with a black cover. "Memorize this in the next few hours. We will be back."

Meanwhile, Titus had run down the hall to the other chaperoned room. He used the duplicate key Ricardo had given him to enter quickly. Waking Mack, he said quietly, "Who would have ever thought our high school football hero would be guilty of treason?"

Mack recognized the voice. "Titus. I can't believe it!"

"Sorry I don't have longer to talk. Take these clothes and hide them under your mattress. In a few hours, you're going to hear several explosions. Drop your jumpsuit, grab these clothes, and put them on quicky. Don't forget to switch shoes with the decoy. Someone will let you out. Follow them to safety, but don't say anything. We'll take care of the details."

Mack nodded.

Titus was gone.

When Ricardo had spoken with President Woodring, he realized that she was going to be the most difficult to remove. After all, she would be immediately recognizable by anyone they would encounter. Colin Lu had been put in charge of that problem. He had a penchant for the bizarre, and said he'd think of something.

"President Woodring, rest assured that it is necessary to take this chance. The One Nation Alliance is scheduled for a world announcement on Monday. They have been dropping hints to the press all week to entice our curiosity."

Santaya grabbed Ricardo's hand. "I'll try. What do I do?"

"Duck when you hear gunfire. Actually, when you hear explosives down the hall, get behind your bed. We're going to try to blow a small hole in the back of the building next to your room with a targeted drone strike. Here's a mask to help with the smoke. Stay low. The mask has a tracker. We will find you," he said, trying to be assuring.

Then he disappeared behind the door that clicked shut.

Soon, the guards were doing their midnight rounds. They verified the presence of all prisoners and noticed nothing awry. The security systems had somehow been revived, so paperwork was sent to their superior electronically. Unaware, a duo of guards was also interchanged with two others who worked the midnight to 6:00 a.m. shift.

"Same old, same old," one of them laughed. "A few hitches in the security cameras again. We need some funding to upgrade the system. Probably will repeat again this week. Maybe the Air Force didn't pay the electric bill."

"We have a few guests coming in early," said one of the new guards. "Major Chaffins will be here to begin protocol for the firing squad today. He's chomping at the bit. He's also bringing in a pastor as requested by Troy Griffins, the Secretary, and Shirley Smythe, who will listen to their last requests and pray with them. Probably will ask forgiveness and all that crap. Anyway, Major Chaffins said to expect them around four a.m. Last rites for the prisoners. Won't do any good. Traitors get what they deserve. Seems Lu gave Griffins a once over as well, trying to get some kind of information out of him. He's a sorry sight."

The guard paused and then droned on. "The pastor plans to see the president as well as the Health and Human Services Secretary. Guess the others too. He is going to be a busy man preparing that crew for the inevitable. I wonder what dead people walking talk about on their way to the firing squad."

* * * * *

At 3:30 a.m., Pastor LeTron Allison, Shirley Smythe's pastor who had privately married Mercedes and Mack, arrived at the Andrews security checkpoint. He had been given permission by the Judicial Tribunal to visit whoever desired his presence before the scheduled executions. Lu didn't mind at all. It showed how generous he was to make accommodation for people of faith.

An Air Force staff car escorted Pastor Allison to the entry where he was scanned for contraband or listening devices. Ricardo had been assigned to accompany him, compliments of Ed Derkovich who had gone into overdrive manipulating personnel assignments. Ricardo was somewhat dismissive of the religious man's presence.

"This way, Pastor Allison. You only have five minutes with each prisoner. We need to prepare two of them for their just demise at noon. Keep it short. No theatrics. Our surveillance cameras will be watching, and guards will be at all entrances. I will accompany you."

They briskly walked down the hall, not bothering to talk. There was nothing to say. Ricardo stopped to chat with the first guard near Mack's room and rested his arm on the soldier's shoulder. The soldier flinched a bit, but stood at attention. The soldier was unaware when Ricardo rapidly injected him with a temporary paralyzing drug. Ricardo unlocked the door and turned on the light.

Suddenly, a torrent of explosives ripped through the silent halls, followed by crashes, screams, and a cloud of billowing debris which turned the scene into a shrouded dust bowl.

Mack was prepared as any good soldier would be under orders. He had been hit by shards of exploding cement, but the cuts were not life-threatening. He grabbed for his hidden gear while removing his orange prison jumpsuit. He also recalled his instructions to change his shoes with the pastor and put on a wig of sandy red hair.

Ricardo crawled into the room, softly calling Mack's name.

"Over here," he said, trying to stand.

Another man following Ricardo whispered to Mack, "Where is your prison suit?" Mack pointed, and the sturdy fellow yanked it on as quickly as he could. He pulled off his shoes and handed them to Mack. "Big feet to walk in," he said, as they exchanged footwear. Then he pulled off his red wig peppered with dust and slapped it on the top of Mack's head. He also had wounds, a few more severe than Mack's. He let out an exasperated cry as he zipped up the suit.

Mack could barely make out his profile, but what he saw shocked him. It was him—Troy Griffins, the real Troy Griffins.

"Nice to meet you, mate," Griffins said, nodding. "Move," he commanded Ricardo.

Pandemonium had broken out. A flank of Air Force guards had quickly reconnoitered down near the end of the prison hallway and were marching briskly toward the carnage, guns drawn. Out of the dust struggled Ricardo and Pastor Allison, looking shaken, covered in dust and debris, and dripping in blood from the impact of flying objects.

The commanding officer said, "Major Chaffins is on his way. We need to get you two to the hospital. "

While they were ushered to the entrance for staff, another larger explosion rocked the hall formerly occupied by Mack. A fire immediately broke out and accelerated at an uncanny speed. The smoke was unbearable. The commanding officer called back to security to order fire-and-rescue squads to the prison wing of the complex.

Screaming fire trucks barreled through the security gates and spread out around the inferno, tapping into designated fire hydrants while unfurling yards of hoses and lifting hydraulic ladders. It was organized chaos.

At the back of the building, a lone truck parked to the side. Smoke billowed from a hole created by a precision strike from a Blues Militia team. Three firefighters poured through the hole searching for their prize, President Santaya Woodring. She was unconscious on the floor, her only apparent wound a deep cut on her left hand.

"Grab her and get her out of here," commanded Titus. They lifted her gingerly, covered her with a blanket, and moved her into the waiting truck. Driving closer to the fray, she was transported to a waiting ambulance in the wings, and was spirited off, sirens blaring.

Ricardo and the pastor were also on their way to the hospital. Ricardo talked to the emergency medic. "All safe?"

"All is well, sir. Should be in Whitsville by noon. We'll be switching vehicles in a minute," he said, as the siren was turned off. They pulled into an abandoned garage and climbed into a government sedan.

"Good," Ricardo nodded. "Any news about the president?"

"None, but Derkovich wanted it that way. Someone is likely tracking any chatter on the airwaves."

But the news was good news.

Mack was lost in the conversation. He couldn't figure out how he had walked out of jail with a wig on his head and shoes that were a size too small for his feet.

"Ricardo," he mumbled.

"Hush, we have work to do." Ricardo gave him a quick injection and laid him down on the cot. "Welcome to freedom, Mr. Gersham. You seem to have nine lives. I know someone who will be happy to meet you again." He said it with seemingly no emotion.

Chapter 41

Santaya Woodring

August 2037

I pray that from his glorious, unlimited resources he will empower you with inner strength through his Spirit. ~ Ephesians 3:16

Santaya's soft moan garnered the attention of the medic. He quickly checked her vitals and shot the driver a troubled look. "Her blood pressure is dropping."

Peeling back her prison jumpsuit, he immediately felt the sticky blood pooling on her left side.

"My God. She has a puncture wound just under her arm! She's bleeding out! We need to get her to a hospital."

The driver looked flummoxed. She'd been strictly commanded to follow protocol in rescuing the president, but the situation now called for independent reasoning.

"We'll deviate and go to Baltimore," she decided. "You need to call our friends to get the surgical team ready. Explain the emergency and keep it generic. We don't want listening ears perking up to an incriminating voice message."

She swung onto the freeway, ambulance lights flashing, then turned them off and proceeded at a less frantic pace. Most likely nothing would seem amiss with all the additional traffic from first responders. She'd be lost in the shuffle.

Fifty minutes later, Santaya was being prepared by Dr. Withers for emergency surgery to remove the masonry projectile lodged between her ribs, alarmingly close to her heart. He was again in his CLF medical office surrounded by trusted staff in the Baltimore warehouse.

The medical team was as bare bones as possible. The fewer people aware of her presence, the better her chance of survival.

Doc Withers spoke briefly.

"Madam President…"

"Call me Santaya," she grimaced. "What's the prognosis? Where am I?"

"Just know you are among friends. We're going to remove a piece of brick that lodged itself between two ribs. After the surgery, you will recover in a safe location. Trust us. All will be well."

As the sedation meds from the IV began to work, Santaya smiled faintly. She wanted to stay awake, but lost the battle and drifted off into dreamland before any further explanation could be added.

The doc's first order was to the head nurse. "Get Arun on the phone. We need help, fast!"

She left the room momentarily and returned with a single use, untraceable cell phone. The doctor conversed in short, clipped sentences for just a few minutes, tossed the phone into a bucket of water, and turned to the surgery table. "God help us," he said with quiet determination.

When Santaya woke from her sedation, she was in an unfamiliar room. There were no windows. The muted light of a simple lamp illuminated a youthful nurse sitting by her side.

"Please stay still, President Woodring," she shared in a low voice. "Your surgery was successful, and you have been taken to a safe house for recovery. God has been with you through this entire ordeal. We've been praying for you and your husband."

"My husband?" whispered Santaya.

"Yes," said the sensitive nurse calmly. "The doctor will fill you in when he arrives."

A few hours later, Santaya woke again with a start. She thought she was hallucinating when she saw Ed Derkovich and her husband DeShaun Davis come into focus. She raised her arm tentatively to touch DeShaun. "Are you for real? How did you find me?"

DeShaun grasped her hand. "Ed, as usual coming to the rescue. How are you feeling, babe?"

"I've felt better. Exactly what happened?"

She noticed for the first time, then, a doctor standing behind Ed. Briefly, Doc Withers described the surgery in Baltimore at the CLF warehouse. "You're in good hands here. I'll hand you over to Ed."

Pulling a chair up to her bedside, Ed Derkovich surveyed her face. He wondered if Santaya would be up for the biggest battle of her life. The times ahead would be tumultuous and dangerous.

"Santaya, we are in trouble, as you know," Ed began. "Your safety is paramount to the country surviving as a republic. Lu has shut down almost all forms of communication and is stymying the legislative branch from moving forward to determine who should be leading the nation at this juncture. Seems he does not even trust the people he handpicked to take over. Our best shot is to get you healed and back in the limelight so that our fellow Americans know you still have their backs and that you are ready to return to service. This is going to take a hefty amount of planning, a bit of espionage, and lots of intervention from the Holies."

"Well, God has done it before," she acknowledged. All in the room nodded at the comment and the nurse whispered, "Amen."

Ed swallowed and moved on with the conversation. "The charge of treason against you has been drafted swiftly and succinctly and sent to the legislative chamber. They are reviewing the evidence. We have a steep mountain with a short timetable to climb. Our only hope is that the representatives believe the information we will present to their body at trial next week. DeShaun is leading your legal team."

"What could they possibly use to charge me with treason?" questioned Santaya. "I have never done any of the people's work in secrecy. My conduct has been stellar… I think."

"Yes, but mine has not," injected DeShaun. He gazed into Santaya's eyes. "Forgive me, love. I have done a foolish thing to enlarge our net worth. At the time, I was convinced I was not hurting anyone, and it seemed so simple and so quick. Why wait decades to accrue millions of dollars. At the same time, I figured that getting rich and rubbing shoulders with some of the world's biggest powerbrokers seemed like too good a deal to pass up."

"DeShaun, what are you alluding to?"

"After we got married, I was approached by an agent from the Justice Department. He was serving behind the scenes as a diplomat to improve our relations with China. He wanted to know if I would be willing to slip what he called 'false documentation of military installations and readiness protocols' to our agent in China, for a fee, of course. The idea was to let the Chinese think they were receiving highly classified documents on our readiness for conflicts, should a major one develop."

DeShaun continued, "What I did not realize was that these were not false documents. They were the real thing. I was able to scan them in the Oval Office to bypass their top-secret status and ship them to the contact in China. That gave them legitimacy as well."

He made a contrite grimace and moved forward. "I messed up. I have jeopardized our country and sold out to some piranhas. Ed caught me in the act and asked me to come clean. He showed me his information on my offshore bank deposits.

"Lu found out about the deposits coming from the pilfered documents and tried to blackmail me so that you would not be charged with their theft. I knew he would eventually get around to using them against you, so I denied his request. Since I would not turn on you, he moved onto you as his target. It always was set up that way. He just had played the charade hoping I could give up more information on you. Now, unfortunately, they are blaming you for what I foolishly did. If I'm as good a lawyer as you think I am, I need to get the charges against you dropped and somehow convince the jury that it was Lu himself who has been sending military plans to our enemies."

The president asked, "Is that why your cell phone had all those secret coded messages? I saw it in the waiting room when you were poisoned and dropped it in my purse. It was suspicious." Her eyes pleaded for an explanation.

"Yes, I am so sorry. I was greedy and shallow. It seemed so simple. The phone you gave Ed clearly shows that I am the guilty party. I deserve to be tried and found guilty as a traitor, not you!"

"We're working on that," Ed interjected.

No one laughed.

Ed pressed on with the conversation. "For now, you will have to disappear for a week. I plan to rally the troops and get the truth out. We'll pirate all the remaining operable airways in a coordinated attack, presenting the true evidence proving your innocence, Madam President. The people will have to choose who to believe, you or Lu. In a few days we will disseminate a ten-minute video featuring you as our star. Center stage. But we need you healthier, proving you are up to the task of returning to the office. In the meantime, we need to distract Lu and clear his goons from D.C."

"Where can we be stashed to stay safe?" asked the president. "And what about DeShaun?"

"He will have to face his own charges. He will plead false enticement by a government agent. The trap was deceptive. But it was also lucrative, which poses a problem. And he was willing." Ed turned toward DeShaun and placed a hand on his shoulder. "God be with you."

"Serves me right for succumbing to greed," DeShaun mumbled. "I am ashamed I fell so easily into their corrupt and treasonous plans. I am a fool. Please forgive me Santaya." DeShaun looked at her with genuine sorrow in his dark eyes.

"DeShaun, I love you darling. Your brokenness convinced you to do something unwise, but we are all tempted by empty places in our hearts. I pray that you will find a way to convince the American people that you intended no harm. God be with you. Stay safe until I get back to Washington. I don't want to have to worry about your well being. Lu has already tried to snuff you out again and amazingly, all he found this week was an empty vehicle, thanks to Ed. He's losing his patience."

The doctor stepped in. "Enough for now. We need to move our patient. It is almost sundown. Make the president comfortable. The truck is pulling up momentarily to take her to the shipyards. Make sure her meds are packed as well," he ordered the nurse.

"Shipyards?" gasped Santaya. "Am I being taken out of the country?"

"Never," Ed rejoined. "We have some international friends who are giving you an all-inclusive vacation. Five stars. You deserve it."

"Tell me it's a private yacht in the Caribbean," she joked.

"Close," laughed Ed as he strode out of the room.

Chapter 42

Mercedes Singleton

August 2037

But I will send you the Advocate—the Spirit of truth. He will come to you from the Father and will testify all about me. ~ John 15:26

Her trembling fingers wildly clawed at the hand over her mouth, as a stunned Mercedes attempted to breathe.

The warm, familiar breath whispered frantically, "Mercedes, it's me, Mack. You must keep quiet!"

Sitting up as though shocked by an electric current, she searched for his somber eyes in the darkness of her father's house.

"Mack, Mack," she sobbed quietly as she pulled his face to hers and passionately kissed him.

With remorse, Mack slowly untangled himself from her embrace. "I can't explain now. I'm writing a quick note to your father. It's all we can do. Grab anything crucial. We won't be back." He slid a small paper onto her bedstand. Hopefully, the generic message would be understood by Virgil and he would realize the necessity of anonymity.

Her eyes locked onto his business-like stare.

"Dad?" she whispered.

"Trust our God. It is better this way."

Grasping her small carry-on duffle bag, Mercedes dumped in toiletries, her phone, some clothes, jewelry of her mother's, and extra shoes. Thankfully she had come to Whitsville with few possessions. She couldn't think straight. Noticing the family picture on the bedstand with her Bible, she tossed it in at the last minute.

Silently, the two of them tiptoed out the door as she gazed back at her father's bedroom. Heaviness fell on her shoulders as Mack pulled her down the street as quickly as she could move.

Outside, the sky was black. "Can't we slow down?" she huffed. "I'm so out of shape." She touched her stomach and smiled.

"No," ordered Mack hastily. With his serious order, she recognized the trouble that disturbed his soul.

They raced a few blocks and then turned onto a footpath which moved in a serpentine fashion up a shadowy hill. Coming out into a clearing, she recognized the destination.

"Mack! This is your old house," she said with surprise. She knew how much he hated the memory.

Walking over to the decades-old, charred remains, he kicked aside some fallen timbers and brushed other debris away.

"Yes," he whispered. With all his strength, Mack grabbed a wheel and began rotating the rusty entry hatch which suddenly opened.

Shining his shaded flashlight down in the hole, he let the word "Good" escape from his lips as he breathed a sigh of relief. "Come here, Mercedes. Watch your step."

With trepidation, Mercedes traipsed over the debris and gazed into the black hole.

"It was my dad's idea to build a nuclear bomb shelter back in the eighties when he built the house. He was paranoid like his parents that the Russians were coming. I thought he was crazy when he showed

Walt and me what was under the house one evening while in a drunken stupor. We had to promise on fear for our lives to never reveal its location to our friends. Dad didn't want people to come here for shelter when the enemy finally dropped the big one on us. We just laughed at his unfounded fear, but he didn't take kindly to our opinion and smacked us hard while again reiterating the need for secrecy.

"When Walt and I were teens, we went down there a few times when we were brave enough, knowing that Dad was at work. It's not much, but now it is a godsend. Come on and follow my flashlight beam. Be careful on the ladder. I'll be right in front of you in case you slip." Mack flung some foodstuffs and a giant water jug attached to a rope down the hole.

"Let me check the ladder first."

Gazing down, Mercedes could faintly see a few musty cots, an antique oil lantern, and shelves of rusty cans. "We have to hide here?"

Mack nodded. "Quick. We're running out of darkness."

He started down the ladder and encouraged her to follow him, allowing her back to press into him with each step. Retracing his path, he grabbed her belongings at the cusp of the shelter and pulled a few boards over the hatch while it dropped into place with a thud.

Darkness enveloped them.

Mack lit the lantern. "We really need an air source in here." He noticed a rusty pipe pushing through the roof. "I imagine my dad thought of that. He was so smart. Just not smart enough to put the bottle down."

Mack grabbed a broom and poked the handle up through the pipe. Dirt tumbled down, but fresh air rushed in. "Thank God." He turned to Mercedes. "Welcome to the Hilton," he said as he bowed with a flourish. "We'll stay here for a day or two until the danger passes."

"Did the Fed Ops track Titus and me?" asked an alarmed Mercedes.

"Yes, they're on their way as soon as daylight hits. General Lu himself is coming. He figures you are the lynch pin to tracking down the president because of your connection to me as a member of her security staff and more so because of his insistence that you are part of the Blues Militia. They have uncovered the computer transmissions you made from Senator Roker's office.

"As for me, I'm golden. Mack Gersham died in the Fed Op drone strike and Troy Griffins, my recent alias, was killed in the strike a few days ago at Andrews. I don't exist anymore." While he was trying to be lighthearted, there was a sadness in his voice.

Mercedes was silent. She knew the kind of man Lu had become: irrational, intolerant, cruel, win at all costs. He was not out for only information. He was out for revenge.

"Grab your jacket," Mack said softly. "Here, sit next to me in this old chair. My dad probably had visions of drinking moonshine down here while the Russians rained bombs down from the heavens. But I get to share this with the love of my life. I will always love you, Mercedes," he said seriously.

Mercedes snuggled in and soon fell asleep. It was cold and damp, but she was exhausted. She couldn't control her drowsiness even though she had a million questions to ask Mack.

Mack, wide awake, prayed softly. He thanked the Spirit for his swift journey to Whitsville in a stolen military vehicle, for his father's crazy attempt at building a bomb shelter, and for a way out of this crisis. He begged God to preserve Mercedes's life no matter what happened to him. Mack knew that Mercedes and their child were a part of God's future plan. He, however, was expendable. How he knew this, he wasn't sure, but he knew it. It was as though the Spirit had tucked that knowledge into a corner of his heart.

"Help us, Jesus," he prayed quietly. "I don't know how we can ever be safe. I know I no longer exist, and if I turn up, it's just going to draw more attention to Mercedes." His jaw was fixed in a sullen grimace.

Mack knew they were to meet with a Blues Militia detail in two days. What transpired after that was not a surety. It would be one day at a time.

The Blues were crafting an attack on the security forces at the White House and other government installations centered in D.C. The elaborate plan culminated in a multilayered attack using false espionage releases and deception. The big question was whether they could get Lu to take the bait. It would be difficult to outfox him. Their best chance was if Lu's current chief of staff became overconfident in his assessment of the dangers stalking the capital city. The Blues were hoping this would signal a strike. The odds were infinitely small.

Chapter 43

Reverend Singleton

August 2037

I pray for you constantly, asking God, the glorious Father of our Lord Jesus Christ, to give you spiritual wisdom and insight so that you might grow in your knowledge of God. I pray that your hearts will be flooded with light so that you can understand the confident hope he has given to those he called—his holy people who are his rich and glorious inheritance. ~ Ephesians 1:16-18

The whirling blades of the chopper spoke of power and force as Lu's helicopter set down in the rays of dawn on Main Street in Whitsville.

There was no fear of vehicular traffic as the number of motor vehicles had dwindled to nothing. Gas stations had long ago disappeared in the revolt of the Freedom First states. No allegiance to the country? No problem. No gas, no electricity, no schools, hospitals or services. Independence from the central government hurt.

Combat troops in full gear poured from the chopper in an organized fashion and lined up in formation, awaiting orders. Other military vehicles flowed and stopped with a flurry of dust swirling around them.

General Lu was visibly disturbed. He had lost the president in the Blues attack on Andrews Air Force Base. His prime specimen, the source of his blackmail campaign, had slipped through his sweaty palms. All he said to his commanding officer was, "Follow me."

Townspeople were beginning to appear on their front porches and along the street, gazing at the unfamiliar sight. Any excitement for these sheltered residents was intoxicating, whether good or bad.

A few of the regulars who hung out at Smythe Hardware store took up their post in the ancient oak chairs lining the porch. Stomping up the steps, Lu pulled the first gentleman to his feet.

"Where is Mercedes Singleton?" he hissed.

"She's been gone for a while," he responded nonchalantly.

Lu slapped his face. "She's back here. Where is she?"

"Listen, General," spoke the local. "Like I said, she went to D.C. and never came back. Left her pa here to fend for himself."

"You goddammed retard. I want her now!"

"Can't help you, sir."

Lu unholstered his pistol and pointed at the forehead of the startled man. He pulled the trigger. Blood and flesh flew over his uniform, the wall, and the other companions. The man crumpled to the floor, his blood soaking into the ancient unpainted floorboards.

The other men jumped up.

Lu grabbed another one. "Where is she?"

"Why don't you ask her pa, Reverend Singleton? We honestly got no idea," he squeaked.

Lu tugged him down the rickety steps. "Take me to his house."

The scared local half walked half tripped up Main Street to Second Street. He pointed up the hill to the Singleton's modest white bungalow. "That's it," he said cautiously. "Reverend should be up. He's an early riser and usually goes down to the school most days to see if anybody needs help."

Lu released the quaking man and marched up to the house, pulling open the door that was still left unlocked.

Reverend Singleton came to the door, freshly dressed, hair slicked down and a tepid smile on his face. "Looks like we have some important guests this morning," he chuckled. "What can I do for you, General?" asked the reverend with strength in his voice.

"Where is your daughter? She is linked to the Blues Militia, and we need her for questioning."

"Well..." began the pastor, but before he could say anything, Lu barged in front of his men.

It didn't take the soldiers long to determine that Mercedes was not in the house as they did a cursory tour of the modest structure.

"Have you heard from her?" Lu demanded. "We tracked her getaway car traveling in this direction. Damn, don't tell me she slipped through our fingers too," he muttered. His countenance was explosive. Fire burned from his eyes.

Virgil sat down on the porch chair and rubbed his chin. He was sure Mercedes had come the night before to escape Washington. Titus too. But now he wasn't so sure that he had not imagined it. How had she disappeared if she had been there? *Dear Jesus,* he whispered to himself. *You brought me another miracle and saved my baby girl and her baby. How can I ever thank you enough?*

Reverend Singleton moved to stand up, but Lu struck him so hard he fell to his knees.

"I said, I need to know where that slut is. She is guilty of treason, old man. Where did she go?"

"In the name of all things holy," Virgil continued, "I do not know. But you cannot be talking about my daughter." He emphasized the word "my." "She is a perfect child of the King. She has beauty and strength from within. She is upright and precious to Jesus. He watches over her."

"God, I hate you religious zealots. One more time, old man. I need facts."

"The Lord has safely removed her from your clutches. You will never find her in your lifetime. He watches over her day and night. Some day she will return here, and I will see her precious face."

"He might watch over her, but not you," growled the general, pulling his revolver.

Virgil looked past Lu to the heavens. "Yes, me too. He loves me."

As the final word passed his lips, the crack of the bullet and the thud of his body were almost simultaneous. Virgil's body was sprawled on the porch floor, looking peaceful except for the pool of crimson blood gathering beneath his chest.

Yelling at his second-in-command, Lu ordered his troops to search nearby homes in the vicinity of the Singleton house. If the townspeople failed to give up information on Mercedes or the Blues, they would be executed.

Sue Ann Forbes awoke to commotion and screams. She had carried on at the Whitsville hospital in Mercedes's absence and took care of the handful of elderly patients as best she could.

Gazing out her upstairs window, she saw soldiers dragging her neighbor Deborah Brookings and her two-year-old son, still in his fireman pajamas, out the door. Sue Ann grabbed her phone and pressed the video button. Her vantage point was perfect and the sound of the demanding questions surprisingly clear. Through the interrogation, Deborah kept trying to coax her young son into the house, but he rebelled at being separated. There were questions with words of Mercedes, Blues Militia, and punishment lifting into the air.

Deborah's face was creased with terror. She tried to control her quaking legs. She could not reveal that her husband had joined the

Blues the prior year and left her to fend for their young son. She seemed evasive and scared. Shockingly, the lieutenant ordered her shot. As the blood poured from her head, the lieutenant pulled the gun from his holster and looked at the small boy crying over his lifeless mother. Without a sound, he pulled the cold metal trigger, and the stillness stunned them all.

Sue Ann wretched at the sight. She was bewildered by the inhumane actions but snapped quickly back to reality. Knowing her house was next, she raced up the attic steps and crawled into the tight hiding space she had crafted years earlier to get away from the abuse of her stepfather. Lined with old metal plates from discarded coal stoves, she had been able to block out her stepfather's lip lash of destructive diatribes toward her and her mother. It was her safe space.

It turned out to be a blessing as the search team did not detect any body images using their thermal cameras. Quickly, she pulled up the video and sent the footage to several of her acquaintances. One of these was Mercedes. Sue Ann prayed, *Lord Jesus, help us. Protect us from the venom of these soldiers. Give me strength to hold onto you. I need you now more than ever. Help our town survive this cruelty.*

She shivered. Her phone vibrated, signaling the video had been distributed to its intended audience. Thank God she was able to record the atrocities happening in Whitsville. Looking at her screen, she saw the symbol that her power had been drained but she sat in awe knowing that despite this, the video had enough charge to record and be sent. Cramped in the uncomfortable cave, Sue Ann sobbed.

General Lu got off his phone. Calling his troops back to their transport, he stated, "We have a lead on Mercedes Singleton. There is an encouraging phone call registered to her on the outskirts of D.C. Pack up the troops. These people have learned their lesson. Consort with the enemy and you will pay the price. They will never give up information anyway. Blood down here is thicker than water. They are too damned stupid to rat on the traitors. I just showed them what happens to stupid." Somehow that struck him as funny, and he smiled a slightly crooked smile.

The aircraft hovered, as though frozen for just a second, then lifted into the air. Its cacophony of whirling blades disturbed the morning peace and dirtied the stiff breeze.

The survivors of the town briskly canvased the homes of their neighbors. Unfortunately, they found several more families massacred in the Fed Op strike. No information on Mercedes was the kiss of death.

Tenderly, they carried the dead to Reverend Singleton's church. Sue Ann assisted and borrowed a phone to continue to take pictures of the carnage. There was no way she could make sense of the utter cruelty of their visitors, especially the murder of the innocent children.

When Reverend Singleton was brought in by the small team of men, she sank to her knees. "The good reverend too? God, strike those soldiers dead!" she whispered with vengeance. "Make their blood roll down the streets and reach the rooftops. Kill them all!"

Softly, she dabbed a wet cloth, wiping what blood she could from the pastor's face, and wrapped him in a handmade quilt someone had carried in from his home. "God help us. Now we are without the reverend's prayers. Oh, my poor friend Mercedes. You must know this. Your poor papa is gone."

Clicking one more photo, Sue Ann sent the next set of pictures to a temporary list of acquaintances. The photos flew into cyberspace.

Within minutes, Mercedes was receiving the treasure trove of data.

Chapter 44

Mercedes Singleton

August 2037

And the Holy Spirit helps us in our weakness. For example, we don't know what God wants us to pray for. But the Holy Spirit prays for us with groanings that cannot be expressed in words. ~ Romans 8:26

Mack was exhausted. Mercedes was past exhaustion. Hours ago, they had viewed in the darkness of their underground vault the horrid videos and still pictures sent to them by Sue Ann. One of those captured the blood-spattered face of Mercedes's father, Reverend Virgil Singleton, lying on the floor of his modest church, surrounded by other victims of General Lu's massacre in Whitsville. The carnage was incomprehensible.

Mercedes had cried for hours after seeing the posting of her father's lifeless body. Mack caressed her as she babbled on about Virgil being the best of fathers, the most dedicated of pastors, and the kindest of husbands. In her eyes, he could do no wrong. She wearied herself asking God questions that had no answers.

A fire of anger burned in Mack Gersham's heart. How could evil be allowed to kill the innocent in such a nonchalant fashion? How could he make Lu and his forces pay for this murder of innocent souls? His anger and frustration were reminiscent of his father's deep, uncontrolled anger.

"Mercedes, when it gets dark, I need to head out for a few miles to contact the Blues. Before we went into hiding, there were plans afoot for an all-out attack on Washington D.C. to reclaim the White House, the Capitol Building, and other government entities from Lu's clutches. We know he'll never let President Woodring legally return to her duly elected position. She will not allow him to hold command of American forces if she returns. While the evidence he has presented to back up his claims of treason are serious, he has not told the whole story, and I am certain the president will be cleared of all charges against her if we can just get the truth out to the public. We have hours of video evidence handed over by the real Troy Griffins which should be enough to bury him.

"If Lu is around, though, she will never get a chance to plead her case. I am one hundred percent certain he will knock her off first. Then he will appoint some crony to facilitate his dream of the Federated States joining with the One Nation Alliance. He will get rid of the vice president and speaker of the house some way. That would be the coup that would place him on top of the governing structure of the ONA."

"Oh Mack. Don't leave me in this steel prison. I'm suffocating. I want to see Dad."

"All right. Tonight, before I leave, we'll walk down to the church," he said thoughtfully. "But it is imperative that you are not seen by anyone, especially the locals. Lu is after you! These people are innocent, but if Lu returns and hears that you were here, more heads are likely to roll."

The day was unusually steamy, and the mustiness of the underground hideout was stifling. Time moved at a maddeningly slow tempo. Mercedes took to pacing back and forth in the enclosure. When the moon finally made an appearance, Mack felt it was safe to go aboveground.

"We'll wait here until about three a.m.," he whispered, as they settled on some pallets leaning against the trees Mack had frolicked in when he was a youth. "I don't imagine there will be any military patrols in town tonight. And I hope the local militia is quiet as well."

Resting her head on Mack's chest, Mercedes finally drifted off to sleep. He tucked his worn jacket over her to keep the dew from soaking her clothes. Despite trying to stay awake and watchful, Mack as well succumbed to a restless sleep. He awoke with a start at the sound of a branch cracking. Sitting up, he detected nothing out of the ordinary as he diligently surveyed their surroundings. It seemed unlikely that anyone would be on this deserted dead-end and overgrown lane. Checking his watch, he noted the time was 2:30 a.m. Time to get moving.

Then he heard it again. He sensed the sound of boots clomping in the damp soil, purposeful walking, silence. Pulling the revolver from under his shirt, he accidentally jostled Mercedes. She moaned softly. He hoped the sound was muffled enough to escape detection.

Then a hand tapped his shoulder from behind. The figure moved around into range. With the full moon shining on them, it was easy to see it was Titus Singleton. "I make a darned good spy, don't I? Any place for me in the president's security detail?" he whispered. "Thought a security guy like you would never be caught sleeping on the job. Especially when protecting my pregnant sister," he continued mischievously.

"Fancy meeting you here," Mack replied. "Weren't you headed up to join the calvary after delivering Mercedes to Whitsville?"

"Just as I got there, I got a call from Ed that I needed to report as part of the chopper crew for Lu's delegation. Interesting trip down. When we landed, I hid in the woods. The first chance I had, I went to the house to warn Mercedes. Lu's son, Colin, gave us the tip. Fortunately, you got to her first. I figured I had better disappear before Dad woke up and saw me. I figured it would just cause more confusion for him."

The cloud of grief covered Titus's visage. He was holding back tears, and his lower lip trembled. "I did not do a very good job protecting him. Lu is an animal, shooting an old feeble pastor like that." Titus spit on the ground in disgust. "I've been praying to the Holy Spirit to take my hatred away. I can't say I'm there yet. If I saw the guy, I would wring his neck!"

Mack raised an eyebrow. This was not the Titus he knew.

Mercedes moved, groaned, and stirred. Her eyes flickered open and she saw her brother. In her mind, she imagined it was just a dream. But just the same she said, "Titus, Dad's dead."

The ghost brother kneeled in the damp earth and leaned in to hug her. He let out a sorrowful sob while the two continued to hug and shudder in syncopation. Their cries spoke of deep despair and loss.

Mack let them have their time together. He knew it was God's way of soothing hearts.

Standing up, Titus wiped his eyes with the sleeve of his shirt and shared, "I just visited him in the church, Mercedes. It's hard to believe, but he looks at peace. There's no place he would rather be than among those he loved so much. Here I thought I was the one who would be dying for my fellow man when I left for China to help my persecuted friends, but it was him. He was God's man to the end."

"Can you take me to see him?" begged Mercedes.

Titus looked at Mack. "Let me chat with Mack for a minute." They moved out of hearing range. Mercedes was miffed that she was being left out of the plans.

Their conversation was brief, but full of detail. Titus was chosen by their leadership team to be the protector of Mercedes and to transport her to a safe place for the next few weeks. Mack was tasked with returning to D.C. with as many of the Blues regulars in the area as he could gather in forty-eight hours. Titus and Mercedes were going to the old farmhouse Walt had been taken to after the drone strike that took his life.

"That is a fitting place to keep my treasured girl," said Mack sadly. Mack thought of the cozy home where he had recovered from his shrapnel wounds. He smiled involuntarily as he remembered working to impersonate his handicapped twin brother Walt who had taken a fatal strike and had later died at the hideout. He had never quite perfected his impersonation of Walt. Walt had a complete dose of goodness, like their mom.

As Titus was turning toward Mercedes, Mack grabbed his coat. "Titus, I need to ask a favor of you. Chances are this will be my last time here in Whitsville. I need you to step in and take care of Mercedes."

"I will do that, Mack."

"I mean long term."

"What do you mean?" Titus said looking confused.

"I'm a dead man walking. Both of my identities in this life have by all accounts already bit the dust. If I show up anywhere, there are going to be lots of questions asked and both Lu's forces and my security staff are going to come looking for Mercedes and our baby. I need to have someone who can raise our child the way that would make me proud. That would be you, Titus. I can't think of a more God-loving and honorable person in my life. Please do me this honor."

Before Titus could object, Mack continued, "And Mercedes must not know."

Turning to Mercedes, Mack walked the few yards to the tree line and grabbed her hand. "I need to leave for a while. Titus knows where to take you. Visit your dad and then get down to the creek. I made contact on the way down here with the Bues and there's a boat waiting. For now, keep yourself healthy and our baby safe." He tenderly rubbed her belly.

"I love you and our baby. You two are the most precious things in my life. I think God has given me far more than I deserve. I'm trying to follow in His steps, Mercedes. You helped me get there."

"But Mack, you are so angry. I'm afraid you're going to volunteer to do something crazy, like try to kill Lu. Don't do it for my father's sake. He would never approve. Killing is not the answer."

Mack's face was set in stone. "Don't worry."

"You are letting your emotions rule. Don't you see that God is not in control when all you can think of is retaliation?"

Mack solemnly replied, "Well, where was God yesterday? Tell me! Think of those videos and photos. The dead kid and his mother."

Pulling Mack to herself, she pressed her body tightly against his. "Mack, you need to trust in Jesus. Let the Holy Spirit shape your thoughts, not your old self. It is hard. We slip into the old nature so easily. But you are a new creation! He will guide you in His ways if you just let Him. Be still and listen to the Spirit speak. Trust that God will bring righteous judgment. I love you. Please stay safe and remember our baby needs you."

Mack relaxed a bit. "I will, Mercedes. I truly will. You are right. I'm back to reacting as the old man instead of allowing the Holy Spirit to direct my thoughts." In sorrow, he gazed down at her hands, realizing he was clutching them way too tightly. "I'm a fallen sinner. I promise I will open my mind to His presence and guidance, Mercedes. I trust Him. I will do what is best for you and our child."

His eyes glistened as he released her hands, his fingertips still entwined with the soft flesh of her fingertips. "Get going," he whispered, as his wet lips brushed Mercedes's cheek. "I will send news when I can. Godspeed."

Mack turned, silently picked up his backpack and water, then headed down the weed-infested lane at a slow jog. He did not turn back to look at his sorrowful wife. It was too difficult. If he had given her the passionate farewell kiss that resided in his heart, he knew he would have lost the strength to leave. It was best this way, for them.

* * * * *

The air in the church was still and refreshingly cool. Mercedes gulped in a fresh breath and snuggled into the comfort of a room that had contributed to so much of her treasured childhood.

But as she walked up the aisle to the front, she began to see the dozens of bodies, bathed in the moonlight that peeked through the back windows. They were cleaned and dressed in their finest, or the best their neighbors could muster from meager wardrobes. Instantly, she recognized her father, near the end of the group. He was wearing his old gray sweater, his white hair brushed smooth.

His facial expression startled her. It was a simple smile, not forced but relaxed and happy. *His last thought must have been "I'm going to see Jesus."*

"I love him so. It's not right he went like this," she moaned to Titus.

"Perhaps it was his time," Titus replied. "God knows he was ready. And he got to see you briefly and to know about your baby. Nothing could have made him happier!"

Mercedes bent down and picked up his white lifeless fingers, still strong-looking and masterful. "I love you, Dad. Thank you for your strength and your faith. You will always be on a pedestal for me because you lived what you loved." She softly cried as she tucked the quilt under his chin and stood up. "Let's get going, Titus. Dad is where he should be." Mercedes took a picture with her mind with the last glance of her beloved father and turned brusquely to leave.

She was surprised by the preponderance of heavenly beings dancing in the back of the church, wings fluttering with soundless movements. Their solemn faces gazed down at the dead as they ascended and descended from the rafters. A musical movement kept them in syncopation. "Glory," fell from Mercedes's lips as she beheld the angelic visitors. "Glory!" She wanted to reflect on their movements, but Titus tugged her through the throng. "Glory!" she cried. "Glory to God!"

Chapter 45

Santaya Woodring

August 2037

For our God is a devouring fire. ~ Hebrews 12:29

President Woodring was given a cursory tour of the cargo ship Chekaru by its amiable Greek captain, Dimitrios Gardis. "Please accept my personal quarters as your home away from home," he stated firmly. "The world stage needs you back at the helm to free us from the clutches of Lu and the destructive cause of the One Nation Alliance. My own country is teetering on the cusp of joining. Our economy is in a shambles. Many consider it a solution. We know better. While they prey on those who think that brotherly love and shared resources is the cure to division and war, they fail to acknowledge human history for the last two millennia. Humankind is driven by power and control, and when that happens, all personal freedoms will be lost in the fray." He paused and rubbed his eyebrow. "Sorry, I just get upset when I see all the efforts of our democratic governments being swallowed by lies and mirages. We need the United States to survive to provide a beacon of hope for the freedoms we have cherished for centuries.

"It's nothing more than the confiscation of power and property," he continued. "My business, my fleet, will be taken and wiped off the balance sheet. These people know nothing about the creation of wealth that benefits all. The ONA are experts at propaganda. God help us."

He reflexively crossed himself and then faintly smiled. "It is not a bad thing to ask God for help, no?"

"I think that might be wise," nodded the president. "I used to think that faith in any god was a sham. Now I'm waking up to the fact that without God's intervention, we have next to no chance of surviving this challenge to the autonomy of the United States of America."

Captain Gardis bowed. "Your meeting will be in half an hour in the crew's galley. You have been requested to wear the disguise provided by our friend. Even my crew cannot be trusted with keeping your presence here a secret." He quietly turned and exited the cramped quarters.

Looking at the petite pile of clothes, Santaya could not help but smile. She riffled through the collection of baker's wear, with uniform, apron and hat, as well as a curly wig. *I had better hone my cooking skills or this crew will starve.*

At half past two the "auxiliary crew" met in the galley. She knew everyone in the intimate group. Ed Derkovich was in charge.

"Sorry, Madam President, but this is just a temporary holding pattern for a few hours. A chopper will be arriving at midnight to take you to a more hospitable location far, we hope, from the public eye. Our headquarters is equipped with technological systems that are current and, so far, under the radar of Lu and his band of insurgents. From our new home we'll launch our attack on Washington. Thankfully, we will not be on the high seas. My system does not care for the rolling waves." Ed did look a bit peaked.

"So just where is this hideout tucked into obscurity? A Chicago high-rise covered with volcanic dust? An old nuclear missile silo?"

"In the Virginias. An old bunker the Blues have resurrected. It was a safe place for government leadership in case of a nuclear attack back in the sixties. It's in White Sulphur Springs, the Virginias. Perhaps you have heard of the Greenbrier Hotel? When the presence of this government safe place was revealed in the nineties, the news made lots of waves and soon it became a tourist attraction. From secret documents our team uncovered, there was also an additional tunnel still in place that was sealed and concealed before the public was allowed in. Our government maps have revealed the secret access points. We now have a battery of computers in this auxiliary command center and our antennae system simply duplicates what was originally part of the composition of signal towers. This small addition does not hold room for thousands like the old adjoining center, but its solitary nature and proximity to D.C. make it ideal."

"Cave camping, Ed! You are a bundle of fun. Can we make s'mores?" The president tapped him jovially. It felt good to laugh.

She continued, "I remember reading about this Project Greek Island or the Greenbrier Hotel when I was a kid. Sounded mysterious and romantic, like a survival movie. Is it still a tourist destination?"

"Thankfully, not," Ed added. "That ended long ago. People nowadays think we have progressed past our nuclear threat era. Little do they know. The hotel has fallen upon hard times. It only has one wing open, and that usually touts foreign billionaires who have siphoned off enough money from their home countries to invest in the States. It is a great place to meet out of the limelight to conduct nefarious business. They also have enough helicopter traffic that we won't attract any attention. It is ironic that after all these years, a president will indeed be seeking refuge in those hallowed tunnels. Who would have thought it would be to escape the dangers of an American military dictator mad with power?"

By midnight, they were lifting off, filing a flight plan as a Greek trading organization meeting at the Greenbrier for a business venture. The president was dressed as a flight attendant and carried bags for a few of the distinguished group as they disembarked. The cases were empty, as Santaya was still struggling to heal from her serious shrapnel wound. The meager hotel staff paid little attention to them. These clients were from another world. They had immense wealth, a choice of lifestyles, and personal power. That lifestyle had long ago been snuffed out by the catastrophic events of the past decade. For those refueling the chopper, assisting with baggage, and participating in the welcome party, life was a daily effort to survive and put food on the table. That was it. Survive.

Turning down the first hall to their reserved rooms, the pilots and the flight attendant chatted amicably about the flight. Santaya was shocked by the diminishment of air travel. Stifled not only by an imploding economy and the pandemic, it had all but disappeared with the newly enacted climate agreement with the United Nations. It did not help that the cost of jet fuel was exorbitant. Air transportation was a world polluter. Aviation fuel was rationed. Former customers were forced to forgo long-distance flights for the sake of the economy. No one flew except those who were exempted—government personnel and the wealthy who were in cahoots with those in power and received exemptions as well. Even the United States Air Force and the Army Air Corps were near extinction. If the world could just reach consensus to coexist, all this could disappear anyway. For now they were crucified on the hill of climate change.

For many, that was an event to celebrate. All that was necessary was to convince the countries of India and China and their satellites to follow suit. Diplomacy would surely win the day.

Changing clothes into comfortable loungewear, the president opened her closet and pulled the latch attached to the back wall. She had been assigned one of the rooms allowing access to their secretive conference center by Ed Derkovick on the trip down. The door opened. Spying the light switch, she flicked it on and closing the door behind her, descended a narrow flight of steps. Into her mind jumped a scene from *The Lion, the Witch and the Wardrobe*. That book had captured her imagination when she was a little girl. Below her, the large room sported an office table surrounded by a dozen chairs. Seated were the inner team of patriots who had dignity and vision to embark on this immense project. Two of the attendees were the pilots, Ed Derkovick and Dr. Simon Hamilton.

Quickly the session began. Ed took the lead. "We are pressed into a tight timetable for reinstating the president in D.C. General Lu will be in Lucerne all week for the One Nation Alliance Conference. Since the First Nations protest has disbanded, he feels he has won a small battle, and D.C. is again safely in his clutches. His spies are still trying to discover what happened to the leadership of the faith communities. Even our contacts are befuddled that the two main coordinators, Arun Polysoing and Bishop Red Raven have vanished in the mist. That was quite a trick getting a hundred thousand people to disappear overnight. We certainly could have used them as reinforcements in the days ahead. Then again, they might be in the way. They are trained to fight the spiritual enemy, but I don't think they would be of much help fighting actual troops."

"How exactly did that number of people vanish into the mist?" posed the president.

Ed Derkovick responded, "Red Raven was sent a vision in the middle of the night to secretly evacuate the participants in God's revival by midnight the following day. During prayer group sessions, people were told to leave as unobtrusively as possible after nine p.m. No one seemed to notice the unusually high numbers of people on the buses and subways, but truthfully, few were paying attention to what was actually transpiring anyway.

Simon Hamilton complimented the process. "That was a miraculous move by our God to disband those protesters without either the press or the Capitol Police noticing anything was afoot. It seems God pulled that out of the history books and relied on George Washington's trick to make his troops disappear after the Battle of Long Island during the Revolutionary War. Keeping those barrel fires going that final night while everyone on the Mall left for home was a godsend! They had so many items to dispose of, from camping gear to printed prayer tracts, that the fires were unusually bright. By all appearances, nothing was afoot. Our friends now have the fire of freedom burning in their hearts. Hopefully they will soon be able to come back to the National Mall without the threats imposed by Lu's henchmen. But now, back to business. Ed?"

Ed Derkovick nodded. "The team has most of our strategy complete," he went on. "Lu has left the National Guard in charge of monitoring the city. Other than the local D.C. police and the Capitol Police, the National Guard is tasked with securing all other government facilities. As you know, General Abrams Sutoski, commander of the Guard, is one of us. We have equipped as many Blues Militia as we can with Guard uniforms and are mobilizing them outside the city in safe zones. They will lead the raid on the Capitol and secure as much as possible. The regular Guard will be ordered to stand down, as instructed by General Sutoski. And our Blues counterparts, led by our own Simon Hamilton or perhaps one of the White House security guards, will smuggle the president into the White House and reinstall her in her official capacity at the Oval Office."

Dr. Hamilton picked up the thread. "We have our tech team mobilized as well. All government satellite communication will be jammed for twenty-four hours. After that, my two government-sanctioned stations will be allowed to broadcast to our citizens, making sure the general populace knows that the president and order have both been restored. Head of communications is Ricardo Medina. He's a whiz at telecom systems and has this nailed down. He has been doing the tracking of militia suspects prior to this for the Fed Ops, so he knows what to look for on their end. I trust his change in loyalties."

A few at the table looked at Hamilton for reassurance. He gave them an understanding nod and continued, "One of our own, Mack Gersham, who has been successfully playing the role of Troy Griffins on the president's security staff, will be returning to duty on her detail. He and his wife have assisted us in gathering a list of enemies of the state who need to be purged for their treason in this plot. He has also shared that you have a particular grievance against the director of the Art's Council, one Kevin McKay, also a former general who is now in the Army Reserves. Do you care to elaborate?"

Santaya folded her hands politely. Looking calm, her heart was racing. Was this the time to finally reveal that Lt. Col. Shamir Wells, the son who was adopted by an American doctor and his wife in the Congo, was flesh of her flesh? Should she revive the scene Mack had shared privately about the execution of Wells and General Marcus Hamilton? It would serve no purpose. But she wanted revenge, and she would have it.

"That explanation is for another day. Right now, we must fine-tune this operation with our friends. My speech needs to be prepared. It will need to cover the most important elements. First, why the charge of treason is false. Yes, my husband was involved with a nefarious partnership with the CCP in China for years, trying to garner influence and wealth without my knowledge. But he was also ignorant of who he was dealing with. I will attempt to plead my innocence and ignorance. I am cut to the quick that Kevin McKay lured my husband into this craziness. He will be charged with treason and must deal with the consequences."

She unconsciously half choked on her last phrase. How had DeShaun been so easily swayed to agree to such despicable activities? Her heart was broken by the fact that he had betrayed her and their country. For what? Money!

"Second," she continued, "we will explain who is in charge. All divisional heads of the military will be relieved of their duties until we can ascertain their loyalty. How is that list of replacements coming along?" she asked to one of the navy officers sitting next to Dr. Hamilton.

"Done, Madam President. Lu's emails were instrumental in ferreting out the enemy. We have information on each individual and are ready to apprehend and charge."

"Thank you," Santaya whispered. More loudly, she said, "I will continue with a full pardon for the Blues Militia, incarcerated journalists, whether they like me or not, media personnel and protesters, as well as the remaining religious prisoners still in rehabilitation camps. We will need a commission of loyal government employees to facilitate this as quickly as possible. It shouldn't be hard to garner their support if we pay them well for their help.

"I am going to charge Lu with treason as well and arrest him when he returns to American soil. We will present proof of his devious attempts to undermine our republic from his dealings with the Russians, his involvement in the murder of General Hamilton, his transport of military documents to the ONA, and the massacre in Whitsville this week. Americans need to see Lu for who he really is. We will not be a pawn for the One Nation Alliance, run by a man who is a narcissist!

"Finally, we need a National Day of Reconciliation and Prayer." All those gathered looked at her quizzically. "I don't know where that came from, but there will be no peace until we learn to live with each other under the constitutional code that forms our Republic. I will attend the rally and seek forgiveness for the role my party has played in dividing us along merely ideological lines and championing the punishment of our so-called enemies. We need to learn to listen to each other and respect the fact that often our citizens see the world through different lenses. America can still be that shining city on a hill. She should be a place we take pride in. Most people of the world honor our rights and freedoms. These must be once again emphasized.

"I have found forgiveness and freedom by getting down on my knees and asking my God to strengthen my love for Him and His people. God is in the restoration business. He came! To this point in history, our constitutional republic, despite her many scars, has prevailed. It is worth fighting for, but we need our citizens to take ownership of her success. We all must step up or we will all sink together.

"And one more thing; we must relieve our citizens of excessive restrictions. We have required them to be robots controlled by the government. Much of that crackdown was by my directive. I see now that creating a police state to quell violence managed to remove what made us the envy of the world—freedom. We will return to our roots at all costs.

"Now we need to seek a higher power than ourselves for success. Our path is clear, but fraught with enemy interference. Please pray with me."

Santaya lifted her hands to her God.

"Holy Jesus, arm us with your wisdom, your protection, your will. Place your thoughts in our minds by your Spirit. Come alongside this noble band and support us. We repent of our independence from you, our lack of love for your peace, our rebellion against your Truth. We lost our way. We thought we could do it all on our own. Your love speaks of freedom, care, and unity. Keep us focused on your footsteps. May we reflect you in the days ahead. Preserve and protect us. Thank you, our Lord. Amen."

"Amen," the gathering repeated.

The task she knew was impossible. They all knew that. Chances of success could not be predicted. But she knew they were in the right and that they were now in God's hands. Restoring leadership to the Lord was the only way. He would have His will done in the days ahead.

Chapter 46

Ricardo Medina

August 2037

And now you Gentiles have also heard the truth, the Good News that God saves you. And when you believed in Christ, he identified you as his own by giving you the Holy Spirit, whom he promised long ago.
~ Ephesians 1:13

Ricardo felt the faint rumble of a phone notification on the private phone tucked in his pocket. Not normally carrying it, he figured it had better accompany him to communication headquarters. Most likely, his former service life would be over by the end of the day. *And to think I will be a mechanism that transforms history today,* he mused.

He glanced at the caller. Colin Lu. Glad this was an Army-issued phone that had not had its security protocols broken into yet, he flipped the phone open. "Yes?"

In a low voice Colin whispered, "General Lu has caught wind of the uprising. He is on his way back from Lucerne. Arriving around noon. We could make short work of Lu and his detail at Andrews. I could use a very accurate missile launcher."

The enticement of killing off his arch enemy energized Ricardo's soul. His hatred for his biological father made his blood pressure momentarily rise. "Wouldn't I like to be done with him," snarled Ricardo. "But balancing that with our advance at zero two hundred hours is not a good idea. Priorities. And the president wants him to stand trial, if we can bring him in alive."

"Damn it," said Colin. "Your people are too principled. Dad would have no compunction killing either of us if he knew what we were up to. Maybe he does. Someone on the inside has squealed."

"I'll pass that on to the president. She is en route to D.C. as we speak. At zero five hundred hours she will be meeting with General Abrams Sutoski of the National Guard. They will be here in the studio to tape a message for the country after our successful sortie in D.C. She will tape two messages—one to be delivered if we are successful, the other if we are not. At this moment, the general and his top aides are meeting with the D.C. police, the Blues militia reps and the CLF to finalize their plans. What a menagerie! I hear the Blues are the advance force. They have been given modified National Guard uniforms including a small blue patch with a black band across the middle. That is how they will differentiate themselves from the regular Guard. From my experience, they will be on top of the Capitol Police before they know what hit them. The big problem is the regulars in the National Guard. Some of them are going to struggle with a change in allegiance from Lu to Woodring. However, I believe the president will be able to sway some of them. I've seen a draft of her speech; powerful stuff."

Ricardo continued. He was in a rare talkative mood, adrenaline pumping. "You know, in the old days, I would have killed Dad without conscience. But now I'm growing a heart of compassion. Darn it. Must be my old friend Danny influencing my thoughts. I just don't hate Dad as much as I used to. Thoughts of him can't eat away at my inner peace the way I let them in the old days. But I still hope he will drop dead."

Ricardo trailed off.

"Well, see you on the other side. I'm on welcome detail for Lu. I hear he'll be under arrest for treason," chortled Colin.

"Make my day." Ricardo smiled into the receiver and then hung up. Whatever the plan was to overthrow Lu's puppet government, things always sounded better and easier on paper. He sighed and acknowledged that his fiery hatred was incrementally fading. Could God and Danny be healing his heart?

Chapter 47

Mack Gersham

September 2037

Therefore, go and make disciples of all the nations, baptizing them in the name of the Father and the Son and the Holy Spirit. Teach these new disciples to obey all the commands I have given you. And be sure of this: I am with you always, even to the end of the age.
~ Matthew 28:19-20

The ride along the twisty roads of former West Virginia was a total blur for Mack. He had made one pit stop to contact Ed Derkovick using a burner phone, giving him a heads up that he was on his way.

Weeks earlier during the demonstrations on the Mall, Ed had retrieved Mack's cylinders with the records of the pilfered armed forces weaponry and paraphernalia. It was amazing the number of depots that had not been discovered by the Fed Op troops in their relentless search for the stolen contraband.

Slowly over the past month, Ed had issued orders for small groups of the Blues Militia to collect items that would be of use in their counteroffensive and had them transported to D.C. Thus far, they had been undetected, as the loosely organized brotherhood had privately prepared for their valiant assault on the headquarters of American government.

Their goal was to rid D.C. of all vestiges of Lu's ad hoc government, remove the puppet leaders temporarily in charge, and reinstall Santaya Woodring to her rightfully elected office. They were hopeful they could secure the objective. The problem would be to hold it. If additional Fed Op forces were sent in as reinforcements, would they break the Blues or would some peel off to support the president? The batting average there was low.

Planning for an invasion with a small expeditionary force seemed frivolous. Everyone in the country knew that Lu would not relinquish his power. Even if he did allow new elections, he would be the puppet master pulling the strings, and he would certainly finagle the push for membership into the One Nation Alliance.

The question was, would the citizens of the Federated States support this revocation of the Constitution, or would they stand firm to hold on to their past form of government and their freedoms guaranteed in the Bill of Rights? Patriotism and fortitude were out of style. The people seemed numbed by the prospect of what Lu's call for unity with the world would mean. And yet the glimmer of hope had grown with the demonstrations on the Mall, as disparate groups of Americans had come to say they believed in the old way of doing things. They were brave enough to step forward to let others know that democracy still exists in the hearts of many.

With an unnatural silence hanging over the assembly, Ed Derkovich started the discussion. Sitting in the cramped space in the safe house in D.C. were Santaya Woodring, Dr. Hamilton, Arun David Polysoing, General Sutoski, Colin Lu and Mack. Mack had raced up the back roads of the Virginias to reconnoiter with the leadership team, arriving just in time to be in attendance. A few others, whom Mack did not recognize, sprinkled the assemblage. There was no time for introductions.

General Sutoski began, outlining the planned attack on each government complex, the White House, and the Capitol building. By running their offensive in the middle of the night, it would be difficult to recognize adversaries who were wearing the same uniform and trained in similar military tactics. They were sure they could neutralize the forces left behind by Lu. The bigger problem would be holding the objective of keeping the president safe and praying for the support of the citizenry of the country.

After the briefing, there was again an uncomfortable silence. Arun David Polysoing spoke. His comforting, direct voice commanded attention. "General Sutoski, this seems sufficient. Your plan seems compact and well-conceived. I know troops are thin. What can we, the CLF, do for support besides praying?" This last line was delivered with a crooked grin.

"I plan to make you a militia. Are your people willing to carry arms?"

Arun gave the question some thought. "Some will. Some will not. Those who do not will probably be willing to work as spies, backroom staffing, providing provisions, meals, transportation, medical care, and communications. We have valuable people who are necessary behind the scenes. We are at your command."

A young, attractive lady next to Ed Derkovich stood up. "My name is Elizabeth Parrish. I previously worked for a NASA subcontractor developing communication systems that operate on different wavelengths other than standard radio bands. Since we have been working to pulse more communications into deep space, we've begun to master sending coded messages in progressive wavelengths. I think this is a workable system for us. There are a limited number of communication devices already developed, but I have diverted those we have to our arsenal in town." She smiled and continued, "My husband has been a Blues Militia member for two years. We know we are the patriots. God bless the USA!"

During the brief break that morning, the president motioned Mack over to the corner of the musty room. "Mack, are you wondering why you're here in the inner circle? I asked for you specifically. Ed concurred. I need your expertise in retaking the White House and have asked that you be in command. From what I hear, it's not going to be a cake walk. Reconnaissance reports that the building's HVAC system has been programmed to flood the building with a deadly gas agent like Novichok that was used on my husband. It will render the People's House uninhabitable for years. We must get to the control center to diffuse the agent before it contaminates the whole structure.

"Lu hates the idea of anyone but himself ruling from that residence. I'm going to prove him wrong. We need to show the American people that we are willing to fight for them. I need the Oval Office to broadcast our return."

The widening eyes of Mack said it all. "Nerve agent? He plays for keeps. Who do I get the other details from and who is with me on the expeditionary team? I assume we are going in with the first wave."

"Even before the first wave," the president shared. "I plan to go with you. Now see Ed about your team. They're already reviewing procedures, but they need your expertise in knowing the White House secrets. I know that as part of my detail you were briefed on the information of our secret entrances. It is time to share this with your team. Enter the underground tunnel at access point B." She paused. "And Mack, I know you have honorably served your country for years. What you are undertaking is extremely dangerous. When I'm back in office, I promise you I will take care of Mercedes and your child if anything should happen to you."

"You people know everything," said Mack. "You also know that any revelation that Troy Griffins exists will cause Lu to search for Mercedes, seeking information. Lu is still after the pirated bonds and diamonds that Griffins stole while they both worked at the Russian embassy. Glad we know where Griffins stashed them!"

The president was turning to leave, but Mack grabbed her arm. "The best thing to happen to me, as far as Mercedes's safety, is to disappear. I love her more than life itself."

"How we love those who love us." She smiled. "Anyway, I always wanted to sneak into the White House through one of those infamous hidden portals."

When the meeting resumed after lunch, President Woodring began the proceedings. The air was thick with the knowledge that this venture was close to impossible. Especially with the word that had just arrived that Lu was on his way back from Lucerne. Their only hope was that whoever had released information on their raid was a low-level player with little knowledge of their invasion plan. It was too late to turn back. Santaya straightened her back and addressed the motley group of patriots. "We stand here on the precipice of success or failure of the dream called America. It was forged through the fires of conflict and sacrifice. It was imagined as the impossible dream, a place of freedom and opportunity, peace and potential. We are hanging in the balance. How we got here is obvious. We need to recalibrate the scales and pray that our fellow Americans hold this love for freedom as we do."

She continued, "I would be remiss if we did not bend our knee to the great Almighty God who enlightened our founders with the idea that mankind could build a country with this foundation. We appeal to Him again as we pray, that our endeavor replicate His objective and may we now ask for His intervention."

With a slight flourish, the president lowered herself to her knees and cupped her hands together in supplication. The entourage followed, watching her every move.

In the ensuing quiet, Arun Polysoing began a mournful prayer to the Spirit. He asked for the Lord to reign in their hearts, to lead their actions, to activate the minds of so many who had given up their faith in the secular world. The clarion call was heard. "Your will be done."

"Amen," stated the assemblage. For a few moments, they held their position, as if glued to the floor. The Spirit wafted over their hearts and minds, attending to their disquiet and their concerns. When they rose, they knew God had heard their supplication, yet they would not know the results.

"God help us," whispered Mack. He could not help himself. All he could see was Mercedes in the mist, reaching out her hands, begging him to come back.

Chapter 48

Mack Gersham

September 2037

And the Spirit of the LORD will rest on him—the Spirit of wisdom and understanding, the Spirit of counsel and might, the Spirit of knowledge and the fear of the LORD. He will delight in obeying the LORD. He will not judge by appearance nor make a decision based on hearsay.
~ Isaiah 11:2-3

The inky blackness of the night enveloped Mack Gersham and his team like a silent tidal wave pouring over them with the premonition of death. Mack shook his head to clear his thoughts and directed the team into tunnel B a half block from the White House.

He had carefully considered the future with Mercedes before his departure from Whitsville. For him, there was no future. When he had volunteered to become Troy Griffins through plastic surgery and an appointment in the inner circle as a security guard for the president, he had unknowingly chosen for Mack Gersham to be forever lost to history.

Mack was gone. For the Fed Ops, he was buried in a weedy plot, decomposing in Whitsville. When Mack enlisted, he had been stone-cold drunk. Needing to give a blood sample, his twin brother Walt had volunteered his blood instead. The switch was enabled by the twins exchanging flannel shirts and a recruiter who was distracted and anxious to return home to his girlfriend. When Walt died, the DNA tests recorded that the body in the grave was Mack Gersham.

Then his alias Troy Griffins, the real Troy Griffins, had reappeared. He had volunteered to stand in for Mack in the Andrew's detention facility and take the consequences of the charges brought against him by Lu. That would be death by firing squad. Griffins was willing, desiring to die with some sort of heroism. He was near death with terminal cancer and this choice was his way of retaliating against Lu and the wickedness he had perpetuated for decades. Fortunately, it seemed, Griffins was killed in the attack at Andrews by a stray piece of cement. Now that his body double Troy Griffins was dead, Mack realized the dangers to Mercedes if he was found alive. Questions would point back to the Gersham boys in Whitsville and by association, Mercedes and her work with Senator Roker. It was common knowledge that she was not only a childhood acquaintance but was also romantically involved with him as an agent inside the White House Secret Service. And she was implicated in downloading Roker's private emails onto her personal server.

On the chilly night flooded with fireflies dancing in the dense grasses, when Mack brushed Mercedes's cheek to kiss her goodbye, he knew it would be forever. For him, it was a difficult but logical choice. Trying his best to be casual, he had kissed her as though he would be returning soon. Not able to bear looking at her for the last time, he had walked away without glancing back.

Mack knew that the lives of Mercedes and their child would depend on his disappearing into the mist for all eternity. If General Lu got hold of Mercedes, he would be merciless. His torture methods were equal to those of the Tower of London, only more maniacal and IT driven.

Pushing through the dark underground tunnel leading into the White House, he took the lead, silently directing his men. Second-in-command, not to his liking, was Ricardo Medina, now considered an adversary to the Federated States of America, if they had been aware of his participation on the team. Soon he would be with the Blues Militia on his next tour of duty. The Fed Ops already had their suspicions, especially because the partner who was tailing him was still missing.

Entering the White House, they encountered no resistance. The hinge holding the secret half door was burned off with welding tools. It had been shielded by an air conditioning unit. The formation crawled into the bowels of the White House. All was undisturbed and at rest.

Mack communicated with Ricardo through his microphone that he alone would enter the control room governing the HVAC systems for the building. They foreknew the dangers. Ricardo considered pressing Mack to let him enter as well, then realized that this request would be denied, so he didn't bother. Mack surveyed the control panel with his glaring pen light for anything out of place. All seemed normal, but he had a strange dread that he was overlooking something.

For safety, the remainder of the team was instructed to continue down the corridor and shelter in one of the safe rooms constructed with steel casings on the walls and ceiling. The other invasion team radioed Mack and Ricardo that they were headed for the Oval Office. "I know where I'm going, Mack." Instantly he recognized the voice, Santaya herself. "I promise to sit in the dark and behave myself until all this business is over this evening. God be with us."

Mack smiled at the president's chutzpah in insisting on coming in with the advance team. She was more than willing to face the dangers to retake her rightful place as president, no matter the consequences. She was the determined leader of the free world and tonight she would stand in that mantle.

Stealthily, Mack searched for any clue that the earlier interlopers would have left in the control box. Using his infrared camera, he noticed no detection of human footprints or fingerprints, so he began to gingerly disassemble the side panels on the largest condenser. Most likely, this would be the source for allowing access to the planted nerve agent, which would then travel throughout the building in the duct system, intentionally killing or maiming anyone within its reach.

An almost inaudible voice spoke in Ricardo's communication ear inset. "Abort."

The shock of the warning hit Ricardo like an unexpected punch in the stomach. Taking charge, he opened the communication channel to the team. "Boss says abort," spoke Ricardo. Briskly Ricardo motioned for his team to move back to the tunnel used to gain entry. Mack looked up at Ricardo through the small door window, giving a "what's up" shrug, and then rose to exit the room as Ricardo raced up the hall to catch up with the president's team.

The ear-shattering sound of metal bursting and the ensuing white-hot fire were seen by Ricardo in his rear camera. Thrown back into the steel-clad room by the explosion, he quickly pulled himself erect and scurried as best he could over the debris while thoughts of Mack and the president raced through his head.

Mack, dead. President, questionable. Ricardo tumbled into the hall outside the Oval Office and behind a curtain, just as a hooded detail with glaring beacons on their helmets appeared. As the detail rushed into the Oval Office, he could hear rapid machine gun fire and saw the president being dragged down the hall, tussling with her captors.

One of the hooded crew said, "Don't bother struggling, Madam President. This time we are bypassing Andrews Air Force Base and placing you in Block N instead. You have no chance now to 'pass go and collect two hundred dollars.'"

Ricardo recognized the voice. It was distinctive and familiar. He crawled down the flight of steps and found the indistinct duct at the end of the landing. Jamming a screwdriver from his multipurpose tool under the rivets, it released fairly easily, and he pulled himself up into the gaping hole. He followed the serpentine path to the parking garage.

Pulling off his gear and any device that might attract attention, he gazed at the crews arriving to quell the fire. Turning, he strolled a bit and then headed in a jog to the safe house, perhaps for the last time. He knew where he must go—Whitsville.

Chapter 49

Mercedes Singleton

September 2037

But you will receive power when the Holy Spirit comes upon you. And you will be my witnesses, telling people about me everywhere—in Jerusalem, throughout Judea, in Samaria, and to the ends of the earth.
~ Acts 1:8

Something drew Mercedes's attention toward the front door as she was clearing the dishes from their meager breakfast. Immediately the door opened and the blinding early morning sun kept Mercedes from recognizing who was entering.

Squinting, Mercedes could make out three figures. One was her brother Titus; the other two were unidentifiable until they stepped into the room. Hopefully they were Blues operatives bringing the most recent news of the events in D.C. after the failed takeover.

She ran to Titus and looked up into his solemn eyes. "Please tell me you have news of Mack," she said. "I am just sick, waiting for any tidbit of information."

Before he could respond, she turned and directed a question at the taller soldier. "What are you doing here?"

Ricardo held his direct gaze at her abrupt question. "I have important news to share with you. I have been sent by Ed Derkovick."

"Thank goodness". She paused and involuntarily touched her stomach as the baby within wiggled with pleasure. "I have been worried to death about him. I knew he was choosing a detail that was extremely dangerous."

"It's about Mack," continued Ricardo. "I regret to inform you that Mack Gersham was killed in the line of duty defending his country."

Mercedes froze. Impetuously she cried out, "No, it can't be. Mack needs to live. I need him. Our baby needs him." She dropped to the floor and began to wail uncontrollably. "Mack" she called in a plaintive sigh. "Come back to me Mack."

The other men just looked on as Titus gently lifted her to her feet and placed her in the feeble kitchen chair. Suddenly she reeled around and demanded answers from Ricardo. "Where is his body? Is he dead or did he just disappear to keep me safe?" She gazed at the floor. Without thinking she blurted out, "I want to bury him next to his mother and his brother."

Then reality returned as no one spoke. Her body drooped and convulsed with the realization that her loving husband, her soulmate and lover, the father of her child was forever gone.

Gulping in air, Mercedes let out another sorrowful cry as Titus bent down and held her in a posture of sorrow and comfort, allowing her to rest her head on his chest.

The small gathering stayed silent as they listened to her tears and her babbling about Mack. There was nothing to say.

Ricardo reached in his pocket. "I have a letter here from Mack. He gave this to Ed Derkovick before the White House raid." Mercedes nodded her head and reached for the missive. Silently, she tucked the letter in her pocket to read privately later that evening.

"Oh, the attack," Mercedes whispered. "Is the president safe?"

"Unfortunately, no. Someone tipped off General Lu's cronies that we were coming. As far as we know, the president was taken into Lu's custody. We aren't sure of her whereabouts. The events have energized masses of citizens who are now protesting Lu's takeover. They are demanding a return to our representative government and release of the president. The temperature is heating up in D.C. Thankfully people are realizing the ramifications of Lu's power grab and are questioning his charge of treason now that the trial of Santaya has begun. We should see her soon during the trial proceedings. He is preparing for a civil war."

Ricardo continued, "There has been a release of some incriminating video coverage of Lu and agent Griffins when they were working with the Russian ambassador during the Middle East War. Apparently, the video evidence suggests Lu was taking bribes of government bonds and diamonds in exchange for military secrets. Of course he is denying the digital exposure as a cheap fake produced by AI bots controlled by his enemies."

"And why are you here, Ricardo? Why aren't you dead in D.C. instead of Mack? How did you turn into a patriot, you spy?" she spit out sarcastically.

"My cover was blown. And I had an awakening." He paused hesitantly. "I have begun to feel purpose in my life. This is a good cause. I want to live the life God chose for me."

Mercedes was stunned. She didn't know whether to believe this or not. God and Ricardo certainly did not fit into the same frame. What did this mean?

Titus interjected, "Mercedes, let's go sit on the porch. You need some time." He lifted her hand into his and pulled her to her feet, leading her out onto the tumble-down front porch equipped with a few ancient rocking chairs and a droopy bench.

They sat stoically for a long time. Then Mercedes started to tell Titus about her memories of Mack and Walt when they came to dinner during the revival by Billy Cramer. In her grief she laughed at the conversation she remembered and the way she felt when the star senior football quarterback had come to their home. "From the beginning, Titus, I think I was in love with Mack. I just didn't know it. He always thought we came from two different worlds, but not really. He just had a tougher life to deal with as a kid, and it made him have a skewed view of what to hope for in the real world. Underneath he was such a warm and approachable man. His hurts had given him a tough veneer, but I was privileged to see through that."

Titus nodded. It was Mercedes's need to talk that kept him silent.

"And my love for him these last few months we've been married has been the best experience of my life. I think deep down he knew our time together was short. That's one reason I think he wanted to get married as soon as we moved in together. He insisted."

"You're married?" Titus looked shocked. "I thought Mack called you the Mrs. to make an honest woman out of you. How did you do it?"

"Mack was insistent that we do what was right in the eyes of God. He and Shirley Smythe figured it all out." She smiled faintly through her trembling lips. "I am so sorry Shirley and the others were killed at Andrews. It was so unfair."

"I don't know how I can live without him," she whispered as her voice quivered.

"I'll be here to help you," Titus promised. "You need to stay strong for yourself and this baby you share with Mack. I know that was his greatest concern when he returned to D.C. I promised to be your guardian if anything should happen. He knew the risks. He also knew if his identity was uncovered, it would point to suspicions concerning the Blues and the old baggage of the real Troy Griffins. It was his one desire that you both be safe."

"Do you mean he chose a suicide job to keep me from danger?" Mercedes's voice rose as the question stuck in her throat.

"He did it for love, Mercedes. It was his choice. He didn't know what the outcome would be, but he knew it was dangerous. We had the information that the HVAC system was rigged before we went in. He chose to diffuse what we were told would be a chemical agent capable of killing everyone in the White House. It turned out to be an incendiary device. He did it for you. That's all he was thinking about."

Titus moved over to comfort Mercedes as she shook with sobs of sorrow. He whispered, "It was Mack's way of saying, 'I love you.'"

There were no more tender words to share. The early morning sun glared down on the dew, bathing them in a deep glow, as they huddled together in tears.

Around the corner, Ricardo and his partner appeared. They signaled to Titus, who extricated himself from Mercedes's embrace. He walked down the rickety steps to speak at a distance to the men.

Ricardo began the conversation. "D.C. is burning as we speak. The rioters have laid waste to several city blocks. We aren't sure if it is Lu's people planted in the crowd, or actual discontented citizens. Probably the first, but Lu will use this to his advantage for sure. Anyway, Lu's troops and the Capitol Police mowed down hundreds last night. We need to return. You stay with Mercedes and move her if you hear from us."

He continued, "I'm part of the Blues now and will be running some sabotage operations against the Fed Ops. I know their systems like the back of my hand. Not sure where this will all end. What I need from you right now, Titus, is a prayer to be covered with God's protection. Can you pray over me and our work to restore our government? We need divine intervention. Really, the prayers need to be for all of us. Can you pray like Danny used to pray, just kind of talking to God?"

Looking confused, Titus said, "Ricardo, when did you become a believer?"

"It took some doing, some searching. I saw people like your parents and Danny who loved something I didn't have. I was hungry and lonely, and frankly, I was just open to seeing if God was real. In the back of my mind, I knew He was, the way Danny carried on conversations with Jesus almost every night. I don't think he was crazy anymore. I've had a few talks with Him myself."

He continued, "The Holy Spirit has given me a peace about myself I have never known before. My old self was filled with hate and anger and revenge. I hated myself, too, and how my mother and General Lu created me in their time of sexual pleasure, to meet his personal needs. The Spirit has allowed me to see their brokenness, too, and now I understand how it happened. I can't say I am a totally new person, but God has a hold of my spirit and that's where I am right now." He smiled awkwardly.

The two men joined the third Blues soldier and wandered down to the creek where a boat was pulled up on the bank. Titus prayed a simple prayer over Ricardo, just talking to Jesus the way he felt comfortable. Ricardo ended with "Amen, thank you, Jesus."

He then added, "One more thing, Titus. Arun Polysoing has sent word to keep Mercedes and the baby safe at all costs. He has had several visions of her and the child leading a children's brigade for freedom. He knows it's God's message, but that is it. He's not sure how to interpret the visions but God has more for her and the child to do. Keep her safe."

Something in Ricardo's face showed concern. Titus was surprised his hard heart cared.

"I'll do that. God help us."

The men in blue shoved the boat into the water, paddling swiftly to their rendezvous location with the rest of their detail. They would then proceed in two military vehicles marked as Fed Op cargo troops.

Titus fell to his knees. God was still on the move, working with His people to press His kingdom forward, heart by heart.

"Thank you, dear Jesus, for saving Ricardo Medina. And thank you for all the people who intervened in his life to show him that there was more than the world could offer. Please, Holy Spirit, cover my sister Mercedes and her unborn child as she works through the days ahead, feeling lost because her beloved Mack is dead. May his soul be with you in paradise and may he right now be praising you and reveling in your glory. We all long to be with you someday. You are a good God."

A slow whirling noise interrupted his supplication. Titus looked up. Hovering over their house above the canopy of trees was a Fed Op helicopter. He was certain it was the enemy. As fast as he could, he raced to the house.

"Mercedes," he called raising his voice. "We need to move out now," he demanded, as she lifted her head, eyes still glistening with tears. "Now!" he yelled, grabbing her hand and running into the house to escape detection. "I know where to go."

Silently she nodded, robotically grabbed her weathered satchel and stuffed in a few personal items, waiting for him at the back door.

"Dear Jesus," she whispered, "hide us from the eyes of the enemy like David in the wilderness. Place your hedge of protection over the three of us. I know you can do this."

The voice of the Spirit responded, "Yes, I can."

The door slammed and they were off into the shadows of the dense forest. No one heard them except a loud cadre of blackbirds that had gathered by the thousands in the surrounding trees overhead. They lifted off and headed toward the helicopter.

God would provide.